Nine schools on two continents didn't make for an easy childhood, so books became the only constant in Karen Guyler's life, even if they didn't help her get out of sports days. Now settled in Milton Keynes, she juggles reading with writing, four children and her husband and a day job – a much nicer mix.

The Only

KAREN GUYLER

www.karenguyler.com
@originalkaren
https://facebook/karenguylerauthor

Book trailer
https://www.youtube.com/user/conmanguyler
© Simulated Film www.simulatedfilm.com

Cover art by Lisa Bonar
statementshome@yahoo.com

ISBN:1500423408
ISBN-13: 9781500423407

For Edith Maude Murkin (1919-1998),

thank you for prompting me

CHAPTER ONE

My bedroom felt how I guessed a sauna would feel. Not that I'd ever been in one, I'd read about them. I'd read about a lot of things that didn't exist anymore. I used to ask Mum to explain them to me–TV, cars, holidays outside England, universities, choices, but she'd get snappy so I gave up. I guess it was hard remembering all the things her generation had lost.

I could never quite understand her bitterness–it wasn't as if things could ever change now and the pandemic taught us if you had your health and someone you cared about, you had enough. At least she'd experienced a bigger life. Maybe that was the problem–we didn't know what we were missing and she was only too aware of it.

The heat was unbearable, pulling sweat out of me where I didn't realise I had pores. The sun shone onto the wall behind me, fading some more the pink flowers and other little girl drawings I'd done when we were moved here. I hardly noticed that expression of hope and act of rebellion that were now just childish doodles but if I could ever have invited anyone round other than Jace, I'd have felt embarrassed about them.

I looked at the window. Maybe having it closed was more suspicious? I didn't want to give our neighbourhood Government Informant any ammunition and I was pretty sure if anyone could see in they probably wouldn't recognise what I was reading. I flicked my duvet over the scientific paper anyway and opened the window.

England's weather had always been unpredictable but each year now seemed to bring more extremes, flooding one week, a grey wall of cloud the next, practically desert temperatures after that. A meteorological Jekyll and Hyde.

I rubbed at the windowsill, flicking off a ribbon of peeling wood stain. Our house hadn't seemed fifteen years old when we inherited it thanks to the previous people's care. These days, after eight years of barely any maintenance – who could afford to paint things now? – it seemed to be ageing in dog years.

I pressed my fingertip against the newly bare wood as if that could cover it up again.

"Maya!" Mum couldn't possibly know what I'd just done.

I flopped back on my bed and unveiled the paper. It was really making me think. I'd be lucky to have read and understood it before I had to give it back to Toby.

"Maya, I need you now for Sebastian." Her voice carried up to me again.

For Sebastian. The one thing I couldn't ignore. I jumped off my bed. No time to return the paper to its safe hiding place, under the mattress would have to do. I raced downstairs to the lounge where everything looked . . normal. At least our kind of normal.

Sebastian lay on the sofa where he spent most of his waking life. Since he first got sick, his world had shrunk until it was practically as small as the germs that made his body turn on itself. How did he stand it, staring at the ceiling reliant on me and Mum to distract him with one-sided conversations? At least I had an escape, I was probably the only kid who looked forward to school. And probably the only one not looking forward to having to leave next Easter.

His hair stuck out in all directions looking too dark and healthy to belong to the rest of him. The Puerto Rican colouring we'd inherited from Mum seemed to have deserted him completely, he looked almost grey against the white of his pillow. He must have a headache again—the curtains and probably the windows were closed.

Why the sudden panic? Mum didn't look up from where she leant over him. The lamplight highlighted more than a sprinkling of silvery strands in her hair. But grey-haired didn't mean anything, not now people couldn't hide it by dying it. She was only forty-two. That wasn't old, not really. Besides the Government's vitamin regime meant she would live longer than Nan, barring another pandemic.

Why was I thinking that? They promised us if we kept the rules there wouldn't be another. And I'd promised myself I wouldn't tempt fate, death, whatever great unseen ruled our lives apart from the Government. Probably the other half-orphaned kids were just as paranoid as me, but at least most of them didn't have a sick brother to worry about too. It must've been nice when everyone had living grandparents and aunts and uncles around them. No need to panic about everyone's mortality all the time.

The air in the lounge felt so thick I had to almost push my way through it. "Mum?"

It was hard to say who looked worse, her or Sebastian. "Finally. Get his Coralone."

"Maybe you should call in sick tonight. You look shattered."

"You know I can't."

Won't was what she really meant. "Did you sleep at all today?" I could read the lie she was going for before she said it. "For God's sake—"

"Don't use that word."

"It's not censored."

"I know that," she flicked a glance at the wall where our house joined our neighbour's, "but certain people don't like it."

Just the vaguest mention of her next door and I wanted to go round and confront her even though we weren't supposed to know what she was. But that would get me into more trouble than I could imagine. I snapped at Mum instead. "You're entitled to be off work if you're ill."

"I'm not ill."

"You will be if you keep going without sleep. I'll bike up to the hospital and tell them you're off. Next door'll just think she missed you–"

Sebastian began coughing.

"It's all right, sweetheart," Mum soothed. "I'm not going for a while then Maya'll be with you."

Like I was every night as if I didn't ever want to go out, do what other sixteen-year-olds did when there wasn't a curfew. Okay, so not quite every night, but it might as well be. She took every extra shift she could. It sometimes felt like she didn't want to be here.

The sounds of Sebastian's laboured breathing followed me into the kitchen. Poor kid, he sounded rough. Which meant we were in for a bad night. The paper I was trying to finish would have to wait.

I grabbed the Coralone from the cupboard above the kettle and rummaged in the cutlery drawer for a medicine spoon. The brown glass bottle felt light. I shook it, trying to see how much was left as I went back into the lounge. Even tipping the bottle completely upside down, only a dribble trickled out, scarcely covering half the spoon.

Mum practically snatched it. "Get the new one."

I tore back into the kitchen. In our tiny house it was only a few steps, but it felt like it was taking too long. I threw open the cupboard and grabbed the new bottle. A kaleidoscope of bright flashes peppered my vision. What was going on? I couldn't see past the flashes, I couldn't hear anything other than the roaring that had filled my mind.

A solid blackness enveloped me. I opened my eyes. I was staring up at a white expanse. Where was I? I could feel the hard coldness of ceramic tiles beneath my head. The whiteness was the kitchen ceiling. Why was I lying on the floor? I'd passed out?

"Maya, what're you doing? Can't you find it?"

Can't find what? My mind groped around the blank the darkness had left behind. The Coralone. I pushed myself up on my elbows. My hand hurt, felt sticky. A brilliant ruby slick emphasised the curve of one of the lines on my palm. But the stickiness I felt wasn't blood. If only it had been.

My hand was lying in a tiny sea of clear liquid, islanding the pieces of smashed brown glass that had held Sebastian's medicine.

CHAPTER TWO

I stared at the puddle of Coralone, more because my brain wasn't working like it should than because I was expecting it might jump back in the bottle. I couldn't believe Sebastian's medicine was spilt all over the floor. But there was no mistaking its cloyingly sweet smell.

In places the puddle seemed deep enough that I could scoop up some, enough to get him through till we could get more. But the bottle was glass. How would I know he hadn't swallowed shards too? I'd be worrying all night about them tearing apart his insides.

"What's taking so long? Tell me that's not the Coralone." Mum said in her 'how could you be such an idiot' tone.

"I'm sorry, I don't know what happened—"

"I asked you to do a simple thing." She snatched up paper from the recycling and began layering the smashed bottle pieces on it. "That half spoonful isn't going to last him all night."

As if I didn't know that. I got to my feet and rinsed the stickiness from my hand. The water stung. "I'll get some more."

"How can you? That was a new bottle. He can't have any now until August."

"It's not so long—"

"Not so long?" She wrapped up the glass as though it were a violent animal that needed restraining. Her wedding ring on the chain around her neck swung violently backwards and forwards. "How do you expect him to go for *any* time without it?"

I didn't but she wouldn't let me finish. She was too busy having a go at me, quietly, so our argument wouldn't upset Sebastian. I wished she'd just yell. Shout. Rant. Scream at me. Quiet fighting festered like a splinter your body wouldn't give up.

She wouldn't let me point out when Sebastian had been discharged from hospital two months ago, they'd given him a bottle of Coralone so he was late starting this new one so it really wasn't long until his scheduled repeat. And we could always get him admitted again if we had to. But when I mentioned it, she was all over me.

"You'd have us watch him get that poorly again? He needs his own Coralone."

"You think I don't know that?" I hissed back. "But they have Coralone in the hospital."

"Taking him to hospital won't help him." Her voice cracked and a look of fear that terrified me flitted over her face. She turned away from me.

"What?" I was almost afraid to ask.

"I'm just trying to keep your brother alive."

And she thought I wasn't? "You think I dropped it on purpose?"

"Of course not." She punched a wad of paper into submission and swiped at the puddle with it. "It's just that—"

"Just what?"

She ignored my challenge, giving all her attention to mopping up the spill. There was no point in trying to reason with her when she was like this.

"I'll be back before you have to go to work." I snapped. "And I'm fine by the way, thanks for asking."

CHAPTER THREE

I yanked the back door closed behind me, slamming it so hard the frame shook. As I marched away, I looked back, in case Mum had come after me. No sign of her but my cut hand had left a bloody smear on the wood that stood out from halfway down the garden. I should just leave it. Serve her right when our neighbour reported it.

But so many years of info-casts about the dangers hidden in spilled blood had been too good a teacher and my feet obeyed their messages, even if the rest of me tried not to. I stopped marching two-thirds of the way towards the back gate. Godamnit. Swiping at the sweetcorn stalks with my good hand, I stormed back to the house and wiped the fast-drying blood off the doorframe, rubbing it away over the forest of weeds that had colonised the unplanted veggie bed.

Damn, the cut hurt. It wasn't worse when I prodded round it so there probably wasn't any glass in it but Steri-strips would have been ideal to picket-fence it together. I looked at the closed door of the house and down at my hand again. It wasn't so bad. I could hide it.

Manoeuvring my bike out the gate one-handed wasn't so easy. Twice I crashed into the fence, jamming a pedal against my shin. I slammed the gate as hard as I'd slammed the back door.

"You trying to bring it down?" Jace grabbed hold of my bike and leant it against his back fence. He wore his around home summer usual – three-quarter length cut-offs, canvas trainers, no socks, no T-shirt. "What's up?"

"Mum, Sebastian, the usual." I flapped my hand at my house, as if that would explain everything. A drop of blood spattered onto the ground. We both stared at it as if it might jump up and bite us. I hid my hand behind my back, looking around in case someone who would report me might have materialised beside us in the back alley. I became painfully aware that the houses that surrounded us could be hiding any number of people who were even now noting what had happened to report on me.

Jace bundled me into his garden as if that might make me invisible. "Why are you outside with that undressed?"

I shrugged. He must be fed up hearing about our arguments. There was a limit to how much self-pity even a best friend should have to listen to.

"Maya, God, anyone could see it. You need a plaster."

"I've got to get to the doctors and back before Mum goes to work."

"You know there's a curfew right? Storm coming."

I looked at the sky. It was the kind of summer's day we only got a handful of times a year and they were ruining it by making us stay in.

"Storm, really?"

His voice dropped to a whisper. "Since when did it matter what we thought?" In another time and place it could almost have been funny that built like he was, Jace felt too threatened to disagree with the weather forecast in public. "The info-casts say there's going to be a storm."

We'd grown so used to curfews being called 'for our safety', we knew the rhetoric as well as the announcers. But they never told us why. Seriously if the weather was

9

going to be that bad, I could tell just by looking out the window not to go out. I didn't need to be told not to as if I were five years old.

"What do we need saving from in a storm?" I asked.

Jace frowned at me and glanced at Dixon's house, our neighbour on the opposite side.

I dropped my voice. "I'm not preaching sedition."

"She'll have someone round here in a heartbeat if she sees that cut."

I sighed. "I'll borrow a plaster. But I don't have a choice about the doctors. I just broke Sebastian's medicine and he's not good."

I followed him to his back door. All along the rear of their house, Esther's potted roses bloomed, a more varied rainbow than I saw anywhere else now that we had to use our gardens for growing food. The roses were really lovely.

"Gran, we have a plaster anywhere?" Jace bellowed. Funny guy, it was against the law not to have a first aid kit.

Although a mirror image of our two bed semi, Jace's couldn't have been more different. It always felt lighter in here, no tension, none of the worry of a long-term invalid. A normal home.

I could smell something sweet. Esther had been baking again. She must use most of her food points on baking ingredients, luxuries like that were expensive and difficult to get. Maybe she bribed Dixon with biscuits and cakes so she could keep her roses. I wondered if she'd made lemon drizzle cake, my favourite. Probably not as she could only get lemons a few times a year from people who grew them in their conservatories. Exotic treats like that were valued more than gold these days.

I could hear the peremptory tones of an info-cast as I followed Jace into the lounge.

"Now that food production has been stable for some time the Government is keen to increase our population." It was the young Father Christmas voice. The Government's anonymity made it easy for us kids to make up faces to fit the voices we heard when the info-casts first started. Most of those imagined faces were still how I saw the different announcers that delivered instructions and rules.

"With immediate effect," young Father Christmas went on, "extra points will be given to pregnant and nursing mothers until the child is five."

Wow, that was generous.

Jace's gran sat neatly, her hands busy with a needle. Just by looking at them you'd never guess they had any genes in common. Esther's hair was grandmotherly white in contrast to Jace's which was almost as dark as mine, even though he was white-skinned. His gran had the same dark brown eyes as me, whereas his were a startlingly pale blue and where he was thickset, almost muscle-bound, and only an inch or so shorter than me, she was tiny, barely bothering the five-foot mark on the doctors' height chart, stick-thin and too frail-looking to have lived through the pandemic.

"Hello, Esther."

"Maya, dear, how are you?" She switched off the radio. "They treat us like so many babies. Now they think we don't know how to prepare for a storm."

"Gran, shush."

"Don't shush me, Jason." It always made me smile to hear her call Jace by his full name, it made him sound like he was perpetually in trouble. "I'm allowed to say what I like, in my own home anyway. Besides you wouldn't report me, would you, Maya?"

"Of course not."

"The Government's just looking out for us." Jace frowned at her until she held her hands up in mock surrender.

"Plaster?" she defused him.

He nodded. "For Maya."

Esther pushed herself up out of her chair and led me to the kitchen.

"It's nothing serious but you know, uncovered abrasions. . ." I tailed off. Everyone knew the mantra.

". . . Carry risk of infection to yourself and others." Esther completed it. She dabbed at my cut with a small square of fabric before smoothing a plaster over it. "It's all a load of old phooey really. Before the flu no one cared if anyone went around with cuts or grazes. You could carry on as normal if you'd been sick or had a temperature. People made their own choices. The Government don't need to know about every cough and sneeze."

I was with Esther on that – the last pandemic before the one that had made everyone so germ phobic was over a hundred years ago and yet the Government had us acting as if we were all carrying leprosy. But maybe their overprotection was why there'd been no reinfection.

"Gran," Jace appeared in the doorway, shoving his arms into a T-shirt. "Maya has to get to the doctors and back before Anarosa goes to work."

"You can't go." Esther closed her first aid kit. "You won't make it back before curfew."

CHAPTER FOUR

"We'll make it." Jace said.

"You can stay here, Jace." The look on his face shut me up.

"We'll make it." He insisted.

Esther nodded as if she'd known she couldn't dissuade him from coming with me.

Even with the plaster my cut hurt so I rested my hand in my lap while I pedalled beside him. I wish I'd grabbed something to tie my hair up with. I needed to cut it, I'd been wearing it up for ages and hadn't realised how long it had got.

"Must have been something," Jace said after a while, "when cars used to zip along here. Imagine going anywhere that fast, sixty miles an hour, some of them, on roads like this. Imagine getting to the clinic in a few minutes."

How could I? The last time I'd been in a car I was only seven and I didn't know to remember it because it would be the last time. One day things were just like they'd always been but then everything changed, I didn't have to go to school and Mum didn't go to work. I remembered the computer stopped working and cartoons weren't on

TV anymore and we had funny things for dinner. Then the soldiers came and they'd been part of our lives ever since.

Here in MK I'd only ever seen army trucks patrolling the city roads. Pushbikes, pedicabs and horses and carts couldn't get close to their speed, however fast that was. "Before the oil crisis apparently there were so many cars on the roads people travelled faster by bike. Except here, they built Milton Keynes for the car."

"I thought it was an overspill from London."

"I guess if they still taught us history we'd know." I'd have liked to have studied history. I'd read just about all the historical fiction the library offered and the past sounded so much better than our present. Champions fighting to free people from oppression, brilliant. Some of the plots were so incendiary I was surprised they hadn't been removed in the Government's purges. Maybe the fact the Royal Family was no longer resident here and most of the books were about their ancestors was why the Government let them stay. They couldn't be anti-establishment if the establishment was no more

I sometimes wondered which country had taken the Royals in, whether it had fared any better in the pandemic. But we'd probably never know, we never heard about anything in the agricultural communes and they were in the same country. We were more an island than we'd ever been.

At least Milton Keynes was still a city, not a ghost town like Liverpool, Manchester, Newcastle, places where urban legend had it that hardly any survivors were found when the Government's re-housing programme began. At least there'd been some kind of population in York when the authorities arrived to move us southwards.

I followed Jace onto V4, one of the big roads that divided Milton Keynes up vertically that, along with the horizontal roads, turned it into a grid. MK was basically flat but it had a fair few slow-rising inclines that killed if you were in a hurry. Or at least they did me at the moment. And we couldn't afford to hang about.

"How's your science revision going?" I asked to take my mind off my struggle.

"Okay, I guess."

"You need more help?"

Jace looked at me and then ahead. "I still can't give you anything in return."

"Jace, don't you listen? I don't want anything. I help you because you're my best friend, practically family." I didn't recognise his expression but it made me feel like I'd overstepped a line. "Sorry, I didn't mean to snap."

Normally when I was with him, I could leave behind the latest saga with Mum. Today wasn't proving as easy, maybe because I'd deserved her yelling at me.

He nodded but pulled away a bit. Changing gears didn't help me catch him up. My legs felt too heavy to match his speed. I'd been feeling like that a lot lately. Nights disturbed by Sebastian were really ganging up on me. I was desperate for an unbroken eight hours sleep, just once or twice.

"We could go through there," Jace waved at the estate on our left, "incline might be less obvious." Sometimes I could swear he was psychic.

With him I didn't mind going through the estates, he could find his way anywhere, even through the redways when the signs were missing. The redways must have been a brilliant idea when people still had cars, a network of paths for pedestrians and cyclists linking the estates together so it was possible to travel around the city without ever touching a grid road. On my own I nearly never left the grid roads – there was a limit to how lost I could get on those.

I followed Jace's lead past kids playing British Bulldog, their shrieks as they tried not to get caught made me smile. A laughing and chatting group of neighbours had gathered in one front garden. You'd never guess we were so close to a curfew deadline. In the next street a handful of young boys were swarming in and over an abandoned car.

"It's my turn to drive now," one whined.

"You can't be in charge till I say so 'cos I'm the boss now." He was told. The wisdom of kids.

Jace stopped at the end of the road, looked at the post as though he could somehow still see the sign it had once held. "Reckon if we go right here and right again we should be back to the grid road."

"Whatever you say."

We turned into a quieter street where the abandoned cars were parked all along the same side of the road. A couple of young girls were pushing beat-up doll-sized pushchairs up and down. We were about halfway along when the sound of an engine coming up behind us made us get on the pavement. The army truck revved past us and pulled up a few houses further up the street. I'd never dared do anything to make me fear soldiers but I touched the pocket where I kept my ID anyway. Stupid really. As if I'd be thick enough to go out without it. Toddlers had learnt to carry their own by the time they hit three.

Four soldiers jumped out and ran towards their target. The first swung something like a stocky black pipe at the front door and it swung inwards. Shouting, gripping guns with lights attached, the soldiers ran into the house.

"Come on." Jace had a sick look on his face. I knew we had to keep going otherwise they might decide to scoop us up too.

We were one house away when I heard a scream from inside, raw sobbing that tore at me and stopped me dead. A soldier marched a man out and pushed him into the back of the truck. I could hear shouting from inside, men's voices, and then a high-pitched wailing that suddenly cut off.

"Maya." Jace urged me to catch him up. I knew there was nothing I could do here, but it seemed all wrong to leave, for us to hurry away so we stayed safe.

"Maya." Jace grabbed my handlebars. "We have to go, now." I looked at the house, the silence was almost worse.

I biked away, wobbling like I'd just had my stabilisers taken off. It had been so long since we'd had a raid in our street, I'd forgotten the awfulness of it. The sudden intrusion of the Government into our everyday lives, the guilt and frustration of being too scared to do anything while the life of someone you knew was destroyed or they became one of the 'disappeareds'. The panic that someone might decide you must be connected somehow so you'd be dragged off too.

I stopped at a crossroads, waiting for Jace to guide me.

"You okay?" he asked gently.

"We're so helpless, aren't we?" My voice sounded as small as I felt.

A gamut of answers played over his face but he didn't know which was the right one. He looked at his watch instead.

I nodded, letting him pull ahead, trying to stop replaying what I'd just seen in my mind, trying not to listen to the echo of the screaming, trying not to think what the sudden silence meant.

CHAPTER FIVE

We had to virtually push through a wall of heat barring the open doorway of the doctors' surgery. The shutter over the dispensary window clattered down, I heard the clicking of a padlock. The receptionist jumped when she saw me.

"The doctors have all left, I'm just closing up." Her face was so red there seemed a real danger she'd keel over before she could get Sebastian's medicine.

Carefully hooking the fingers of my cut hand over the front of my shorts so she wouldn't see it, I handed over my ID card. "Maya Flint, I need a repeat prescription of my brother's Coralone." I hoped I sounded business-like enough that she'd just give me what I'd asked for.

"If I can't help you in two minutes," she said, "you'll have to come back."

She read my ID and typed something on a keyboard. Her chin folded in on itself when she looked down until she had soft cushions of skin filling the gap between her chest and jaw. She must struggle to stay within acceptable weight guidelines. "Patient's date of birth?"

I told her, added our address and Mum's details.

She tapped away again. "He's not due a repeat yet."

"I know. But I accidentally broke his current bottle so

I need his next one early."

"Did you bring the bottle with you?"

Taking broken glass out in public? There had to be a law against that. "I thought it wouldn't be allowed."

"Without it I don't know that you did break it." The receptionist peered at me as though I might have my intention written on my face somewhere. I could feel myself flushing. "Did you bring your brother?"

"He's too sick."

"How sick is he?"

Sick enough that he needed his medicine, sick enough that he couldn't come and get it himself. How sick did he have to be?

"He's pretty poorly." Jace stopped me getting us both in trouble.

"Who're you?"

"Their neighbour, Jason Anderson." Jace flashed his ID.

"Why have you come?" The woman pulled herself up on her chair. His size did that to people, made them feel defensive. Sometimes my height did it too. There weren't many of us girls who topped six foot, makes some people think they can stare. Which would have been bad enough on its own if I didn't also have to contend with not being in the social loop at school, making me almost as much a pariah as if I were a teacher.

"My friend's upset because she feels bad she broke her brother's medicine. Could you just give him his repeat now? He can make it last till the regular one's due. I know you want to get going. If we could just take the Coralone, we'll get out of your way." Jace flashed his best smile. How did he not have a girl friend? I'd never really noticed him fighting girls off but he had to be, looking like he did.

The receptionist looked around the empty waiting room as though checking no one had sneaked in who might report her. She tapped on the keyboard again. Her face creased into a question. "I can't give you any."

"Please, he needs it to survive." I felt so desperate I might even have promised I'd become a Government Informant if it got the medicine.

The woman mopped her forehead. "You're not hearing me, I can't give you Coralone."

But that couldn't be right. She had to help because if she didn't, I didn't know where else to go.

"Why not?" Jace asked.

Her tone became altogether more human. "Look, I might have been able to find a way but there's really nothing I can do. Now I have to go."

"We understand, thanks for your time." Jace held out his hand as though he was going to shake hers but he connected with the box of forms on the counter and knocked it onto the floor. "I'm so clumsy." He made a gesture with his other hand, deftly knocking a pot of pencils after the forms. "Would you look at what I've done, here, let me help you."

With surprising grace he was around the receptionist's side of the desk, gesturing to me with a glance at the computer screen.

"I'll help too," I got his hint, "make it faster."

As I rounded the desk I glanced at the screen. I vaguely remembered playing computer games in York but it felt so alien to my life now, sometimes I wondered if I'd dreamt it. It was kind of scary to see information about Sebastian but not to know where it had come from. When I could persuade Mum to talk about life before the pandemic, she'd mention something called the Internet, where people could talk to each other from different sides of the world and find information about anything in seconds. All the scientific papers and research I could ever dream of reading just a few key clicks away. It sounded like magic.

I scanned the screen. At the bottom a sentence blinked at me. Could computers make mistakes like that?

But the words reappeared on the screen in the same

formation, spelling out the same ridiculous message –
Coralone withdrawn.

CHAPTER SIX

Standing outside the surgery, I watched the receptionist walk away in tight hurried steps. There really was no help here.

"We need to get going." Jace straddled his bike.

"I can't go home empty-handed."

"You'll have to." He checked his watch. "We'll get caught out if we're not really fast as it is."

I knew he was right but leaving felt like giving up. "Sebastian needs his Coralone."

"Can your mum get some from the hospital?"

"How can she? Even though she works there, it'd still be stealing." And there was no way she would ever steal again – the Government had seen to that the first time.

I wanted to kick my bike. Instead I yanked it out of the rack and pedalled off as if a bottle of Coralone was dangling just out of reach and would be mine if I could only touch it. The burst of speed didn't last long. After only a few minutes I was struggling again.

The roads were deserted.It felt surreal, seeing and hearing no one else. Sometimes I wondered if everyone obeyed the Government as fervently as me, if I was weak never questioning anything, blindly doing what I should.

But looking at the empty streets, it seemed everyone else obeyed them too. Well, not quite everyone, Toby operated under his own rules. The curfew siren shattered my thoughts, perfectly timed as if it were reminding me that just thinking about a black marketeer was wrong.

Nothing was physically different from five seconds ago, yet somehow everything felt changed, as if unseen eyes were watching us from within the tangle of bushes on the roundabouts and the verges, unseen hands waiting to grab at us.

"Now I've got you in trouble, Jace, sorry."

"They haven't caught us yet." He bent over his handlebars and pedalled harder.

A couple of rabbits darted out in front of me. Swerving to avoid them, I managed to ride straight through a mound of fresh horse manure. Great.

I was so busy keeping my feet out of the pile as I careered around the roundabout, I nearly crashed into Jace. "A little warning next time you stop?"

"Listen."

Against the silent backdrop of no people, all I could hear were bird calls. Oh, crap. Not all. I could hear an engine.

"It's coming from behind us. Hurry." Jace yanked his pedal round ready to ride off.

"We can't outrun it." The way my legs felt I couldn't have outrun Sebastian.

"We have to try."

"They'll catch us. But if they don't see us, they won't be looking for us."

"What're you talking about? Of course they're looking for people, that's what the Army does during curfew."

Now wasn't the time to get into what I thought the Army should be doing. The sound of the engine was getting louder, the patrol closer.

"We can hide in there." I nodded at the roundabout.

"Soldiers might patrol the verges, but in there we should be safe."

There was no time to argue. I wheeled my bike across the grass and tried to force it into the bushes. They pushed back. After years of neglect the city's greenery had blossomed into a shield that would defeat even the most determined fairy tale prince's efforts. "Need your muscles, Jace."

He was beside me instantly, shoving his bike, then mine into the resistant foliage. I forced myself into the unyielding twigs and leaves. It was like fighting cats, everything I touched scratched back.

Then I was in amongst it, watching the world through a living mantilla. Jace wriggled in beside me, I shuffled sideways so he could fit in the tiny gap too.

Only a handful of breaths later the jeep we'd heard pulled around the roundabout and drove up the grid road. Keep going, keep going, no one breaking curfew here. Every second I expected it to stop but it carried on, crawling away from us.

Was that it? They'd gone? But then I heard movement behind me and a soldier strode past us. I laid a hand on Jace's arm and signalled with my eyes. I hoped he got it, I didn't dare breathe, let alone whisper a warning. Luckily the soldier had no reason to be quiet.

"You gonna have a kid now?" He threw the question in our direction and for a crazy second I thought he was talking to us.

"Already sorted, mate. Lyndsey's due January, thought we'd better not leave it too long, you know before Ben gets too old." Another soldier materialised from the other side of the roundabout. "You?"

"Extra points are extra points. Andrea won't fight me on that, another one should mean a bigger house too."

It seemed wrong that they were discussing having kids while patrolling the streets, looking to capture other people's children to lock up.

The first soldier turned a slow circle as he walked away, his gun aimed. He passed level with us. I looked away quickly, trying not to acknowledge how pathetic my defence was, if I couldn't see him, he couldn't see me, trying not to think that he could probably hear my heart banging against my ribs, desperately pretending that the bushes in front of us were so impenetrable we were invisible to him.

"What?" his partner asked.

The first soldier clicked something on his gun and fired a shot into the bushes. My heart stopped but he'd aimed left enough to miss us. He was shooting at our bikes. The bullet grazed the metal of one of them but the splintering of the branches it also hit seemed louder. Please let it be enough, please let him think it's a trick of the light.

"It's nothing." The soldier adjusted his gun again and they walked away from us.

Don't turn round, keep going, I urged them away.

As the distance between them and us increased so my senses returned and I could feel Jace's body heat layering warmth on my front. The sound of his breathing filled the silence.

"Sorry." I whispered when we couldn't see the jeep or soldiers anymore.

"Why?"

"Getting you stuck out in a curfew with me."

"I can think of worse places to be." His gaze was so intense I looked away, making a big thing of rubbing a scratch on my arm, smearing a string of blood droplets. I seemed to be having real trouble keeping my insides inside today.

"Looks like someone's tried writing on you." I pointed at his scratched forearm, looking my joke at him but my smile died beneath that gaze.

Everything outside the green cocoon dropped away, the worry about Sebastian, the soldiers, the need to get home. Everything dissolved into only our breathing. It felt as though there was only Jace and me in the whole world. The intensity of the moment had its own gravity, pulling me in towards him.

But then he looked back at the grid road and became all business-like. "Patrol's gone, I don't hear any others. Maybe now's a good time to make a run for it."

What had just happened? Had we been about to kiss? No, that was ridiculous. Best friends didn't kiss. It was a reaction to the danger we'd been in. Were still in.

"Maya?"

"Oh, yeah, sure, we need to get going."

"Fast."

A magpie on the verge chattered harshly as we shot past it as if underlining the fact we were breaking the law. Even the wildlife was co-operating with the authorities.

Jace reached our estate first and had disappeared by the time I turned in. Good. He'd be back safely. All I could hear over my ragged breathing were the sounds of my bike, the click of the gears, the hum of the tyres. It seemed as though the entire area was holding its breath.

My legs felt like they were going to give out. I needed to be faster but I couldn't push myself any harder. What was wrong with me? I was so late now Mum would be livid. I braked to round a corner and came face to face with a soldier.

CHAPTER SEVEN

"Hey, you!" The soldier recovered from his surprise at finding someone breaking curfew by pointing his gun at me. I pulled up so fast trying to keep as much distance between me and it I nearly went over the handlebars. No, no, no. I couldn't be caught now, I was so nearly home.

"Over here." The soldier pointed at the ground in front of him as if his order wasn't enough.

I glanced at the rusting cars at the kerb, would their bodies protect me from his bullets? The new jagged graze on the sound metal of my bike answered that. I didn't seem to have a choice.

I got off my bike and nearly fell over. My legs felt like they belonged to someone else. I hoped he didn't notice how wobbly I was. I took a deep breath. I couldn't pass out in front of him, I'd be quarantined forever, if he didn't lock me up first, and Mum would be fined for letting me out in such a state.

I gave him my ID. He checked it, again and again judging by how long it took him. He was probably new to deciphering the codes. We'd never figured out what the rows of numbers meant, they seemed to be different for everyone.

Another soldier joined him and glanced at it too.

"Out during curfew without authorisation," he said. "We'll have to take you in."

They were going to arrest me? What about a warning, a slap on the wrist and sending me home scared? They couldn't take me anywhere, Mum needed to get to work. I had to get home.

I gripped my bike harder and the pain gave me an idea. "I need medical treatment. I cut my hand. I don't know the rules for getting help in a curfew."

"When did this happen?"

"Earlier, I couldn't get it to stop bleeding—"

"Where are your parents?"

"My dad's dead." I couldn't help jutting out my chin in defiance of the lie I always told about him.

"Your mum?"

"At home. Nursing my sick brother."

They both took a step away from me as though they'd rehearsed it. It was almost funny.

"What's wrong with him?"

"Have you reported his illness?" They shouted over each other.

"I know the law. Maybe I should go home, get my hand looked at tomorrow."

"Let's see."

I held my hand out and could almost see the thoughts running through their minds that their uniforms and authority and guns were no match for a microscopic germ. As if whatever germs were running through Sebastian's body would come out of mine too. As if I might pass them on to them. As if I might start a new pandemic and they'd be shot for letting me.

"I'm going to give you a pass giving you permission to go to hospital." The first soldier spoke so quickly his sentence came out as one word. That meant they weren't going to arrest me? My legs felt wobbly again.

His partner produced a slip of card. Regulation

Government pale pink, an 'I'm-your-friend' kind of shade, non-threatening. He scrawled something on it, copying my details from my ID onto the pass before handing them both back to me.

"Thank you." I got on my bike and pedalled off before they could change their minds.

"Hey!"

What now?

"Isn't the hospital that way?" He was pointing where I'd just come from.

No! I needed to get home, the opposite direction to where he wanted to send me.

"I know a shortcut through there." I gestured towards my road.

"Best stick to the main routes, you don't want to be surprising any more patrols."

It didn't take a very high IQ to work out that I couldn't win. I'd talked my way out of one nightmare, straight into another. And worse, Mum couldn't go to work now. She was going to kill me.

CHAPTER EIGHT

All the way to MK General I argued with myself. I needed to go home so Mum could go to work. But not showing up would be noticed. 'We'll have to take you in.' I never wanted to hear those words again. Just the echo of them kept me pushing the pedals round.

It was as eerily quiet at the hospital as the streets had been. No pedicabs waiting, no people milling about. Only bikes presumably belonging to the doctors and nurses and an ambulance waiting for its next call-out in what used to be the car park.

A wave of chemically clean scent took my breath away as I entered Accident & Emergency. From every available inch of wallspace posters screamed at me in different coloured urgency: 'germs are everyone's responsibility', 'cover your mouth when coughing and sneezing', 'uncovered abrasions . . .'.

"It's the same thing no matter how many ways I say it, no ID, no treatment." The receptionist looked past the man she was arguing with and waved me over.

"I told you, I rushed out without it because I'm hurting. See." The man removed the rag he held against his head. Blood welled up, filling the gash at the edge of his scalp. "Sort me out then I'll get my ID."

The receptionist pursed her lips together, lines furrowed outwards from them like a child's drawn sunshine. "In a curfew? You can't just wander around the streets."

"She did." He pointed at me. "To have just arrived, like."

"ID?" The receptionist asked me. I handed it over with the pass. "See, she has ID and a pass from the military." She smiled at me as though I'd been responsible for her getting everything she wanted in life.

"Look, love, let me be seen by a doctor, real quick like and I'll be out of here." He spoke with a strange accent I wasn't used to hearing.

"What's the problem?" The receptionist asked me.

"I cut my hand." I held up the offending injury.

"How?"

"On a glass bottle."

The man banged on the counter, making her jump.

"I need to be stitched up, you stupid mare." A globule of spittle landed near the keyboard. Surprisingly her glare didn't turn it to ice.

"I have called security." she announced. "We all know that to be outside without ID is a crime." She slapped a paper-wrapped package on the counter. "Pressure bandage. It'll stop the bleeding enough that you can get your ID."

"For the love of God woman, a couple of stitches is all I need. Would you have me bleed to death for your petty rules?"

Her gaze snapped straight onto his. "I do not make the rules, that is the prerogative of our Government because they know what's best for us."

"Trouble?" A security guard materialised at the desk.

"No ID." The receptionist went back to her typing.

"Let's go." The guard was probably, twenty, even thirty years older than the man and about four inches shorter. If the man resisted, there probably wouldn't be anything the guard could do about it.

"I'm not going anywhere until I get stitched up." The man swatted away the guard's hand.

"You don't do as you're instructed, then you'll need more care than stitching but you won't get that either."

"You threatening me?"

The guard patted the nightstick on his belt. "All the threat I need. No ID, no treatment."

"The Government has to supply what I need. I need stitches."

"You'll need that to get back home." The receptionist handed me my ID and pass, completely ignoring both men. As I reached out to take them, the man ploughed into me sending me flying. We landed in a tangle, him half on the floor, half on me, whooshing the air out of my lungs. The smell of bleach mingling with disinfectant was stronger down here, enough to make my eyes tear up, make me cough.

The guard raised his nightstick and brought it down so fast I heard it whistle through the air. The force of the blow that hit the man made me duck away from it. He let out a yelp. I pushed at him to get him off me but he was too heavy.

Like a fully-wound clockwork toy the guard pulled the nightstick up and smacked it down again and again. The man dropped his rag in the scramble to get his hands up to protect his face, his neck. He scrabbled to get away from the guard's fury, pushing himself more onto me, his heels drumming out a cry for help on the floor that everyone ignored.

"Stop it!" I couldn't bear it any longer.

"You're not telling me how to do my job?" The security guard panted, turning his vicious tone my way. "Do I have to deal with you too?"

"No, please, I just meant that's enough. He'll go now, won't you? Please, just do what they want, you're only going to end up more hurt."

The ribbon of blood trickling down the man's face splashed onto my top. I stared at it as if I could see the germs he carried. He pushed himself up and limped out. If a patrol stopped him, he'd be straight back with a soldier's gun directing hospital policy to keep his blood where it belonged. As improved as our lives apparently were, things would be a lot better if they hadn't thrown out compassion and common sense along with crime and thinking for ourselves.

The guard glared at me "I'll be back for you shortly."

He snatched up the bandage and followed the man out. I grabbed my ID and pass and sat down amongst the witnesses.

What were they all looking at? I hadn't done anything wrong. But the more conscious I felt of their stares, the hotter my face flushed. They were the ones who should feel embarrassed and awkward, not me, because they'd pretended nothing was going on while a man got beaten up. Okay, he shouldn't have come out without ID but he clearly needed help. How was beating him up a fair way to remind him not to do it again?

If the Government cared so much shouldn't the default be to treat him first and then worry about who he was? I didn't get the big deal about ID anyway - he was hardly likely to be one of those illegal immigrants that people used to be so worried about. From what I'd remembered and had read, anyone who had a tie elsewhere in the world couldn't get out of the UK quick enough when the pandemic started.

The woman sitting opposite stared at me as though I'd bled all over her. I didn't stare back in case that antagonised her into reporting me for having blood on my clothes. It was my favourite top too. Mum would insist on binning it now.

Mum. God, she was going to go ballistic. Stuck at home waiting for me so she could go to work. Maybe she'd have used Jace's radio to say she was poorly. That didn't count as an emergency but she'd probably get away with it because of the curfew and her nurse's protected status.

I felt more wobbly and sick now than when I'd passed out. It must be the shock of it, that was all and the panic that I either had to face the security guard if I stayed sitting here, or the gun-toting soldiers on patrol if I left now.

CHAPTER NINE

I couldn't stop replaying the scene of the man being beaten up in my mind and him cowed and bleeding overlaid everything I looked at, everything I tried to distract myself with. Even the guard's threat was diminished beneath the visual reminder of the violence.

I tried to sidestep it, concentrating on something innocuous about the man. His accent. That's where I'd heard it before, the day we'd been moved south.

Mum had been in the kitchen that morning, crying into a pile of folded tea towels. In all my eight-year-old wisdom, I'd thought she must really love them and didn't want to leave them behind so I took my least favourite doll out of my suitcase and slipped one in her place. One doll less wouldn't matter, I had plenty of others.

It had seemed like a game at first, packing my favourite, then my next best things. But there'd been a lot of next best things so my suitcases were full of dolls and books and a sketch pad and the little turtle made out of a shell from somewhere far away called the Caribbean that Nanny and Grandad had bought me as a present.

Then Mum said the dolls and books had to stay because I needed to pack my clothes. I wouldn't take them out so she'd shouted and tipped the suitcases up until everything fell out, and a book landed on the turtle, snapping its wobbly head off its body. I remembered crying while she emptied my wardrobe into the cases and zipped them shut so I couldn't open them.

I'd cried until a lady with blonde hair in a soldier's uniform appeared in the doorway. "Are you ready to go, love, to your new house?"she'd asked in that strange accent. "Don't be upset, it's dead exciting, moving house."

"I don't want to leave my books behind." Just the thought made me want to cry harder.

"There'll be books where you're going and I bet you'll have a pretty room like this."

"With pink flowers on the walls?" I sniffled a bit less.

The lady smiled. "If that's what you want."

"I like flowers."

"Me too. Are these your cases?" I nodded. "Come on then."

I sat on the bottom stair where the lady told me to wait while our cases were carried out. Seven I counted. Two for me, two for Sebastian, two for Mum, one for our house things and then our duvets, all rolled up. We seemed to be leaving lots of things behind. If I told Mum, she'd sort it out.

I crept off the stair and peered into the kitchen where I could hear her getting cross. "I need to leave a forwarding address."

"Sorry, love, but we don't know where you're going until we get you there." The lady soldier checked her papers. "You're a single mother, not likely to expand your family, that'll have a bearing on how big a place you'll have."

Mum made a huffing noise. "I know I can't expect to have anything like this house."

"You're not down for agricultural placement."

"I know that too."

The soldier looked at her papers again. "The only

other thing I can tell you is that London's nearly full so by the time we get down there they'll probably be re-housing in the satellite towns."

"It's just that I don't know that my husband died of flu. It's something I told the kids to protect them."

Even remembering those words was enough to make my stomach do the lurch it had when I'd heard them the first time. Daddy wasn't dead? How could that be? He had to be otherwise he'd be here with us, moving house. And I'd seen Mum crying a lot and that's what people did when people died. I'd cried for him too but Sebastian had been too little to really understand.

"If he comes back when we're gone, how will he know where to find us?" Mum spoke so quietly I had to listen really hard. "I need to at least leave a message so he can track us down. Please, I'm begging you."

"Love, I want to help, I really do. But once this area's evacuated, everything will be shut down, like all the other empty cities and it'll be declared a no-go zone. The Government's good at record keeping, if he wants to track you down, he can."

Daddy was alive somewhere? The words had felt strange in my mind, like saying the sky was green and the sea red.

Why had Mum lied? Telling lies was bad – she reminded me often enough. If she could lie, maybe the soldier had too. I ran back upstairs, shoved my absolute favourite books into the first backpack I grabbed, put it on backwards and zipped my jacket up over it. If I bent over slightly, no one could tell. Mum was too busy with the soldier and Sebastian to notice. I picked up the broken turtle and put his body and head in my pocket.

The lady soldier did lie - when we got to our house in Milton Keynes my room wasn't pretty and there weren't any books anywhere. When I complained Mum snapped that I should be grateful I had a proper bedroom. They'd converted the garage for her, after all no one had cars anymore, so what was the point of a garage? A waste of resources, a crime against the country.

I lay in bed that night, listening to the noises around me, feeling the way the new house was different.

What felt like hours later, Mum came in and lay down beside me. "This can be a pretty bedroom, Maya. You can paint whatever you like on these walls."

"You won't get mad if I draw on the wall?" That didn't make any sense.

"Not in here. I might not be able to get paint anymore because it costs lots of pennies, but I'm sure we can get crayons and pencils."

"I brought some of my books." I blurted out. She didn't sound mad anymore, maybe she wouldn't mind.

She kissed my forehead, wrapping me up in a cuddle. "I'm glad you did."

"What happens if Daddy wants to find us? Can the Government tell him where we are?"

Mum let out a long breath and pulled me closer. "It seems the Government can do whatever they want."

"Has he gone even further away than where Nanny and Grandad went on their holiday before they went to heaven?"

"I don't know."

"Why did he go away? Doesn't he love us anymore?" She was quiet such a long time I thought she'd fallen asleep. "Mummy?"

"Sometimes people do things you wish they didn't. And when someone hurts us, it's really hard not to get mad at them and want to hurt them back. But you have to remember if you haven't walked in their shoes, you shouldn't really judge them."

"Daddy's shoes wouldn't fit me."

Mum had laughed, a hiccupy sad little laugh. "No, my smart girl, they wouldn't."

"I'm sorry about your bedroom."

"Me too."

"I can draw flowers on your walls, if you'd like?"

She kissed me again. "I'd like that very much."

My smile at the recollection melted as I heard my name being called, when I realised the nurse calling me was my mum.

CHAPTER TEN

Mum was here? Was Sebastian so poorly they'd already admitted him? We almost collided rushing to get to each other.

"Is Sebastian all right?" we said together.

"Jason's sitting with him." she said. "He told me you were round the corner, to go so I wouldn't be late."

I owed him again. I'd thought it odd he'd biked off like that, but now I understood. He really was the best friend ever.

"How's Sebastian?" I hardly dared ask but the panic that had written itself over Mum's face when she called me had already relaxed away. He couldn't be so bad.

"That half dose seems to have settled him down. Why are you here?" I held up my plastered palm. "Come through and I'll look at it."

She entered a code on the keypad and the door clicked open. Just hearing us, no one would know we'd rowed the last time we spoke. I guessed her being back to normal was because she was at work doing the job she loved. She was lucky.

I couldn't even daydream of doing what I wanted and to make things worse, everyone at school could hardly shut up about career decision these days.

We had the rest of our lives doing what they said, what was the point in wondering about the 'what ifs'? We were only likely to end up disappointed. I knew I would be. Nothing would match going to Science Academy. Being amongst the teams of the brightest in the country working to engineer new medicines to treat the sick, new inventions to get our lives back to something approaching what they had been before everything fell apart. In the words of Sir Isaac Newton, 'standing on the shoulders of giants'. Did those scientists realise how lucky they were?

I'd be like my dad. If he was still alive he'd be doing something he didn't want because there was no use now for the architect he'd once been.

I pushed thoughts of career decision away because it always ended with me getting in a state about the 'what ifs' for Jace. I'd never said anything to him but I worried that the military would want him. He looked threatening enough without a weapon, how could they not? Which would be all wrong considering he was the gentlest person I knew.

And, being totally selfish, how would I not go crazy if he got sent away? He was the only person I could talk to.

A moaning came from my left. Through a gap in clumsily-closed curtains, I could see a white-haired lady clutching at her blanket. The metallic clanging of something dropped shattered the murmuring of restrained conversation, made me jump.

Mum led me to an empty cubicle and washed her hands. I let her fuss over my cut for a few minutes, not wanting to upset her again.

"You're probably borderline for stitches. Does it hurt when I do this?" She pressed around the wound.

I shook my head. "Steri-strips are fine." I finally forced myself to ask the question. "Did Jace tell you about the doctors?"

"That you couldn't get a new bottle?"

"That I saw a computer message saying supplies of Coralone had been withdrawn. Why would it say that? There are lots of people like Sebastian who need it to—" I censored myself. I'd just thought the message was messed-up but the look of shock on her face really scared me.

"What is it, Mum?"

"There's been some kind of mistake, that's all." She sounded sure enough, but she looked all at odds with what she was saying. "Computers are only as good as their operator. I'll sort it out in the morning." Something in her tone, a desperation I often felt from her over Sebastian made me feel worse than ever. I opened my mouth but didn't know what to say.

"There, I'm done." Her efficiency saved me. "Let's get you some dressings."

She led me down the corridor away from the treatment area, following red arrows on the floor to the Dispensary. Venetian blinds pulled shut behind the glass reinforced the 'closed' sign.

"Mum." I lowered my voice, even though I couldn't hear anyone near us. "There's Coralone in there, isn't there?"

"Of course—what does it matter? We can't take it."

I looked up and down the empty corridor. "What about borrowing a little bit, just a few spoonfuls?"

"And then what? A few more? Whatever way you try to justify it, it's still stealing." She covered her left hand with her right. I hated that she'd caught my glance at her personal reminder that the Government didn't tolerate stealing. "I brought you up better than that." she said as if she had never been caught and punished.

She punched numbers on the keypad and the door clicked open. "Of course I've thought of that but I'd be caught and sent away and you'd end up in a community home. And that kind of place would kill Sebastian. Believe me if I could, I would, even after . . ." She put her hands behind her back. "But there's no way we can take it."

"What about me? They don't search the patients, do they?"

She sighed. "Just trust me that we cannot steal it. I need to be here to care for Sebastian. There's no one else to fight for him."

She hugged me. Since I'd shot up our hugs had gone backwards, with me feeling sometimes like I was the adult, and that Mum took comfort from me. It felt odd but it was okay. We didn't hug often but we both needed to feel the warmth of another human's touch. Everyone did.

"I'm sorry I shouted before. I just worry."

The understatement of the century.

"I wish you didn't."

"It's what mums do. I'll get your dressings."

Even though she rushed off as if a cure for Sebastian was behind the Dispensary door, I noticed her tears. Although I wouldn't have thought it possible, I seemed to have made things a whole lot worse somehow.

CHAPTER ELEVEN

What was that noise? My alarm already? Wasn't it still the middle of the night? I opened one eye and was almost blinded by the sunlight streaming into my room. Yep, morning.

I kicked at my top sheet, trying to disentangle it from around my legs, pulled at my vest top to unwrap it from where it had corseted me when I'd rolled about. I always seemed to move around as much when I slept as I did during the day but last night appeared to have been worse than usual as I'd fought the replays of the raid we'd witnessed.

All through my shower I couldn't help rerunning it. What could those people have done to make the Government respond in that way? And had four armed soldiers breaking into that house like they had really been necessary – who would stand up to one? And that guard last night hadn't tried very hard to get the injured man to leave before he started with the violence.

The Government might be looking out for us but sometimes I caught myself thinking that they didn't need to always be so heavy handed. Most of us lived our lives from a position of fear as it was.

I poked my head around Sebastian's door, half dreading what I might find. But he was asleep how he always slept, like a hospital patient in a straight line, arms neatly by his sides. Thankfully his breathing was regular, unlaboured and he was only slightly flushed, not burning.

"Atta boy, keep fighting." I whispered.

Even though the kitchen window and back door were open, no breeze stirred the thick air. No storm yet then. We could enjoy one more day of sunshine. The smell of freshly made toast taunted my hunger.

"Thought I heard you." Still in her nurse's uniform, Mum pushed a plate of toast towards me. A globule of rich yellow butter nestled on the top piece, swimming in its own little sea. The sight of it made my mouth water.

"Butter?" It was more a sigh than a question.

"Esther gave us some yesterday. I know how much you like it."

"Thanks." I bit into the toast, licked at the warm stream that ran down my chin. Heaven. Not least because it reinforced that she loved me. Because she'd never told us, sometimes in the routine of our lives it was easy to forget she did, until a gesture like this reminded me. For her to allow what was practically contraband in the house was a huge deal. I knew she wouldn't have any and she'd be jumpy until we'd eaten it all, as if she expected a GI to be able to see through the walls and arrest her for breaking food regulations. I knew why she was always so careful to obey the rules but she never questioned anything – I swear if the Government told us to stop breathing, she'd try.

She rummaged in the cupboard above the kettle. The space where Sebastian's Coralone always stood accused me with its emptiness. I looked away, watching Mum getting out our vitamin pills instead.

"This is so good there shouldn't be a law against it." I reached for the second piece.

"Government food guidelines aren't really laws."

"If they won't let us have something what difference

does it make if it's a law or not?"

"They're only trying to help us stay healthy." She put three different coloured pills by my plate.

"I know, they taught us about the obese population at school. But they should trust us to decide for ourselves. We don't need to be nannied about everything."

"Maya!" Mum gestured at the open window and door, mouthing the words, 'she'll hear'.

I shrugged. "That's hardly anti-Government."

She shot me a dark look. "And who do you think would be the judge of that? You?"

I changed the subject. "Do you want me to stay home to mind Sebastian so you can sleep."

"No, Maya, you have to go to school."

She opened a jar and scooped out two preserved plums for me.

Whenever plums were first harvested their sharp taste was so welcome after a year without them but it was always the same, we got fed up eating them before they were replaced by apples and pears and we got tired of them before they were done while we waited for next year's berry crop. Most of the summer had been so grey and dull September's blackberry crop would be rubbish, again, and it had already been three years since we'd had blackberry jam. I could hardly remember the taste of bananas now and what I wouldn't give for my favourite, passionfruit.

I knew the Government's insistence that it wasn't safe to try and re-establish contact with anyone elsewhere in the world was once valid. But still? We'd had things really bad here and we were recovering. If the rest of the world had got away more lightly than us, wouldn't they be mostly back to how they'd been before the pandemic? Or were we the only ones left?

I pushed that last thought away, as I always did when it surfaced, and concentrated on my plums.

The food might be monotonous but at least lately

we'd had enough. It was almost as if mum hadn't been punished. Taking her finger hadn't been enough for them, they kept taking from her every month in the form of reduced food and clothing points, reduced cash. For someone who abhorred stealing, the Government seemed to do a lot of it.

But somehow she'd found a way to get by. I shouldn't begrudge her the extra shifts I had to babysit Sebastian. It wasn't much of a life for her. Unwilling to make friends because her one shameful lapse marked her to everyone as someone not to be trusted. Working and sleeping and working and sleeping with no end in sight because Sebastian wouldn't be able to work. If he even reached the age of career decision.

"Promise me you'll sleep." I mumbled around my last mouthful.

She nodded.

"What about getting the Coralone?" I almost cringed as I said it, hoping the mention of last night's disaster wouldn't set her off again.

She stacked my clean plate in the dish drainer. "Esther's offered to sit with Sebastian, I'll go to the doctors then if I have to I'll see if I can borrow some from the nearby families."

"I thought I'd try the Restons, they're on the way to school."

She nodded. "Thanks. Take your pills." She disappeared into her bedroom.

When I was sure her door was closed, I pulled a crumpled envelope from my backpack and slipped the pills inside to join my week's ration. Sliding the envelope away, I blobbed sun block on my arms, rubbing it in as I walked down the garden. The sun already felt strong, as though it would burn me even before I got the cream rubbed in. On days like this I could believe the Government spiel about global warming. It was much harder in the winter when it rained or snowed for days and the sky disappeared behind a grey wall for so many months we forgot it was blue.

Jace appeared at our back gate. "What's all that anti-Government propaganda I could hear from your house this morning?"

"It wasn't anti-Government anything, it was common sense."

"You should be careful of open doors and windows, you don't know who's listening."

I picked up my bike and winced.

"Still sore?"

"Been better." I looked at the dressing, no sign of any blood, at least the Steri-strips were holding.

Jace took my bike and pushed it out the gate, leaning it next to his. "Why're you up so early? I know you don't mind exams but this is keen even for you."

"I've got something I need to do before school. I may have another way to get some Coralone."

"Are you asking Toby?"

I sighed inwardly at the careful tone in which Jace always spoke about him. As far as I knew, they'd never met so it couldn't be that he didn't like him personally.

"No." At least not now. But if this plan didn't pan out, I would be.

I dropped my voice. I knew Jace wouldn't like me asking him this but I didn't have anyone else to ask. "What happens to people who steal?"

He looked utterly horrified. "You're not—"

"Of course not. I just wondered if you knew." I was really asking why Mum had been so adamant she wouldn't borrow any Coralone. If we put it back it wouldn't be stealing and if it would save Sebastian's life . . . I didn't get it.

"Because we all know not to steal I'm guessing the punishment would be worse than taking fingers like they used to, a hand maybe, the person . . ." He picked at the grip on his handlebars. I don't think I'd ever heard him say the word 'disappeared'. He struggled to talk about the

48

barbarism in our lives as if he expected it to touch us if he mentioned it. He looked at me as though he might read what I planned through my eyes if he looked hard enough. "Maya, you can't—"

"I'm not, really. I just wondered."

"Don't. Ever."

I smiled, tried to lighten the moment. "I won't even think about it. Promise." The word slipped out. Damnit, now I was breaking a promise to Jace.

CHAPTER TWELVE

"You took off in a hurry." Jace caught me up easily as I biked away after school. My legs still ached from the hard ride to and from the doctors last night.

"Had enough today." It seemed easier than explaining it all to him.

"But that test was okay, wasn't it? And if I thought that, you must have aced it."

Jace, the master of irony.

I hesitated. What would he say if I told him the truth that I'd fallen asleep during the exam and then in the panic of worrying about Sebastian and only having half an hour to finish the paper, I accidentally answered the questions at the level at which I'd been studying on my own, answers light years ahead of what we'd actually learnt?

After years of pretending I was averagely intelligent, I'd let the mask slip and now whoever read my answer paper would fast track me to Science Academy.

I wanted to scream. The unlucky breaks life had been dealing me had derailed into outright cruelty. My dream for so long was now just within my reach. But I couldn't take it because I couldn't leave Mum to cope with Sebastian by herself.

"Maya?" I tried for a smile but Jace could see right through me. "You worried about Sebastian?"

"It's always Sebastian." God, it wasn't Jace's fault. He was the last person I should be snapping at. "Sorry, today's been . . . hard."

"You want to talk about it?"

Yes, I really did but the minute I opened my mouth I knew I wouldn't be able to hold it all together. I shook my head and we rode on in silence.

As we approached the roundabout leading home, I dropped back letting Jace take the exit on the right while I rode off left.

"Where you going?" He caught me up again. "You know there's a curfew again, right?"

The air felt warm against my skin. There was no way the few clouds filtering the sunshine into a hazy wash of light could bring a storm worthy of a curfew.

"I won't be long." There was no way I ever wanted to be out late enough to remotely be worried about a curfew deadline again.

"Is it something for Sebastian?" Jace asked. "Maya, you're not?"

Why did he have to ask me directly? Now he'd be upset with me. "I'm going to Toby's because I couldn't get any Coralone this morning." Donna Reston had been way sicker than Sebastian, I couldn't bring myself to ask to borrow as much as a spoonful.

"You're going to get in trouble, you keep going there."

I braked. We were on the flat and still I felt breathless. I couldn't ride and have this argument at the same time. "I don't *keep* going there."

"At least once a week, that counts as keeps going. How long do you think you can do that before someone reports you?"

"I'm only tutoring his daughter, that's not really anything criminal." I couldn't quite look at him. Not

51

wanting my next-door neighbour or Mum to know proved I knew it wasn't absolutely okay.

"You put yourself at risk once a week for what?" Jace asked.

I pulled in a deep breath, hoping forbearance would be right there amongst the oxygen. I got plenty in return for tutoring Jessica but Jace would never understand, he'd get angry over me putting myself in danger for something he considered unimportant. And telling him would feel like betraying Toby and even though it was Jace, the only person I completely trusted, a secret only stayed that way if only the participants knew it.

I was being selfish too. I didn't want to do anything that might persuade Toby to stop getting papers for me. I didn't understand why they were contraband. They'd left more books available at the libraries than they'd taken away so what difference could reading old research make? But all I had to go on was what I was told, mostly not enough about mostly the wrong things. The Government was the ultimate control freak.

A group of 'popular' girls from our year rode past us, ignoring us both. It was like we didn't exist. Well, me anyway, one of them turned round and looked at Jace. He didn't seem to notice.

"I know you don't like Toby, Jace, but right now he's probably my best hope to get more Coralone." I pulled my pedal round, ready to ride off.

"But you don't know if you need to see him. Your mum probably got some today."

"What if she didn't?" And if she hadn't there was no way she could ever entertain visiting a black marketeer, so this was down to me. "And even if she did, we could do with a spare, in case what we saw on that computer is true."

I hated the look on Jace's face, as though I'd hurt him on purpose. I didn't know what it was with him and Toby. If anyone was to blame for the black market, it was the

Government who had created the niche for black marketeers when they got so tight with food rations. If they'd kept everyone on the points system they'd brought in when our economy crashed instead of reintroducing cash, the black market would never have begun. And now Toby was a lifeline for my sanity – I might not be able to be a scientist, but I could at least read like one.

"I'll see you back at home, I won't be long." Don't give me a hard time, I almost added.

"I'll come with you." He had his stubborn look on.

"Actually I was kind of hoping you'd let Mum know I'll be back a bit late?" I did need to get a message to her, it wasn't really a lie.

"You'd rather go on your own?"

"I'd rather she knew I won't be long, after last night . . ."

I could see the argument he was having with himself playing out over his face "Okay, I'll tell her."

"Thanks, Jace. I really appreciate it."

I felt conscious of his gaze on me as I pulled away but resisted the urge to turn around because I couldn't bear to see his disappointment in me reflected on his face.

CHAPTER THIRTEEN

The gaggle of populars had congregated at the turn off to Furzton Lake. Why there? Now I had to ride right past them. I always felt so awkward and geeky near them, conscious they would be laughing at me, talking about me, and not in a nice way. I tried to pretend I hadn't seen them but I was a lousy actress. Each of my movements was stiff and wooden, easily fodder for more laughing. My face had only just stopped burning when I got to Toby's road but it flared up again when I realised Kevin Fook was walking across the front garden of the house next door but one to Toby.

Not that he'd notice me, despite having sat behind me in the stupid exam today. We moved in totally different orbits, he was a popular, I was a nerd, we were like a doctor and a flu carrier. It was stupid me even fancying him. Especially if by some major miracle he noticed me and asked me out, how could I ever go anywhere with him when I had to look after Sebastian?

His sister had been at the same pain clinic as Sebastian last year. I could pop in and see if Mum had visited them after I'd seen Toby.

I'd scarcely dropped my bike outside his neighbour's

than she'd materialised beside me. "You can't leave that there."

"It's not actually on your property."

"What if I want to go out? I might fall over it."

I looked at the expanse of road between the woman's house and the other side of the street. Four pedicabs could have lined up side by side across it, at least where there weren't any rusting cars. She was scrawny, she could have easily fitted in between the gaps left either side of the cabs. But I only said "I'll just be a few minutes."

"That's all it'll take for me to report it."

She'd report something that banal? Surely that wouldn't warrant a follow-up visit by a Government representative to reinforce good citizenship? But when it came down to it, I didn't want to take the chance.

I dragged my bike to the end of the road. "Can you walk around it now without falling over it?" I muttered.

There was nothing wrong with her hearing. "There's no need to be sarcastic, young lady. Teenagers, you're all the same."

I sucked in a deep breath and forced my feet to take me past her up Toby's path.

"Don't think I haven't seen you going in that place." She spat the last two words as though Toby's house was responsible for every wrong in the world. "There's only trouble there. You should stay away."

I walked up Toby's steps. "Thanks but I can make up my own mind about my friends."

"That man's no friend of yours. Consider yourself warned, I can't be responsible for what the authorities do about people who won't toe the line."

I stopped. People spying on each other was so wrong. I wouldn't argue with her, even though she had everything backwards. I climbed the rest of the steps.

"Going in there will only get you a whole boatload of trouble." she went on.

I knocked at Toby's door, spelling out with body

language that I wasn't listening.

"It's coming, sure as this storm." Would she just stop?

The door opened and I nearly flattened the person on the other side in my hurry to get in and close it behind me. All the doors on the ground floor were shut, bringing an early night to the hallway, perfectly camouflaging the dark skin of whoever had answered the door. I could hear the faint whirring of an air conditioning unit. The coolness felt delicious on my skin.

"You're supposed to wait to be invited." Toby said.

I cringed, I didn't ever want to do anything to upset him. "Sorry, I thought your neighbour was going to follow me in."

Toby looked through the spy hole in his front door. "You want more papers already? Girl, you gotta learn to read slower."

"I brought the last one back."

"Can't take it today. You need to go." He peered through the spy hole again.

"Can I just ask you something quick for my brother? He needs some Coralone, his medicine."

"See what I can do. Cost might be an issue. You're the second person to ask for it today. Seems it's a seller's market."

"I'll pay the highest for it. I've got these for you anyway." I pulled out the envelope containing my vitamins.

"Not today, bring them Friday. I can work on getting this medicine but you need to understand what I'm saying here, no teaching can settle that cost. We clear?"

I ran my thumb and index finger down the side of my envelope. Sebastian needed his medicine, and he didn't have it because of me. What I might have to pay was kind of irrelevant.

One of the first times I'd come to tutor Jessica I remembered seeing one of Toby's guys throw a bucket of water over a sticky mess at the bottom of his steps. A sticky mess that looked a lot like blood. I shivered, the memory pulled goosebumps up on my arms, across the back of my neck. Even the Roman charm that I never normally noticed because I wore it every day, suddenly felt cold against my skin. I couldn't trust that Toby wouldn't take payment like that but I had to believe I might be worth more to him in other ways. I probably didn't want to know about them either.

"We're clear," my voice caught. I tried to swallow my fear away.

His lips pulled back from his teeth, part grin, part grimace. "Almost on schedule. Out the back. Army's here, I'm about to be raided."

CHAPTER FOURTEEN

Toby opened a door to a room that seemed to lead directly into the sun. It was actually a kitchen in full sunlight, packed with shiny gadgets. "Right out the gate and you're on your own. You never was here."

"Will you be okay?" I asked.

He laughed. Bizarrely now that the authorities were about to knock at his door, he'd visibly relaxed. "'S all a game we play. They know their rules, I know mine. But they won't be kind to anyone they catch from here so run fast."

I shot out of the back door, through the gate into a narrow strip of wild hedgerow. Who'd have thought this was here? Toby probably cultivated it on purpose. Brambles and bushes snagged at my arms and legs, trying to hold onto me. I crouched down below the level of the fence and forced my way through. This was creepy, déjà-vu from last night on the roundabout messed with my sense of reality. I'd never been so up close and personal with nature as in the last two days. More scratches to explain away.

Shouts from behind me. I flashed a look in their direction but the greenery hid my pursuers. As long as that worked both ways. The fence on the right became a gate. Toby's obnoxious neighbour. I crouched lower, wanting to pass the woman's boundary as invisibly as possible.

Was that why she'd kept on at me? She'd been trying to warn me? Which made her amazingly brave or idiotically stupid. If Toby knew who'd reported on him . .

Tearing and snapping of foliage behind me. The soldiers were fighting the many-tentacled greenery too. I heard shouts of 'stop!' I kept seeing the jagged scar scored in the metal of my bike. My skin had never felt so fragile, my body so vulnerable. If their bullets did that to metal . . . I struggled through gaps that weren't there, wrenching myself free of the twigs and thorns that snagged me.

I felt rather than heard something zing past. A crack from behind. They were shooting? They were shooting at me?

Another gate appeared on my right. The shouts were louder now, bolder, as if they knew they'd catch me. If they fired now . . . I threw myself through the gate.

Bare-chested, Kevin Fook looked up from his sunbed. I tried not to look at his six-pack but suddenly I couldn't look at anything else.

"Hi, Kevin, sorry to just barge in. I'm Maya, from school." He laid back down again and shut his eyes even before I finished blushing. At least he didn't notice me looking for non-existent locks. Tremors of movement bobbed the fence. I only had a few seconds. Desperation shattered my normal Kevin-induced awkwardness. I practically hurdled the veggie beds, swung my backpack off and knelt down beside him, facing the gate. The recently turned earth moulded itself around my knees like a warm blanket.

"Can you do me a favour?" I asked.

"Depends." He didn't even open his eyes.

I couldn't believe I was going to say it until I heard the words come out of my mouth. "Kiss me."

"What?" He opened his eyes then, wide, and laughed.

He sounded a bit nervous. But how could the most eligible popular be nervous of kissing me?

"I heard at school that you're the best, just wanted to see if it was true." Where was this coming from? Up until now I could barely think of him without going bright red and now I was being so bold? The certainty of being arrested was a wonderful motivator.

Kevin pushed himself up on one elbow "You heard that? In your face, George." He laughed at his best friend, the one most girls drooled over. "I could show you, you're pretty hot for a nerd."

I heard the gate latch rattle. They were here.

I leant over the distance between us. My heart beat hard against my ribs as though looking for a way out but it was nothing to do with him. In all the scenarios I'd imagined of this moment, not one had involved the military. Or had him kissing me to cement his prowess. I was shaking so much there was no way Kevin wouldn't be able to not feel it. Hopefully he'd just think I was overwhelmed by him.

Our lips met as the gate opened and a soldier burst into the garden. That ought to do it. Long enough for him to misread the situation perfectly. I pulled away, leaning backwards, tucking my arms behind me to hide my scratches.

"What now?" Kevin's anger tailed away when he saw the soldier's gun pointed at him.

"We're looking for fugitives." The soldier looked around the garden.

Kevin spread his hands. "No one here but us. Can't you see I'm trying to get it on here, mate?"

The soldier looked at me and back at Kevin. I returned his gaze as though I was just a kid with nothing to hide. I hoped.

"ID."

Oh God, how could I show it without the soldier seeing the scratches on my arms? And as soon as he saw them . . . I pretended to rummage in my backpack for my ID, trying to hide my arms, frantically juggling scenarios, shuffling closer to Kevin and the shadows beneath his sunbed. While the soldier was checking Kevin's I flicked mine onto Kevin's legs, hoping he wouldn't question what I was doing. Kevin held it out for inspection.

Another soldier burst into the garden. "Next door's clear."

The first nodded. "Who's inside?"

"My mum and my sick sister."

The soldier gestured with his gun at his partner and then at the house. "Check it out."

The second soldier hesitated but did as ordered. My backwards stance was killing my wrists, the cut on my palm throbbed, pins and needles were gathering in my legs, I wouldn't be able to sit like this for much longer. I tried not to let the effort of holding the position show on my face.

Just as I knew I had to move, the second soldier came back. "As he said. No one else here."

The first soldier threw our IDs at Kevin and they left. I waited half a minute in case the bramble hedge's solidity past Kevin's gate gave me away, then eased my arms forward, stretched my legs out in front of me.

"One thing Jasmine's good for. So where were we?" Kevin tossed my ID to me.

I pocketed it. "You were on your sunbed and I was going to see Jasmine."

"But what about showing you I'm as good as people say."

"I'm sure you are, but I really did come here to see your sister." From the look on his face, he truly didn't believe me.

I stumbled as I walked towards the house. Fight and flight had flown off, leaving me with legs that had apparently forgotten how to hold me up.

"If my mum asks, I am weeding the veggies." Kevin

called.

I knocked at the back door suddenly fighting tears. What was wrong with me? I'd got away from the soldiers, Toby would get Coralone and in the meantime Jasmine might have some I could take home right now. Why was my body behaving like everything had fallen apart?

CHAPTER FIFTEEN

I stood outside the head's door. My stomach still felt as though it were trying to knit itself into something. If I'd felt sick since my exam yesterday worrying about this summons, that was nothing to how I felt now I'd actually been called here.

What if they offered me a place at Science Academy right now? Everything I ever wanted since I first heard its name there for me to take. Would I be strong enough to turn it down?

"Maya, I think Miss Pattershall wants to see us *in* her office." Mrs Randle rapped at the door and opened it, gesturing me in ahead of her.

I'd never been called here before. I would have expected her office to be as primly groomed as the head herself but papers were strewn in erratic piles everywhere, books stacked haphazardly on every surface. Miss Pattershall sat behind her desk, her hands clasped. The lines on her face wrinkled together in well-practised furrows – she looked as though she'd just been offered sweeping the streets as career decision.

Two Government Inspectors stood behind her, their shirts and ties a better match to the cooler weather today now the grey ceiling of cloud had returned. People were already joking that the last two days had been our summer. The Inspectors stared at me too. This would happen the week they were here. I could feel a flush crawling over my cheeks. Had I turned green? Grown an extra head? Were they all just going to stand and stare? This wasn't awkward at all.

We heard a tentative knock and Mrs Randle opened the door.

"Sorry I'm late, I had to find a baby-sitter for my son."

"Mum!" Oh no, that was the worst thing they could have done. She was bound to make a scene. She'd think I aced the test on purpose. Why had Miss Pattershall dragged her here?

Mum still looked a bit spaced out, like she had last night when we were comparing blanks with borrowing Coralone. It still freaked me out to think of how sick Jasmine Fook and Donna Reston had been, and they had Coralone. Mum had spent practically the whole day visiting all the families she could physically get to to see if anyone could spare any. But she'd found the same as me and neither of us could begrudge that no one would share a drop.

And both of us were too frightened to ask where that left Sebastian.

"Do you have anything to say for yourself?" Miss Pattershall asked. She didn't seem very excited or pleased.

If she wanted me to explain how I'd got hold of the texts I'd used in my exam answers, I wouldn't rat Toby out. I shook my head.

"Not even to explain how you did it?" Same clipped response as though she didn't have time to finish her words properly.

I couldn't answer that either. I might have admitted to tutoring someone if the Inspectors hadn't been in the room, their gazes practically branding me, but I couldn't say anything that might lead them in Toby's direction. I shook my head again.

"Maya, it'll be easier if you tell the real truth—" Mrs Randle began.

"For goodness sake. Tell the head what she wants to know." Mum now looked as angry as when I'd dropped Sebastian's medicine.

"I would but I don't understand what she's asking."

"Let me spell it out for you." Miss Pattershall ground out. "I want to know how you cheated on your science paper."

What was she talking about? "Cheating, what cheating?"

"Don't play the innocent with me. Your academic performance at this school has been remarkably sustained. Roughly ten per cent higher than the pass mark in every subject, in every exam, and suddenly in a burst of genius, you're answering science questions with information the teachers are struggling to understand. In all my years of teaching, I've never seen anything so reckless, only a few months from career decision. You do know what kind of jobs they assign troublemakers?" Miss Pattershall stopped to draw breath.

'Cheat', it was the only word I could hear. I would never have dreamt they could be so wrong. How could they even think that? Didn't any of them know me at all? "I didn't cheat, I would never do that."

"Explain these answers to me then."

"Maya, tell the truth." Mum thought I'd cheated too. Brilliant.

I stood straighter, pretending I wasn't hurt by their mistake. "I am telling the truth, why would I need to cheat – I could answer those exam questions years ago."

"Take off your dressing." One of the inspectors nodded at my hand.

Did he think I was that stupid? "So you can fine me for having an undressed wound in public?"

"For our purposes we can overlook that."

"It's okay, Maya." Mrs Randle was the only one still speaking kindly to me.

I unwound the bandage, pooled the gauze in my good hand and held it out.

"And that." He pointed at the pad that protected the Steri-strips. I peeled it off. He peered at my hand. The cut still looked angry, the Steri-strips stark against my skin. "Is this the dressing you had on yesterday?"

"Of course not. I know the rules."

"But only abide by some of them apparently. It seems to run in the family." He'd noticed Mum's hand. I could feel the shame burning on her face from where I stood. "Do you still have yesterday's bandage?"

Mum looked even more mortified. "It'll be in our rubbish."

"I'll need to accompany you to collect it."

This was ridiculous. "I can save you the trouble." I snapped. "I didn't write answers on my bandage. Don't you think Mrs Randle would have noticed me unwrapping it in the middle of the exam? Wouldn't you have noticed?"

"Enough," Miss Pattershall said. "You're suspended—"

As hard as 'cheat' was to hear, it was nothing compared to 'suspended'. "But I haven't done anything wrong."

"Then tell me how you came to be in possession of this knowledge and how you got it into the examination room." Miss Patershall said.

I bit the inside of my lips, holding in the truth I wanted to shout out. Miss Pattershall pushed herself to her feet to deliver her verdict.

"You're suspended, you're banned from all further exams and from the school premises. When we confirm that you've been cheating you will be expelled. You should know that I would have expelled you already but Mrs Randle persuaded me to take a softer approach.

Congratulations Miss Flint, you have successfully crucified your career decision."

CHAPTER SIXTEEN

Finally I turned into our road. Pushing my bike home one-handed would have been bad enough on my own but walking all that way feeling the menace the Inspector represented marching along behind made it ten times worse. The pedal smacked the back of my calf again. Godamnit, if it did that one more time, I'd ride home and sod his orders.

I fed my bike through our back gate, the clumsy rebandaging of my hand that I'd managed making it difficult.

"Stay here while I retrieve the evidence." the Inspector said. He followed Mum inside.

Evidence? Was this going to develop into a criminal trial?

I slumped down on my backpack and stared up at my bedroom window. There didn't seem any point in looking at my books.

That guy shouldn't have the power to go through my stuff without me being there. I didn't know if the rumours were true but surely he wouldn't plant anything on me. I was just a kid accused of a petty crime, hardly worth any bother. He didn't need to send any more of a message to the school community – news of my suspension at assembly tomorrow would be enough deterrent.

My backpack made a lousy seat. I shifted my weight to the right, to the left, stood up, sat down on the path, stretched my legs out, forced myself to sit still. I didn't want to let him see this was bothering me.

Thank God I'd never shown Mum where the corner of my bedroom carpet lifted up from the gripper rod, where I hid the papers from Toby. Up until now she'd never questioned why I kept my room so clean and tidy. I hoped the inspector wasn't telling her the real reason that I didn't want her finding anything secret or contraband or both. Best she didn't know that.

What was he doing up there? Had I left anything out of place this morning? No, I was sure it was all as it should be, my hiding place camouflaged by the overspill from my bookcase. But what would happen if he found it?

I kept myself still, resting my chin in my hand. Keeping the stroppy teenager look on my face was getting harder every minute. The concrete leached cold into my legs, the sunbaked warmth from yesterday vanished completely.

Mum appeared at the back door. "He's gone, you can stop sulking."

I snatched up my backpack and marched into the house. Mum had put the kettle on.

"You think I'm sulking?" So much for my self-control, my hope not to argue today.

"Aren't you? Cheating, Maya? How did you ever think you could get away with it?"

She really believed I'd cheated. I couldn't tell what hurt more, having sacrificed my dream or Mum being so ready to doubt me. Maybe it was all rolled up into the same thing. "You really don't know me at all, do you?"

"Do you know how embarrassing it is to watch a Government official rifle through our rubbish, through our home because you think you can buck the system?"

She threw the tea strainer on her mug and dumped a spoonful of herbal tea in it.

"I'm being falsely accused of something I'd never do and this is all about *your* embarrassment?" I took a deep breath trying to hang onto my calm. "What did he do?"

"Took away your dirty bandages, searched your room."

I was halfway up the stairs when she yelled, actually yelled, me back. "You see what happens when you do what you want? God only knows what you've done to your career decision. We were counting on your income, how selfish can you be?"

I marched back into the kitchen. "Selfish? How can you call me selfish?" I swallowed hard, hoping I could beat the angry tears that threatened. "Do you know how I aced that stupid exam? I studied hard, on my own, like I have been for the last three years."

Mum slopped boiling water into her cup, sending as much over the worktop. "I don't know of any sixteen-year-old who would study that much."

That hurt. She really didn't know me. I might have hidden the scientific papers from her, but all she ever saw me do was homework or read. "What else can I do when I'm stuck here practically every minute I'm not at school? I can't have friends like everyone else, I can't go out. I study, so I'm smart. Smart enough to go to Science Academy."

She looked up from mopping the spill, the shock on her face real.

"I hid it from you, from everyone. You heard Miss Pattershall. I've been very careful not to do anything exceptional because I know I can't go, because you need me here. I've sacrificed the only thing I've ever wanted for you so don't call me selfish."

"We all have our duty to bear, you're not the only one who's made sacrifices." She scrubbed harder at the spill.

"Looking after Sebastian's not a duty, he's my

brother—"

"We're a family. Families help each other." She threw her tea into the sink with such force it smacked against the metal. "I'm going in early. This conversation is over. You won't mention Science Academy again. Chasing things you can't have will only make you unhappy."

My room was a mess, my duvet heaped on the floor, my mattress half off the bed. He'd emptied the bookcase and thrown my books everywhere. Drawers were open, the contents hanging half out. Clothes in the wardrobe were ripped off the hangers, what little childhood memorabilia I had was tipped out. All that was missing was graffiti scrawled over the walls. The Inspector had even left behind the smell of him – a waft of stale male sweat. It made me shudder.

I closed the door and pushed my dressing gown against the crack at the bottom. It might slow Mum down if she decided to continue the argument. I moved the books in the corner out of the way and scrabbled at the carpet. Thank God he hadn't found the paper. I pressed my fingers to it then covered it up, stacking books on top of the replaced carpet, returning most of the rest to their shelves so the tidy pile didn't look out of place. I could repair the other damage later.

Suspended. The word came from nowhere, catching me like a blow to the ribs. Miss Pattershall had suspended and wanted to expel me and Mum believed the worst of me. Just because of that I wanted to go to Mrs Randle and tell her the truth, ask her to put me forward to Science Academy. I pulled in a deep breath that did nothing to ease the hole within me.

I hung up my early warning system and opened the door, listening to how the house felt. Mum had gone. I checked the cupboard above the kettle but there was no brown bottle in there. Still no luck.

Sebastian lay on the sofa looking up at the ceiling.

"Hey, Rocket, how you doing? Had a good day?" I

asked.

"Auntie Esther came in to sit with me."

"That's nice." I felt his forehead, warmer I thought than before. "Did Mum get you more medicine?"

"No."

"How do you feel?"

"Shaky, bit strange."

That would be the lack of Coralone. I tried not to see Jasmine's or Donna's faces when I looked at him.

"Strange good or strange bad?" I asked.

"How can strange be good?"

"Sometimes it is, like the planets Rocket visits. They're strange but in a good way."

"I don't like books about Rocket anymore, they're babyish."

I didn't mention the Rocket book on the table next to him. "You're getting so grown up. You'd better not grow taller than me." It was a game we played but today he didn't want to take his part. He looked a little wild-eyed.

I sat on the edge of the sofa. "I'm sorry you heard Mum and me arguing. It didn't mean anything," I rushed on, hoping he wouldn't catch the lie. "We were just venting, you know, getting out our frustrations but it wasn't right to do it where you could hear us."

"Is it better to say those things when I can't hear them?"

Damn, he was sharp. "No, of course not, that's not what I meant. But you know what I said about going out with friends, I didn't mean it. I like staying here with you, you know that, right? Without you I wouldn't be smart."

I tried a smile but it faded beneath the hard stare he'd perfected as a baby. He must realise I couldn't abandon him, not like Dad had, not like Mum appeared to be doing to me. Finally he nodded. I felt such a surge of relief fill me, it made me feel a little shaky.

"Cool. Now, hug, dinner, then game?"

Sebastian smiled. I hugged him, thankful for where I

was and with whom for the first time that day. And for that moment I wouldn't fret at how I seemed to be destroying everything in my life because nothing else could possibly go wrong.

CHAPTER SEVENTEEN

This was a bad idea. A really bad idea. If Miss Pattershall found me outside my form room only a day after she'd suspended me, no prizes for guessing what she'd do. I'd say what I'd come to say and go. I tapped at the door and walked into the classroom.

"Maya!" Mrs Randle looked surprised and horrified.

"I know I'm not supposed to be here. I waited till now so no one would see me."

"Come in quickly, before someone does."

As if me shutting the door was a catalyst, the lights went out. Storm clouds plunged the classroom into an early dusk.

"Again!" Mrs Randle rummaged in her bag. "It must be getting bad out there. I've got candles, hold on."

A scraping and then the hissing flare of a match lit up her face. She tipped the candle sideways letting melted wax drip onto her desk and pressed it into the liquid pool.

"Why are you here, Maya, you'll only make things worse for yourself if Miss Pattershall sees you."

"I know." I'd tried all day to talk myself out of coming but it seemed I could be pretty persuasive. "I don't want to get you into trouble. I just wanted, it's important to me that you know the truth."

Mrs Randle gestured at the front desk. "I know you didn't cheat."

I sat. "You do?"

"I see how you carefully word your answers so that you don't appear to know all the topic. Playing to not seem over intelligent, that's a real skill." Mrs Randle looked at me over the candle flame, her grey eyes gentle. "Why wouldn't you tell Miss Pattershall the truth?"

"It's all kind of irrelevant because I can't go to Science Academy. My mum needs me to help take care of my brother."

"Sometimes you need to put yourself first, Maya. You only have this one life, such as it is. Being noble isn't all it's cracked up to be. You need to look out for yourself, because in all probability no one else will." All well and good but all well and impossible. "It would be such a waste for you not to go. Have you ever thought what you'd like to do there?"

Wasn't it obvious? "Find a cure for my brother." I whispered.

"Scientists get paid the most because they're the future of our country. I'm sure it could be arranged for you to send your mum money to pay someone to mind him. The obstacles you're putting in your way can all be surmounted."

"It isn't an option for me." I couldn't let myself believe there could be a way. Hoping and then losing it would be worse than resigning myself to not going at all.

"Isn't it your duty to help rebuild your country?"

The political rhetoric wasn't something I usually heard outside of info-casts. "Like I said, I don't have a choice."

"I may not have one either." Mrs Randle put a pile of exercise books into a cotton bag. "I can't let you throw your future away through a sense of misguided loyalty. It's not your place to care for your brother at the expense of your own life. I'm going to tell them the truth."

I knew I had to tell Mrs Randle not to but I couldn't form the words.

The classroom door slammed open.

"No one move!"

The warning wasn't really necessary. I was frozen trying to process what was happening. Two thin beams of powerful torchlight swathed through the gloom making me jump when they travelled up my face. The dim by comparison candlelight was enough for me to tell the torches were attached to weapons being wielded by two soldiers.

Soldiers, here at school? That wasn't right. Oh God, were they here for me? I lifted my hands into the air, surrendering. One advanced, his torchlight swinging from me to Mrs Randle. The pendulous beam seared the back of my eyes. Bright dots in my vision blinked themselves onto him.

"Up against the wall."

I followed the gesture of his torchlight, pressing myself into the wall as though I were trying to meld with it. He put his hand between my shoulder blades, holding me there.

They were going to arrest me? I'd imagined if Miss Pattershall had caught me here, she'd have had me thrown off the premises and expelled, but arrested?

"Jennifer Randle, you're under arrest under section 3 of the Right to Detain Act. You are required to co-operate with the authorities, choosing to remain silent will harm your defence and make you subject to further charges. A Government lawyer will be appointed to you. Do you understand these rights?"

Mrs Randle? They were arresting Mrs Randle? I spun around. The soldier slammed me back into the wall. "Did I say move?"

"No, sorry."

The cold hard metal of his gun dug into my skin.

"That convince you better?"

"I won't move again. Sorry, I'm sorry."

Oh God, what if his finger slipped on the trigger? The tiniest movement from me might be all it took. I could hardly breathe in case my ribcage moved. I willed my heart to stop racing in case the heartbeat-sized tremors through me were too much movement. Don't shoot me, please don't shoot me, I screamed in my head. I don't want to die. Please don't shoot me.

The snapping closed of handcuffs cracked the silence. I couldn't let them take Mrs Randle in my place. "You're making a mistake." My voice didn't sound like me at all.

There was an ominous click from the gun pressing against me. I tensed against it, suddenly desperate for the loo. My knees were giving way.

"Did I say speak?" The soldier stood too close, pinioning me against the wall. I could smell a primal body scent from him, a cloying sweetness on his breath as if he'd not long eaten something sugary.

"No," I shrank away from him and his gun. My mind still screamed please don't shoot me but my mouth said something completely different. "You shouldn't be taking her, it's me you want."

"Don't you know, the military doesn't make mistakes." He breathed on my neck. I felt a wave of nausea so strong I had to bite my lips together to hold it in. I felt clammy and wobbly, just like when I'd passed out.

"Can I leave a message for my husband?" Mrs Randle asked.

"No." the other soldier snapped.

"Please, he won't know where I am. This student here, she can—"

"I said no. You don't want to upset me making me repeat myself. Let's go."

"Please, it's me you want, not her." I wasn't sure he'd hear my broken whisper.

"Sarge." The soldier took a half-step away. It took

everything I had to stay upright. "We got the right one, yeah?"

"Jennifer Randle, twenty-eight, 5' 7", brown hair, grey eyes. I only see one in here like that. Let's go."

I heard scuffling across the floor.

"This one?" The soldier behind me asked.

"Nothing about her."

The gun pushed deeper into my back, then melted away. I folded to the floor but waited until the sound of boots had disappeared before I dared look round. I was alone.

I shuffled around until my back was against the wall and hugged my knees. Mrs Randle arrested. What could she possibly have done? She was so kind and genuinely wanted the best for people, how could she have done anything bad enough? She wasn't just my favourite teacher, she could have been a friend. What would happen to her now?

I pulled in a wobbly breath and another, trying to keep my stomach contents where they were. Should I tell Miss Pattershall? If she saw me on her precious school grounds, she might well call them back to take me too. But Mrs Randle's husband needed to know. The poor guy would be waiting for her, with no idea what had happened.

I stared at the flickering candle flame, letting it lull me into a trance-like state where there was nothing. No worries about my teacher, brother, mother, my future. Just the dancing flame. Peace of a kind.

Some time later, the lights burst back into life, stabbing at my night vision. When my sight readjusted, I got up and blew out the candle. My cheeks were wet, my head ached, I was filled with a dragging kind of dread. The exercise books Mrs Randle had been packing up were spilled everywhere. My hands had stopped shaking enough that I could get them into her bag. I'd go to the office, maybe the secretaries could send one of the runners to Mrs Randle's house to tell her husband, maybe I could get there before Mum's shift started - not knowing, having to guess what happened to the 'disappeareds' among us had to be the worse thing of all.

CHAPTER EIGHTEEN

I peered round the corner of Toby's road. It had been two days since he'd been raided and the street looked how it usually did. Quiet, unassuming, a distinct lack of anything military. A couple hurried down the road, their torchlight bobbing around on the pavement as they cast glances at the clouds boiling in the restless sky. When it broke, it was going to be a storm you wouldn't want to be out in. Score one for the Government meteorologists.

The couple turned out of the road, leaving me alone. The city had virtually put itself under curfew - no one wanted to get wet. I knocked on Toby's door. And waited.

Light peeked out from behind cracks in the lounge curtains so someone was there. Come on, Toby, what're you doing? Mum would be fretting that I wasn't already home so she'd know she'd be on time for work. It must have been incredible when people had phones and could speak to each other whenever they wanted from wherever they were. I rolled my shoulders, trying to get rid of the feeling of the gun still pressing against me. What if Toby was still being held? What if there were soldiers waiting inside to arrest anyone who came here? A little paranoia was healthy but I was being ridiculous, surely? Still shocked by Mrs Randle's arrest. I hoped the last secretary had gone via Mrs Randle's house like she'd promised. I hated that there was nothing else I could do for her.

I lifted my hand to knock again but hesitated. Because there could be soldiers in there? Or of whatever price Toby asked for the Coralone? Knock or leave, simple choices. I forced myself to knock. When the door finally opened, I let out the breath I'd been holding. It was only Frank, Toby's cousin, not a gun or scrap of camouflage in sight.

"Is Toby about? I asked him to get me something and wondered if he had it yet?"

"He's just back. Come."

I followed Frank into the lounge.

"Maya!" Jessica jumped up and practically threw herself at me. "I didn't know it's Friday."

I squatted down to hug her back. "It isn't, I just needed to ask your daddy something."

"I've been practising."

"I know you have, you keep this up and you'll win another prize off me." Jessica giggled. I traced her braids with my finger. "These are pretty."

She shook her head and the beads at the end of her braids knocked together. "They're new."

"Hey, baby, upstairs now, Maya'll see you Friday." If Jace could have seen the look of fatherly love on Toby's face as he watched Jessica scamper out of the room he'd get over whatever it was that made him dislike him. As Jessica's thumping footsteps faded away, Toby spoke. "You got away okay the other day, without saying anything?"

I nodded. "Were you all right? I wondered if they'd hold you."

He let out something approaching a laugh. "I pay the price, they let me stay right here. They take me away, no way they get their money."

"They blackmail you?" Even with everything I'd seen

of the Army recently, it shocked me. I'd assumed the soldiers I'd come up against were simply following orders but blackmailing meant they were corrupt. The system responsible for law and order and justice could be bought and sold. The injustice of it made me want to cry.

"You're so naïve, Maya? Just the price of doing business."

"It sounds a lot like blackmail to me."

"I told you, just a game we play."

On a skewed board, where they made up the rules as they went along.

Toby took his jacket off. "You here for your bro's medicine? You think I work that fast?"

"I know you do."

He nodded, acknowledging how good he was at tracking down pretty much anything. "Not good news."

"You couldn't find any yet?"

"I couldn't find any."

A ghostly finger tracked down my spine. "I don't understand."

"Nada, zippo, zilch. No Coralone anywhere. Got the network hooked on it but nothing. Seems like the supply dried up."

The message on the clinic's computer had been right? What now? I'd tried everything I could think of to get more. What else could I do?

CHAPTER NINETEEN

"Sebastian's in a lot of pain." I interrupted mum getting ready for work. "Jace can message the hospital over his radio, get him admitted—"

"No." She reacted so violently to my suggestion, she knocked over her tea. The red liquid ran off the top edge of her dressing table like a blood-soaked waterfall layering a pool of second-hand colour onto the carpet. "Godamnit." Hearing her say that was more startling than the destruction.

"It's not fair for him to suffer like this." I ploughed on. "We could get him taken in now and he'd be back on Coralone within the hour."

"I said no. We'll care for him here."

I could see where I got my stubbornness from. But this time she was wrong. "But we're not. In May—"

"That was May. This is now. And don't you dare defy me, Maya. I make the decisions."

"But Mum—"

"There are things about the hospital that you have no idea about. You'll just have to trust me."

"Tell me then so I understand."

She shook her head. "All you need to know is that

hospital for Sebastian isn't a choice."

I really didn't get it. Why was she not begging Jace to call it in? I wanted to sweep everything off her dressing table to join the tea puddling on the carpet.

Somehow Sebastian got through the time to his pain killer. I fed him two spoonfuls, giving him a drink to wash away the taste. Even in the candlelight he looked terrible, burning up one minute, shivering the next, shaking, sweating, an endless nightmarish cycle. I'd never seen him like this. Surely if Mum saw this, she would get Jace to call for an ambulance.

"Do you feel a bit better?" I asked after a few minutes. He shook his head. "The medicine'll work soon and you will, okay?"

He looked at me, so trusting. How did he not hate me for putting him through this? I felt so helpless but I stroked his hair, mopped his brow, did acupressure on all the points I could remember that might help while we waited for the numbing of the medicine to kick in.

And eventually I could see his face relaxing. "Better now?"

He nodded. He opened his mouth a couple of times as if he was going to say something.

"What is it?" I asked.

"I won't be here much longer. Then you can go out with your mates."

"Sebastian, don't say that."

"Why not, it's true. Mum won't talk about what's going to happen, but you're more honest than that."

God, for an eleven-year-old who'd spent more than half his life indoors, he was really perceptive. "I don't want to go out with anyone. I want to be right here with you."

"But every day isn't fair." he protested.

"It's not really every day and besides there's nowhere I want to go." And who would I go with? My name had never made it on to any invite lists.

"You'd find something."

I tried to steer him away from the depressing stuff. "You know Mum won't talk about the future because she worries."

"It's not fair for me to have to live like this, ill all the time. No one would want to, if they had a choice." His honesty was painful.

"Medical research is working on a cure." The lie felt huge in my mouth. All the Coralone in the world didn't seem to be making the kind of difference he needed. I'd spent months puzzling over his condition, because he should have shown some improvement. But with debate stifled, I had no hope of finding out anything meaningful. And then there was the barely hidden rumour that the flu vaccine itself had been the cause.

"A cure?" Sebastian kicked the blanket off his legs. "Yeah, and I can fly."

"Why wouldn't they be looking to cure you?" I folded the blanket and laid it over the sofa arm. "The Government wants everyone working."

"So me and everyone else like me are a huge pain in their arse."

It was the first time I'd heard him swear. "Does Mum know you know words like that?"

He fixed me with his hard stare. "I'm sick, not a retard."

A huge wave of sadness quashed my smile. Sebastian was funny and clever and deserved a chance to live a life away from his bed and the sofa.

"Maya, if I ask you something you have to promise not to tell Mum."

"Sure."

"No, really, you can't tell her."

"I promise, on pain of being thrown into the dungeons of Muller of Akek." I quoted from his favourite book.

"Seriously." Even as he demanded my promise, I was struck by how different he looked. As if he'd stored up some growing up and cashed it all in on one day. "Maya?"

"Seriously."

"If the pain gets worse will you help me stop it?"

"Hey, of course, but I've given you all the pain killers I can for now."

"I mean for good."

Was I hearing right?"Sebastian, do you know what you're asking?"

He nodded. "Like I said, I'm only sick."

"I can't—"

"I don't want you to do anything, just get me pills, that's all. There's no one else I can ask, Maya. Just you."

I shook my head. "No."

"You're the only one who can help me. I don't mean now, but later, if it gets too much." He caught hold of my hand. "Please."

"Sebastian." His name came out all croaky as though I hadn't spoken for years.

"You don't have to say anything now, just think about it, okay?"

How could I? How could I think about such a terrible thing for even one nano-second?

"I just, I worry that one day I won't be able to stand it anymore. That I'll be, that it'll be . . ." his voice tailed away. He tried again. "If you got me pills, I could just go to sleep."

My attempt at stifling a sob burst out of me in a painful hiccup.

"Just say you will?" His face was so hopeful, I couldn't bear to deny him anything. Saying I would think about it, could there be any harm in that? Just making him easy in his mind. I didn't need to tell him there was no way I could do what he asked. "Please?"

"Okay." My whisper scarcely reached my own ears. "I'm just thinking about it."

But it wouldn't come to that, I wouldn't let it. I would do the undoable before it came to that. "Jace is going to sit with you, Sebastian, just for a little while, I need to go out."

To do the unthinkable – that much I could do for him.

CHAPTER TWENTY

I wasn't so much sheltering from the rain as hiding behind a tree. The hospital main entrance was closed as I'd expected, so Accident & Emergency was my only option. I just had to hope Mum was on a break or already busy. And if that wasn't pressure enough, I still hadn't come up with a reason to be here. Because all I could see was Sebastian's face, all I could hear was him—no, I couldn't even think about that. I needed a clear head, I couldn't let my fear for him cloud my mind.

I put my hands in my pockets as if looking for inspiration as to how I could get to the Dispensary. One hand gripped my torch, the other grazed something small and cold. I pulled it out, my pocket mirror.

Opening the gift on my sixteenth birthday, I'd looked at Jace in confusion.

"It's a handbag mirror," he'd said, "women use them to check their make-up."

That much I got but not why he'd given it to me when make-up wasn't available any more. "It's lovely, Jace, thanks."

"It used to be my mum's."

"I can't take it then." He didn't have much to

remember his parents by, I couldn't keep one of his most personal mementos of her.

He curled my fingers around it. "If she'd met you, she'd like you, Maya. She'd want you to have it. I know you don't wear make-up, but when you look in the mirror, you'll just see what a lovely person you are."

I'd thrown my arms around him, the first time we'd been so physically close for a long time. As boy/girl best friends, we didn't do the 'hello',' goodbye', 'I'm so excited/depressed' hugs I saw girls at school sharing. Once we'd hit puberty hormones and awkwardness and painful self-awareness had grown into too big a gap to bridge with physical contact. He'd returned my hug awkwardly, but I'd wanted him to know how much I loved his gesture.

I slipped the mirror back into my pocket, decidedly not looking in it. I didn't feel very lovely right now. But I had to do this because Mum couldn't. I stroked the little finger of my left hand. I wouldn't miss it if I was caught, she managed well enough without hers.

Career decision. The words sounded as clearly in my head as if Miss Pattershall was standing right beside me. Yes, caught for stealing would be catastrophic for my career decision. The trick was not to get caught.

And if nobody saw me taking the Coralone, I could maybe pretend that I hadn't broken my promise to Jace. I really wasn't liking myself at all.

Quick in, quick out. I pulled in a deep breath, stretched myself up to my full height. It was a trick I'd learnt as I'd shot up and past most of my classmates. How could I feel intimidated when I was six feet tall?

As I approached the reception desk, I could feel everyone's gaze on me, feel them scrutinising me as though they could read exactly what I planned to do. I pulled my spine straighter.

"Can I help you?" the receptionist asked.

"Yes, please—" I broke off, trying to remember what had happened to me the day this nightmare began but I'd been so busy trying to see past the blue flashes of light, I had no real idea. Perhaps in the half-light of the emergency lighting I might get away with it.

I let my knees sag and crumpled to the floor. My head banged the tiles harder than I meant it to. I tried not to let the pain be mirrored on my face.

I heard a shout, voices. I could feel the world shrinking as people crowded me. Did they believe I'd fainted? Would it be enough to get me through the keypad-locked door to the treatment area, where the drugs were?

No one said anything, no one touched me. Lie still, breathe normally, in, out, in, out, eyes closed. What was going on? The urge to peep was almost irresistible.

Then I could feel something solid sliding beneath me, clipping together under my spine. Something rigid around my neck. Movement, practised hands lifting me up and I was on a gurney, being pushed along. And then I heard it, the soft beeps of a pass code being entered on a key pad. They were taking me through to the treatment area. So far, so good.

I counted another sixty seconds before I opened my eyes. I could see white ceiling tiles. I couldn't move my head. I couldn't move at all.

CHAPTER TWENTY-ONE

"Hello, there," a face appeared in my line of sight. A nurse, not Mum, thank God. "Can you tell me your name?"

"Maya."

"Do you have ID, Maya?"

I tried to nod but gave up. "Jacket pocket, right hand side."

She unzipped my jacket and took out my ID. After a few seconds, I felt it being returned.

"One of our nurses is called Anarosa Flint. Do you know her?"

"Why can't I move?" I sidestepped the question.

The nurse picked up on the panic in my voice, not realising its actual cause – that I'd suddenly become a lot more conspicuous than I'd intended. That lying here was adding too much time to my 'slip in, slip out' plan.

"It's just a precaution. You're immobilised on a backboard to minimise further injury until we can X-ray you."

X-rays? No! How could I stay hidden from Mum like this? I scrabbled at the collar around my neck. The nurse caught hold of my hands. "We need to keep that on."

"I'm fine, really."

"I'm sure you are, but the collar stays on for now. Do you have family?"

I couldn't have her asking that either. "I'm fine."

"We won't contact them unless you have to stay in. We need to keep the channels free for casualties in case the storm steps up. Someone will take you down to X-ray in a bit. Then we'll be able to make you more comfortable."

She vanished from sight and there was nothing I could do except wait.

Finally a man's face popped into my line of sight, making me jump. "Just taking you to X-ray, love. Don't worry, won't be breaking any speed limits." He was grey-haired, as old as his joke. The only thing that moved fast enough now to be remotely troubled by speed limits were the freight trains that transported food and supplies to and from the agricultural communes.

The power still being out worked in my favour at X-ray. The radiographer decided one shot was good enough. He disengaged me from the board and collar and helped me into a wheelchair.

"You may not have damaged your spine but you've cut your head."

"You can tell that from the X-ray?"

"From the bed." He pointed at the red stain on the pristine white covered pillow where I'd lain. He pulled on gloves and rummaged through my hair as though he were looking for nits. "There it is, not much more than a nick, but the head really bleeds. You'll probably need a stitch." He produced a swathe of gauze. "Here, hold this on it. It'll do until they sort you out."

I held it as he showed me. He slipped my film down the side of the wheel chair, pushed me outside the X-ray suite. "A porter'll be along to take you back."

Left alone, I rested my elbow on the armrest of the chair, keeping pressure on my cut. Instant karma. That would teach me to lie so outrageously.

The corridor opposite was virtually dark. Only two emergency lights on in the whole span but enough to light up the sign at its mouth. Dispensary.

There was no sign of the porter. Of anyone. Now was my chance.

The closed sign hung at the window again. Excellent. I keyed in the number I'd seen Mum enter and was rewarded with a tiny click that echoed out of all proportion. I slipped inside and crept to the closest shelf. Picking up the first packet of pills and shielding the glare of my torch, I read Naprexalene. Walking the alphabet backwards I found the shelf with the 'C's. Ca, Ce, I ran my finger along the labels. Co. Conivarton, Coralone.

Coralone. I slipped a bottle into my pocket and I pulled forward the one behind it. As easy as that and no one would even notice I'd been there. It took me only a few seconds to retrace my steps out into the still dark and empty corridor.

I'd done it, thank God. I had Coralone for Sebastian.

The roaring in my ears and the blue flashes hit me so quickly I'd scarcely thought 'not now' than the darkness took over.

CHAPTER TWENTY-TWO

Voices breached the darkness that filled me.

I tried to think around the blank that had invaded my head, tried to remember where I was, what I'd been doing, but my brain didn't seem to have returned as quickly as my consciousness. I remembered flashing lights, a roaring in my ears and a blackness. A clinically clean smell I recognised played with my perception of time. Bleach and disinfectant. A floor. Accident & Emergency a few days ago. I was lying on the floor in the hospital again.

"You can't move her, we need to find out why she keeps passing out. She'll have to be admitted." A woman, her voice urgent.

"She's my responsibility now." A man said.

"Because she isn't where she's supposed to be? You don't know that she's done anything wrong." The woman again.

I felt someone patting my jacket pockets. Oh no, I didn't want anyone doing that.

"I do now." The man's voice, triumphant. I felt him tugging the stolen bottle of Coralone out of my pocket. "Tell me she didn't take this from the Dispensary. I knew she was trouble when she was in here couple of days back."

I knew I ought to be jumping up, defencing myself, but my arms and legs felt as though they had tonne weights attached to them.

"I'm getting a doctor, you can't move her." I heard the woman moving, the squeak of her shoes on the floor.

"The maintenance of law and order is paramount over all other considerations." The man argued.

"Not over her life it isn't."

I heard a brusque sound that could have been a laugh. "It might have been that way once, but it sure ain't now. People know to respect the law. Do you want a return to when you had to lock everything up? When the crims just took what they wanted from you because they didn't feel like working for it?"

"Of course not, but for goodness sake, she's just a kid."

I felt rummaging in my pockets again, my ID being withdrawn this time.

"Says here she's sixteen." the man said. "That's adult enough for the law. Jail's where she's headed, no comfy hospital bed for her."

The implications of what he said made my head spin, even though I was lying on the floor. A gasp escaped me before I could stifle it.

"Maya, can you hear me?" the woman asked. There seemed to be no choice but to open my eyes. The nurse from earlier was kneeling beside me. The corridor was still dimly lit by emergency lighting. "Do you know where you are, what happened?"

"No." It wasn't far from the truth – my brain was taking a while to catch up to my present.

"It doesn't make any difference." I recognised the security guard from three days ago when Mum had dressed my cut. "You're under arrest—"

"What's going on?"

Oh God, no, now this was really spiralling out of

control. Mum wasn't supposed to know I was here. So much for my quick in, quick out plan.

"Found this one stealing." The guard held the bottle of Coralone up like it was a trophy.

I knew exactly when Mum recognised me, everything about her changed.

"Maya! What's happened? Why aren't you with Sebastian?"

She knelt down and the chain holding her wedding ring, worn like that so she didn't draw attention to her hand, slipped out from the confines of her uniform and swung forwards, accusing me.

I pushed myself up into a sitting position, trying to distance myself from the guard. "Jace's with him—"

"Your head's bleeding! I need to get you to the treatment area." She held out a hand to help me up.

"She's not going anywhere." the guard said.

"What're you talking about, Fred?" Her hand floundered halfway between us. "She's hurt."

"She's a thief. Maybe it's in her genes." I wanted to smack the smirk off his face. "I found this medicine in her jacket."

"She wasn't taking it. I asked her to get it for me. I had a patient I couldn't leave." Mum took hold of my arm, sure in her lie.

"You asked your daughter to wander around the hospital while her head's bleeding?" Fred got to his feet.

"She wasn't bleeding before."

"And you gave her the access code to the pharmacy? Isn't that grounds for dismissal? You were obviously prepared to break the rules before," he nodded at her hand, "but I know the rehabilitation worked, I know you wouldn't do it now." Hacking off her finger was rehabilitation? "She's been caught stealing. I have to arrest her."

Arrest me. The little finger on my left hand throbbed. I'd never noticed it before, not really, but now it felt so vibrantly alive, so much a part of me and they would cut it off. I felt my stomach contract. I sucked in a breath, another, trying not to throw up.

I thought I'd reconciled myself to my potential punishment but I had expected to get the Coralone first, to make the sacrifice worthwhile.

Mum stood, grabbing hold of the guard. "Because you know me, you can't do this. You know I need her to mind Sebastian for me."

"The law's the law, you should know that better than anyone." Even without his vicious display the other day, I wouldn't have liked him. He was a man who loved his job too much.

"Please, there must be something you can do."

"You know me, Anarosa, I'm a reasonable man." Really reasonable. Every time I looked at him, all I could see was the vindictiveness on his face while he hit the man without ID, over and over. "But I can't ignore this."

Fred grasped my arm. "On your feet."

I couldn't. I felt all wrong. I put my head on my knees. The sudden thwack of his nightstick on the floor made me jump.

"Next one'll be on you. Get up."

I staggered upright. He produced a pair of handcuffs. "Hands behind your back."

Should I do what he said? I looked the question at Mum. She'd aged ten years in the last ten seconds. Her face was greyer than Sebastian's earlier, her breathing shallower.

The guard yanked my hands behind me and I felt the cold grip of the metal handcuffs as he locked them. I towered over him but the feel of the metal, the image of myself as a convict cowed me.

"You're under arrest under section 2 of the Right to Detain Act. You are required to co-operate with the authorities, choosing to remain silent will harm your defence and make you subject to further charges. A

Government lawyer will be appointed to you. Do you understand these rights?"

The same question Mrs Randle had been asked.

"Her head wound needs attention," the other nurse said.

"It's not spouting, looks to me like it can wait." The guard pushed his nightstick into the small of my back in another echo from yesterday. But even though the nightstick couldn't shoot me, it somehow felt worse than the gun. "Let's go."

I twisted against him. "I'm sorry, Mum, I didn't mean for this—"

"Now." The stick pushed harder.

"How could you have done something so stupid?" Her face was too painful to look at. "You know better, I've brought you up to know better."

"You didn't see Sebastian, you don't know . . . You wouldn't get him admitted. What else could I do? I had to make everything right again."

"And this was your plan?" she shrieked. "You should have left it to me."

"But you're not doing anything."

"You don't know that."

The pressure from the guard's nightstick was unbearable. I had no choice but to walk forwards.

"Mum—" Panic hit me with all the force of an army truck. Bands constricted my chest. The cut on my head throbbed and went numb in waves, I couldn't seem to make my feet work together.

"NO!" Mum's scream dissolved into sobbing like nothing I'd ever heard before. I risked a look backwards as the guard steered me around the end of the corridor. She'd collapsed on the floor. The nurse was trying to comfort her.

No matter what came next for me, nothing would erase that terrible memory – it would haunt me forever because I'd put that awful look on Mum's face.

CHAPTER TWENTY-THREE

Fred marched me through a maze of semi-dark corridors stopping at a locked door. He fished one-handed for his keys, holding my right forearm, his fingers digging in harder than necessary.

'Security'. I read the sign on the door over and over while he messed about, willing it to change to something less frightening. He got the door open and pulling me into the room, pushed me down onto a chair. My head flung backwards and hit the wall with a squelchy kiss.

"Stay." He unlocked a wall-mounted cupboard behind the desk, the torch in his hand drawing erratic patterns on the walls and ceiling as he worked. He took another pair of handcuffs down from a hook. "Can't have you getting any ideas about wandering off, can we?"

I felt him thread the second pair through the chain of those I already wore and handcuff my bound wrists to the chair. "Might take them a while to get you."

"Where?" my voice cracked. I coughed, trying to pretend it was only a tickly throat. "Where am I going?"

"Jail."

"But what about my family?"

"Should have thought of that before you decided to

steal."

"My brother's dying, I was trying to save him." I felt the world shift sideways as I realised the truth of what I was saying. Sebastian was dying and it was all my fault. And now I'd probably never see him again.

Fred shone the beam of his torch directly into my face. "It's no good trying to play the sympathy card with me, it won't work."

I blinked at him, shadowed behind the bright light. I'm sure it wouldn't, from what I'd seen of him, I bet he didn't have a heart to touch. I hated that I couldn't hold back my tears, hated that he could see how much this was affecting me.

"Why am I going to prison? Why aren't you just cutting off my finger?"

He burst out laughing. A real belly laugh, the kind to make your eyes water, your sides ache. It made me feel sick.

"You kill me." He wiped his eyes. "I can do that if you want, could even get your mum to assist, how would that be for poetic justice? But the Government don't need to be so dramatic now. They only used that deterrent at the beginning when people were used to being criminal."

I was sure Mum had never been a criminal. She would never talk about what she'd been punished for but losing that part of herself had been a deterrent all right. It maybe even explained why she was angry all the time.

"Can you give a message to my mum please?" I pretended that my voice hadn't cracked. It was really hard to ask him for anything but there was no one else.

"Kinder to just accept your fate and go."

Maybe it was, but I wanted her to understand that despite everything I loved her and never dreamt my last ditch plan to save Sebastian would come to this.

Surely she could understand why I'd done it and not totally condemn me.

CHAPTER TWENTY-FOUR

I'd been on my own a long time when the door to the security office opened and a sunlight bright beam of light blinded me.

"This her?" A voice I didn't recognise.

"What do you think?" Fred followed him into the room. "Thought I wouldn't see you till after the weekend."

"We've got three others on a run now up from London, one more won't hurt. You done all the paperwork?"

"Do I look like I don't know what I'm doing to you?" Fred's torchlight outlined the questioner, a soldier, dark blond hair cut short over his ears, not much older than me. "Found her outside the Dispensary in possession of a bottle of restricted medicine."

"As I was unconscious, someone could have planted it on me." I'd done a lot of thinking while I'd been by myself.

"If we still bothered with trials, it might matter. As it is, you had stolen property on you and that's good enough for the law. The bloody smears you left on the bottle you stole and the remaining one in the Pharmacy are just a bonus." Fred directed his baby torch beam behind my head. "Blood on the wall from your head wound, on your hands, on the bottles, even without bothering with all that forensic stuff, case closed."

"This is a hospital, there are lots of people here who are bleeding."

"His evidence is enough to convict," the soldier said.

"What about the lawyer you said I'd get?" My voice was getting higher, more desperate. I'd really expected them to listen to me, for some consideration to be given to the circumstances. But they were just going to take me away?

Fred laughed. "Amazing what people still believe."

"What about justice?" I thought the soldier would join in with Fred's laughter, but in the echo of his torchlight he just looked pained.

"Unlock her," he said. "I've brought my own."

Fred obliged. I rubbed at my wrists, tried to stretch out the kinks in my arms.

"In front this time." The soldier demonstrated. I didn't want to help him lock me up. I didn't want to be taken away, I wanted to go home. I wanted this to be a normal boring night where I babysat Sebastian and in the morning went to school and everything was as it had always been. I couldn't do this, I couldn't go with him. Who knew what would happen to me if I did?

"Please." I whispered.

"Are we going to have a problem here?" The soldier shone his torch on the huge gun slung across his chest. "Do I have to get heavy?"

"No." The word was little more than a squeak.

"Good. Wrists in front."

I shrank away from him, from the touch of metal around my wrists again. I pressed my lips together to stop the scream building within me from escaping because if I started, I didn't think I'd ever stop.

"I'm putting leg irons on you but don't try anything stupid. You kick me, he'll hit you."

I knew Fred would be only too happy to. The soldier bent down in front of me and clicked leg irons around my jeans. He pulled me upright. He was taller than me by at least four inches.

He scooped up the paperwork and with his hand on my shoulder, directed me out the door. I shuffled along, the leg irons chinking as the chain between them pulled taut and then relaxed again. As much as I might want a less hurtful last image of Mum, I hoped she didn't see me like this.

Even as little as a few days ago, I would never have believed I could ever do anything so against the rules. Now I'd been reduced to a criminal, to be shunned by everyone as soon as my wrist was tattooed. Maybe we were all capable of more bad than we expected. Maybe it was as simple as being asked to pay the one price we each couldn't. I'd never realised before that we all had one. I'd found mine in Sebastian. I couldn't stand by and do nothing and watch him die.

CHAPTER TWENTY-FIVE

An army truck was waiting outside the hospital, a hulking presence, dark on dark. The soldier adjusted the pressure on my shoulder to steer me towards the rear.

"Sit on the tail-gate, swing your legs up and rotate yourself in." he directed me.

I shuffled across the concrete in baby steps. But even those ate up the distance to the truck far too quickly. "I can't do this, I—"

"You don't have a choice. The other soldier with me, he won't," he dropped his voice like he was sharing a confidence, "he won't be understanding at all. You really don't want to upset him. He doesn't play by the rules."

I shivered. Every muscle and nerve ending, every fibre and blood vessel within me had tightened. I felt as if I would snap into tiny pieces. The soldier manoeuvred me up to the open back of the truck. It yawned at me like the mouth of a monster ready to devour me. I couldn't get in there. I couldn't leave MK, they couldn't seriously be sending a sixteen-year-old to prison. 'Everyone mattered' that's what the Government's latest initiative said. Didn't that include me too? But how could I matter if they were sending me away, punishing me for something I'd been driven to do because they hadn't provided for my brother?

I half-turned away, my mind screaming at me, do something, don't get in the truck, just run away.

Hands grabbed my jacket, wrenching me onto my back on the tail-gate so unexpectedly I let out a yelp.

"We haven't got all night. You're up front." The man inside dragged me further in.

I rolled away from him aiming to roll right out the back again but with my hands and legs bound I was useless.

"A hand here, Evan."

Between them they dragged me up to the front and pushed me onto the wooden bench that ran down the length of the truck. One pinioned me to the side while the other did something at my feet. I'd never felt so helpless. I heard the chinking of a heavy chain on the floor, the clicking of a lock.

"Now you won't be going anywhere." The other soldier sat on the bench opposite me. Evan was apparently the driver. I heard the cab door slam and an impossibly noisy engine roar to life. The truck accelerated out of the hospital car park taking me away from everything I'd ever known and everyone I cared about.

It was really happening. They were really taking me to prison. I should have been kicking and screaming, throwing myself out the back of the truck. Shouting that what I'd done was a small crime, petty, it didn't warrant prison time.

The universe only ever gives you what you can bear. I remembered our neighbour Auntie Carol saying that all the time when I was little. But then Uncle Malcolm died from the flu and so did Charlie and him only three and she never said it again. I didn't think I was strong enough to bear this.

"Hey, I asked what you did." The soldier kicked my foot, toppling my thoughts off the tightrope I'd been trying to balance them on since we'd started driving. That way I didn't think about everyone I was leaving behind,

Jace, Mum, Sebastian. Oh, Sebastian.

"I won't ask again." The soldier tightened his grip on his gun.

"Took some medicine to save my brother's life."

"Took? Don't you mean stole?"

I looked up and down the truck – the woman next to me and the two on the other side seemed to be ignoring me as much as they ignored each other. I hoped it would stay that way.

"Stealing, how did you ever think you'd get away with it?" The soldier seemed amused.

"I didn't, but I expected a fair trial." I didn't mention I'd only expected them to take my finger, my naivety seemed to be providing enough entertainment as it was. Mum had said something about being sent away but I hadn't understood it then.

He laughed. "They stopped them years ago. Guess they didn't put that out on the info-casts then? You want a trial?" Now he was mocking me, but I couldn't help rising to his bait.

"It should be everyone's right, things aren't always black and white, sometimes they're just different shades of grey."

He laughed again. "So when you're not stealing, you're quite the philosopher. They will not like you in prison. Tell you what, you want a trial so bad, I'll give you one. A trial. By sex."

CHAPTER TWENTY-SIX

I pushed myself back in my seat against the inside of the truck. Was he crazy? I might be a nerd and therefore incapable of having a boyfriend, but my first time should be special, with someone I really cared about. Not with a brutal man in the back of an army transport. Soldiers were supposed to uphold the law, he couldn't seriously mean it.

He shone a torch into my face. I lifted my hands to shield my eyes from the stabbing light, to protect myself from him. He couldn't mean it. He was just trying to shock me, to scare me. He was doing a great job.

I tried to get further away from him but there was nowhere to go. I tried not to think about Evan's quiet admission about him, about the soldiers who blackmailed Toby. This man was the law, supposed to be one of the good guys, supposed to protect. But if he wouldn't, what would I do? What could I do? He was the one with the gun.

"Ours is the only justice you can get now. You don't look thrilled. You think I'm too old for you? You can always have Evan."

He jerked his gun in the direction of the cab. As if in answer, Evan hit a pothole, jolting us, rattling the chain woven between our leg irons. My stomach had gone into freefall, a wave of sick dread crawled through my insides. My nerves had tightened so much I was shaking.

"It's a good idea though. How about you?" The soldier spotlighted the woman chained up next to me, the two on the opposite side. "Whoever gives me some action, I'll see about letting go."

"If you'll actually let me go, I'll give you more action than you know what to do with." Before my neighbour had finished her offer, the soldier was playing the beam of his torch over her. Above her handcuffs, I could make out two lines of tattooed numbers circling their way around her left wrist. She was probably only in her mid-thirties, young to be locked away forever.

"See why you want off this trip." The soldier had noticed them too.

"What does it matter to you why? I'll make it worth your while, that's all you need to care about."

"Think I might prefer her though." He flashed the torch back at me. I flinched away from him again. No, not me.

"She probably doesn't know anything. But I can show you a real good time." The woman pushed her shoulders back and her chest out.

"Evan!" He banged on the partition separating us. "Pull over, we're taking a rest stop."

"We're only about an hour away—" Evan shouted back.

"I don't care if it's a minute, we're stopping."

The truck slowed. The soldier ran his torch beam up and down the woman with the prison tattoos. He was practically licking his lips. He'd apparently forgotten me. And as awful as I felt about it, I couldn't help feeling glad she'd offered.

With a reverberation like a dying breath, the engine stopped. The silence that rushed to fill the space had a sound of its own.

"What's so urgent we had to stop?" Evan appeared at the open back. Squinting in the other soldier's torchlight, his blond hair looked almost halo-esque.

"Unlock their leg irons, take them out."

"You know we're in a no-go zone, right?"

"And it's where I'll be leaving you if you don't do it."

I heard the metallic chink and click of keys and padlocks then the chain tethering us to the truck floor slithered out the back. I followed my neighbour down the truck, shuffling my feet forward like an old lady. Despite my long legs, I stumbled as I jumped down. Evan grabbed hold of me, steadying me. "Line up against the side with the others."

The wider expanse of empty darkness outside made it easier to see. A brilliant latticework of stars filigreed a sky that showed no sign of the thunderstorm that had engulfed Milton Keynes earlier. The truck was parked in the middle of what had once been a motorway. A couple of car corpses rusted to the right. More solid shapes in the darkness ahead and behind marked the place where their owners had been forced to give up their flight when they'd fallen sick or ran out of fuel. Although the verges were camouflaged amongst the shades of darkness, I knew they'd be creeping towards each other, slowly carpeting the crumbling tarmac with grass and seedlings now that humans had withdrawn from here.

This was the first time in eight years that I'd travelled out of MK and so fast, I had no idea where we were. All I knew was that with each revolution of its wheels, the truck had taken me further away from Jace, from Mum and from Sebastian.

I swallowed hard. I knew I couldn't cry here, as much as I wanted to lie down on the ground and sob for him. I couldn't think that I'd never had the chance to say sorry for letting him down so catastrophically. I couldn't think about him at all here.

"Evan, you're on guard duty. I've got an itch to

scratch. Undo her." The older soldier's order brought me crashing back to my nightmare present. He didn't mean me, did he? It had to be the other woman he was talking about, didn't it? I was shaking so much my handcuffs sounded like they were tap dancing. I was breathing as if I'd just run a marathon but still I couldn't pull in enough oxygen. The world was going fuzzy at the edges. Was I going to pass out again? Maybe it'd be better if I did, if I just didn't know what was going to happen.

I wanted to run, anywhere, to get away from here, to face up to whatever was in a no-go zone rather than stand here, but my legs were shaking more than my hands. I leant against the side of the truck.

Get out of here, run, hide! My mind shrieked at me, peppered with obscenities I didn't know I knew. But no part of my body was obeying my commands. I'd turned into a jellified mess.

"You made us stop here, put us all in danger, just so you can get laid?" Evan sounded completely incredulous.

"Stop bleating, you can have a turn after me."

"I don't think with my trousers."

The sudden thwack of the older soldier's fist connecting with Evan's face rippled outwards into the silence. "You'll think how I tell you to."

"Yes, Sir."

"I can't hear you."

"Yes, Sir." Evan's response was barely louder than before. Was a no-go zone so dangerous that a gun-toting soldier didn't want to make his presence known?

"I'm not going to say it again."

"Yes, Sir!" Evan's shout echoed away from us, a rallying cry to every wild thing. He unlocked the other woman's handcuffs.

"Come on, baby." she said. "I'll show you a real good time."

The other woman. Evan had unlocked the other woman. The tsunami of relief that overwhelmed me made me feel even weaker and even more wobbly. I didn't know how I was still standing.

The older soldier leant in as he passed me. I tried to take a step away from him, but the side of the truck held me. "Brilliant idea of yours. Listen and learn, I might decide to thank you properly when I'm done with her."

CHAPTER TWENTY-SEVEN

Evan stood in front of me and the two remaining women, his gun trained on us. I tried to ignore the sounds coming from inside the truck. But if the soldier kept his word, did it matter? The woman would get what she wanted. Perhaps I would have done the same in her position. The world was altogether a different place from what I'd thought just a week ago.

The wave of nausea I'd been fighting overwhelmed me. I leant forward and threw up. I still felt like a puppet with a maniac in charge of my strings but at least my stomach had mostly stopped doing somersaults. Now I was terrified and embarrassed. I could feel the other women looking at me, Evan's gaze on me. I tried to straighten my spine but the effort was too huge. I just wanted to sink into the ground and disappear.

A bark split the otherwise blanketing silence. Evan spun around moving his gun across the verges of the old motorway.

"They won't attack for a while," he turned back to us. "They were pets once but they're not used to us now. This generation's probably never seen a human. Doesn't mean they won't attack though - you need to help me keep watch."

Would I notice anything before the dogs sprang at us? The trees were only shades of black on black.

"Why did you steal?" Evan glanced at me before turning his attention back to the tree-line.

"Apparently it doesn't matter."

Minutes ticked by measured by the erratic barking of feral dogs. My nerves were still screwed up from the run-in with the other soldier. I could hardly concentrate on something as simple as watching, even though it might save my life.

The older soldier finally rounded the back of the truck, leading the tattooed woman by her elbow.

"Dogs are getting closer." Evan reported. "We need to get on our way. Sir." The older soldier didn't seem to notice his sarcasm.

"Load up the others. You're free to go." He told the tattooed woman.

"You can't let me go here." she protested.

"I'm letting you go, that was our deal. You didn't say where. We're going north, civilisation's that way." He pointed back the way we'd come. "You can always come with us."

The woman glared at him and then she was off, jogging down the motorway, close to the crash barrier, her white T-shirt standing out in the darkness. She'd got her freedom. I was glad. She'd taken the soldier's attention away from me after my big mouth had got me in trouble. I'd always feel grateful to her for that.

As the soldier watched her running away, I passed behind him, wanting to get back in the truck before he remembered me. I sat on the tailgate, lifted my legs up, trying to get in on my own this time. I jumped so hard at the sudden sound of the gunshot I almost fell off it. A dog had come that close?

I looked around but saw only the tattooed woman faltering as though she'd walked into an invisible wall. She staggered sideways, a stumbled zigzagging from right to left, then fell over. The soldier had shot her?

"Sloppy." He looked at his gun.

"Sir?"

"Need some practice at live target shooting. Should have felled her straight off."

"I meant why did you shoot her?" Evan asked.

A howl that sounded as if it was just the other side of the truck layered tension onto the exchange between the soldiers.

"You didn't actually think I'd let her go, did you? How would that look on the report? As it is I stopped a potential runaway. I should get an award." He reholstered his weapon.

"Why did you let her go if you were going to kill her?" Evan ground out.

"I'm a man of my word. I said I'd let her go, I didn't say I wouldn't shoot her."

"You're just going to leave her there?" Evan sounded as appalled as I felt.

"The dogs'll finish her off. Look on the bright side, none of these others will give us any trouble."

He was right about that. I couldn't get back onto the hard bench quickly enough.

CHAPTER TWENTY-EIGHT

An hour away from the prison Evan had said we were when he'd stopped the truck. Only another hour. I let my eyes close. Sleep might be too far away to catch - the dread of each passing second too nauseating to let me relax – but emotional exhaustion was happy to smother me.

I tried not to let myself think of the countdown to our arrival. But even that was better than thinking about that poor woman, left on the road to be fought over by a pack of wild dogs. What if she was only injured? What a horrible way to die. And it was my fault. If I hadn't opened my mouth to complain, we wouldn't have stopped and the woman would still be sitting next to me.

The truck shuddered to a halt dragging me back to the present. Even over the banging of my heart I could hear men's voices, bolts being drawn, the clink and clank of metal against metal. Bright lights outside almost blinded us, it was as if someone had tethered the sun to the back of the truck. Someone laughed. How could anyone be laughing now, here?

Evan unlocked and unthreaded the chain that held our leg irons attached to the floor.

The other soldier stood up. "Don't think about doing

anything stupid. You all remember the lesson from earlier."

He waved us out of the lorry with his gun. Evan grabbed me as I tottered off the back, steadied me as I landed. I blinked away the intrusion of the artificial morning, blinked to shake off my disorientation. The women in front of me shuffled their way to the open gate.

My legs wouldn't move. I looked up, up, up at the prison walls. They'd really meant it, they'd really brought me to jail. Even in the gateway, the sort of no man's land between so-called civilisation and life in there, the walls soared above me, closed in on me, suffocating. I couldn't go in there. What would happen to Sebastian if I went in there? I couldn't, I had to go home. I belonged at home, I was just a school kid, I didn't belong here.

I took a step backwards and another straight into the unyielding bulk of Evan. Even through my jacket, I could feel the solidity of his gun, held across his chest.

"You can't show weakness here." His voice was low. "Even if you're falling apart inside, you can't let anyone see that. It's different in there from outside. Take a step."

I still couldn't move. He pushed his gun against my back, but it wasn't a threatening gesture. He was trying to give me the impetus to move.

"Problem?" A shout from somewhere to my right.

"No, Sir." Evan's reply made my ears ring. "You have to pretend to be strong." He pushed a little harder. "If you don't go, he'll make you. And you don't want that."

No. I didn't. I forced myself to take a baby step and another until there was clear space between us. One step, another. One at a time. It sounded like such a platitude. But it got me from the army vehicle through the gate into the prison. I wanted to turn around and acknowledge Evan. But I knew if I did I wouldn't be able to stop myself running back towards him. I'd end up being shot before I'd ever set foot inside. The way I was feeling right now, maybe that wouldn't be such a bad thing.

CHAPTER TWENTY-NINE

"There's only one real rule in here."

The warden put her pen down on her desk, straightening it until it lined up exactly with the files in front of her. Cropped blonde hair straying into grey, wearing a neat suit, she looked less like a warden than anyone I could have conjured up in my imagination. But as she looked at me and the other new arrivals, I understood how she came to be given her job. Her eyes were cold, the corners unworried by laughter lines.

"The rule is that you belong to me." She looked at each of us. I felt a chill run down my back as her gaze nailed mine. "I'm not like the Government. I won't pretend I'm not screwing you over. But as long as you do what you're told, we won't have a problem. You do something that makes me haul you back in here, you should be scared, really scared. Let me spell it out for you so there are no misunderstandings."

She adjusted her pen, dragging out her pause. "All that the Government says about 'everyone matters' doesn't apply in here. Your food and cell privileges will be paid for by your families outside. They don't pay, you don't eat, you don't get a bed and the only person who will care is you.

You get the first day free while the system is updated. After that," she spread her hands, "it depends on how badly you might have fucked people around."

I tried not to look shocked. She had deliberately sworn yet neither of the guards standing behind us so much as flinched. Outside no one would actually say that word. Evan was right, things here were very different.

The warden allowed something that could have been a smirk to cross her face. "You don't play by my rules, that's your choice. But you, Jackson, you screw up, your sister pays the price. You, Flint, your mother and you. . ." The warden raised her gaze from her file and stared at the woman on my left. "You don't seem to have anyone out there. You'll have to bear the cost yourself, but I'm sure we can settle on something that will be equally as much a deterrent. You've already got a problem, who's going to pick up your tab? You'd better start being nice to people."

"Excuse me."

The warden's glare dropped several degrees into Arctic territory. She looked at Jackson's wrists, hidden beneath the long sleeves of the tracksuit jacket they'd given us all.

"Newbie, ma'am." One guard explained.

"No one's said how long we'll be in here." Jackson said.

The guard drew his nightstick. My shoulders clenched, my back tensed. Was he seriously going to hit her for just asking a question?

The warden held up her hand. "You probably still believe in parole boards and time off for good behaviour, don't you? Did you not listen to me?"

I found myself nodding even though she wasn't looking at me.

"I don't like to repeat myself so listen harder. The only real rule in here is that you belong to me. So I decide how long you stay because every time you cross the line, or disrupt things, I add more time to your sentence. For example, for questioning me, I've added another day to yours." She smiled but it was so cold it only felt threatening. "Actually I've added another day to all of your sentences just to make sure you're all listening."

I tried to cling to what Evan had said, 'show no weakness' but I could feel tears of rage prickling. Where was the justice here?

Although all the rules we lived by sometimes wound me up, I had always felt the Government was looking out for us, maybe too much like a strict parent at times but at least they'd protect us as they promised. That illusion had been cracked on the motorway and the warden wasn't saying anything that would repair it.

"It doesn't sound like much, does it?" she went on. "A day. But if you've served years that one day will feel a lot longer than twenty-four hours. Imagine how another week would feel, another month. Being here when you could have been back home."

The tears spilled over and ran down my cheeks. The rage had evaporated, leaving behind only fear. I wouldn't wipe the tears away, the only defiance I had was to refuse to acknowledge them but the warden looked satisfied. Trapped in a purgatory at the whim of a sadist, maybe the woman who'd been shot on the motorway had got the better end of the deal.

CHAPTER THIRTY

Bracketed by two guards, we new arrivals were led to the main prison block. Every movement echoed back to me off the painted brick walls. Although my cuffs were gone, my wrists still felt phantom metal clasped around them. The track suit I'd been given felt hard against my body. Even the air seemed to be rubbing at my skin, chafing.

My head throbbed. Just a nick the radiographer said, but the shower I'd taken after they'd processed me seemed to have washed half my body's blood supply out of my hair. I was surprised the red water hadn't got me into trouble.

My hand felt bare without its dressing but at least the Steri-strips had worked. I was healing on the outside at least but I couldn't help curling my hand up so I hid the injury. Despite what they'd said, I didn't believe there wouldn't be consequences leaving it undressed but I hadn't had a choice.

"Breakfast." The lead guard stopped by the open door of a large room. "You all get fed today, no cost, make the most of it."

I followed the women over to where food was being served. The low ceilinged room bounced conversations back down to the talkers in an endless game of verbal ping pong. If I closed my eyes, I could have been in the school cafeteria, the chinking of plates and scraping of cutlery sounded exactly the same. But it was slightly off, only female voices babbled around me, I carried no backpack, there were no cooking smells hanging in the air, Jace wasn't beside me.

Jace. I couldn't think of him right now. Show no weakness, I was trying my best although I wasn't doing very well. My eyes were probably red-rimmed, marking me out for what I was – a kid scared witless.

I shuffled along with the queue, every movement made more self-conscious and awkward by the weight of so many stares on me. I pulled my spine straighter, held my shoulders back, my confidence-boosting trick not working. I wanted to shrink into the floor, to be as unnoticed as the crumbs at my feet.

"Fresh meat." An enormous woman with close cropped hair barged into me. I gripped my empty tray tighter. I wanted to look away but I couldn't stop staring at her. She scarcely came up to my chest but she was almost as wide as she was tall. There was so much of her sideways. I'd never seen anyone that big before.

"What you looking at? You want some?" She had three bands of numbers circling her wrist. The highest one curlicued up her arm, the size of one of my thighs, in a clumsy spiral design.

I stepped backwards, away from her, bumping into the tray rack.

"Thought not." She glared at me and walked off.

The woman serving breakfast threw two pieces of toast on my tray and handed me a bowl of something that could have been cereal. "You get fed today, newbie. Tomorrow's up to the warden." She scooped a tablet from each of four bowls and held them out. "I don't got all day. Take."

I held my tray out and she dropped the pills on it.

"Water there." She jerked her head towards a serving rack on her right stacked with cups. I balanced my tray against my hip and the rack and took one.

I looked around the dining room. A lot of faces were still looking at me. I headed for one of the few free places by the door. The guard in the doorway glanced at me with a bored expression.

I sat down and stared at my dry toast. Who was having the butter we'd had at home this morning? Was Sebastian even still at home? Stop it! I couldn't keep thinking about them. The list of those I cared about was short but each one meant more because of that. Blocking thoughts of them was probably the only way I could hope to survive for now.

I took a bite of cold toast, trying to ignore how much my hands were shaking. It was like eating cardboard. Probably it wasn't that bad, I just had no appetite. I picked up the vitamin tablets – what was the extra one for? – and slipped them into my pocket. Except I wasn't going to see Toby. I swallowed the pills, expecting the knot in my stomach to throw them back up again. I took another bite of toast and a gulp of water to ease the lump down. I couldn't eat it. I held out the second piece to the woman sitting closest to me. "Do you want this?"

She moved quickly, half-standing and snatching it, like a snake striking at prey. She'd eaten the whole piece before I'd managed two more bites, watching me all the while as though I might change my mind and take it back. I tried the cereal. The milk tasted funny. I stirred it around a bit, not sure if I could manage that either.

Someone sat opposite me. Late twenties, long dark hair, brown eyes, slim and long-limbed, she looked a lot like I might at that age. Her skin was darker than mine, maybe because she'd been outside a lot. Probably had to pay for sun cream here. On her arm the same spiral tattoo I'd seen on the huge woman curled up from two bands of prison numbers.

"Where you from?" she asked.

"Milton Keynes."

"Where're you really from?"

"I was born in York."

She tried again. "Where are your people from, Venezuela like me?"

Something made me not say Puerto Rica, where my great grandparents had come from.

"Milton Keynes." I said stubbornly.

She let it go. "You shouldn't give things away. Everything here carries a price."

"I didn't want it, she did."

"You need someone to look out for you, show you how to survive."

Yes, I did. I needed someone on my side, but I wasn't sure she was it.

"Whatever you're charging, she can't afford it and she's not interested." Someone behind me answered. I looked around, straight into the grey eyes of Mrs Randle.

CHAPTER THIRTY-ONE

How much longer? It felt as though I'd been sitting outside the doctor's surgery all day. I wanted to go to wherever everyone else had gone so I could talk to Mrs Randle. I had so many questions for her, it would probably take me all night to ask them.

I stretched, not quite daring to stand up, trying to work out the kinks in my back, relieve my numb bum. The other new arrivals had long gone. Why was it taking so long for me to be processed? I draped my tracksuit jacket over the chair next to me. Even the tiny splodge of cotton wool taped to the inside of my arm from where they'd drawn blood made me feel hotter.

It was quieter here. A little removed from the main prison block, the continuous clanking and locking and unlocking of doors barely registered.

"Flint."

Finally. The guard led me into a small consulting room off the main infirmary which could have been any doctor's surgery anywhere, if it weren't for the bars at the window.

The woman sitting at the cluttered desk wasn't wearing a white coat.

"Why haven't you been taking your vitamin tablets?" Her gaze was direct, searching.

I looked down at my hands, crossed my legs, uncrossed them. Stop it. Whatever I felt she couldn't actually read my mind. "Of course I have, I'm—"

"It's pointless lying to me, Flint. The tablets have a protein in them that leaves a marker. Your blood doesn't have it, so you haven't been taking them for quite some time. You want to tell me why?"

"It doesn't matter."

"It wasn't a request."

The guard came a step closer.

"I've been trading them." I said quickly.

"For what?"

I hesitated but maybe the doctor would understand. "The chance to read scientific articles and papers."

She let out a harsh laugh. "I've heard some rubbish in my time but please, are you mocking me?"

"No, it's the truth."

"Even if I believed you, who would want to trade you for them? Everyone has vitamins, where's the market to sell them on?"

I often wondered that. Why Toby took my pills when he got his own, legitimately, and when everyone else had them too. They had to be useful to him somehow because he wasn't into charity. I'd never thought too hard about it, because if I did I might have to stop trading them with him and then I'd only get enough credit tutoring Jessica to get a paper once a month. My reasoning made me sound so shallow and selfish, I was embarrassed I didn't know.

I shrugged. "I only know someone wants them enough to trade with me for what I want." I felt my face burning, now I'd look as though I was lying.

"To read scientific research?"

I nodded.

The doctor sighed. "Your tests show a clean bill of health, except that you're anaemic."

"Anaemic?"

"You've been feeling tired all the time, maybe breathless, experienced palpitations, perhaps passed out?"

I nodded. Anaemia, that was what had made me so worn out, made me pass out? I felt a weight I hadn't realised was there dissolving. I wasn't sick, the fainting was nothing sinister.

The doctor unlocked a cupboard behind her, chose a bottle of pills and handed me a tiny white one. The coating on the tablet was sweet and slick. It slipped down easily even without water.

"You obviously did a lot of growing. Do you have heavy periods?" she asked.

"Sometimes."

She made a note in her file, the scratching of her pen on the paper the only sound in the bubble of silence. "That could explain the anaemia. Although it probably wouldn't be a cause on its own but coupled with not taking your multi-vitamin . . . I'll have to keep an eye on you. If you faint again, I might have to do something more drastic. The warden will want you fit for work."

I'd stopped listening. My mind had got caught up on 'coupled with not taking your multi-vitamin'. I'd made myself anaemic? If I'd taken my pills instead of trading them, I wouldn't have passed out in the hospital and wouldn't have been arrested? If I'd taken my pills, I'd never have passed out and broken Sebastian's Coralone in the first place?

The weight slammed back into place. I'd done this. All of it. Sebastian was at risk because of my selfishness. His death would be my fault in more ways than I could ever have imagined.

CHAPTER THIRTY-TWO

"Not yet." Mrs Randle stopped the deluge of questions I'd been desperate to ask before I voiced one. She handed me a tray and I followed her, collecting something for dinner that could have been stew. We sat an empty table near the door.

"No one likes these seats because the guards can overhear their conversations." Mrs Randle explained the spaces. "What happened, Maya, why are you here?"

"I was caught taking a bottle of medicine for my brother. Without it he'll die but—" my voice caught and I looked down at the food that was no more appetising than breakfast had been. "I failed him."

"One thing I've learnt is that recriminations don't do any good. You have to make peace with the past, so you can move on."

"Maybe I don't want to." I gestured at the door and the guard. "This is no future that I'd want. Stuck in the past seems the best place to be for me, with my brother alive, my mum—" I stopped. My mum still loving me sounded such a childish thing to say.

Mrs Randle looked at me with the same expression of empathy that she'd shown in Miss Pattershall's office what felt like years ago. And yet she probably wasn't much further along riding the shock wave of being arrested and jailed than me. I changed the subject. "I tried to leave a message for your husband, Miss."

"I don't think you need to call me Miss anymore, Maya. I'm not your teacher now. My name is Jenny."

"Why did they arrest you, Mi-Jenny?" Her name felt all wrong in my mouth.

Mrs Randle glanced at the guard who didn't seem to be paying us much attention. "'Acting to undermine the Government's power and authority' were the words they used but they meant subversion."

"Why would they say that about you?"

She lowered her voice still further. "Because I don't accept that the Government should have so much power over us all, I don't accept that we shouldn't have control over our own lives. And I'm not prepared to do nothing about it." She smiled. "You can close your mouth, Maya, but you ought to put some stew in it first, the food is almost bearable while it's hot."

I did what I was told. Mrs Randle guilty of subversion?

"Why did they know to arrest you?" I asked around a lump of meat.

"A Government Informant I wasn't careful enough of I guess. I don't really know. It doesn't matter. I'll do my time here, I'll learn everything I can and when I get out, I'll be more careful."

"Being here, being punished like this, won't stop you?"

"Only if me being here changes what goes on out there. I have another crack at making things right before I have to leave it to others. I may be subversive but I'm not stupid, I have no desire to be caught for a third time and locked up for good."

I noticed the tattoo around her wrist as she spooned up her stew. One row of numbers that looked red raw and had been weeping. My wrists felt bare in comparison but I couldn't have much longer until they gave me mine.

"Does anyone ever escape from here?" I asked.

"The theory is no – that's why they only use prisons in no-go zones. It would have been nice if they'd just locked us up in Woodhill in Milton Keynes, wouldn't it? Makes you wonder what they're using Woodhill for. A building designed to keep people in is also very good at keeping people out."

She chewed a mouthful of dinner. "There's lots of things the Government have got us to accept without question. Why do they need to call curfews anymore? It's not as if anyone's going to riot again. Is it just a control thing or is there something going on they don't want us to know about?"

Mrs Randle took another mouthful. I'd never met anyone so willing to question the Government's motives. But she was right, curfews couldn't be to stop the spread of infection because we could all move freely around the city during daylight and germs didn't only work a night shift.

"It's like a microcosm of society in here. You can have anything, if you can pay for it, just like outside."

"How does that work?" We were miles from anywhere.

"You've seen the women with spiral tattoos? They belong to a gang. The gang has a network of people and resources on the outside they can reach, even from in here."

"Could they get medicine to my brother?"

Mrs Randle laid a hand on my arm. "You don't understand what you'd be getting into. They'd own you, worse you'd be beholden to them for the rest of your life, you could never say no to anything they asked of you, not now, not ever, no matter what it was, no matter how many laws you might be breaking – even if it leads to a third strike for you. If you're in a gang, you can't say no.

'That woman this morning," she went on, "that's what she was doing, trying to recruit you."

"Who do I have to talk to?"

Mrs Randle spooned up the last of her dinner. "You're going to do this with or without me, aren't you?" I nodded. "Okay, I'll take you but please, Maya, think this through really carefully."

"I will. I just need to ask."

CHAPTER THIRTY-THREE

Mrs Randle led me over to a group of women at the opposite end of the canteen, furthest away from the guards. The big woman from that morning intercepted us. "You got no business here."

"We're here to see Patrice." Mrs Randle said.

The tall black woman slightly apart from everyone else threw a jug of water with such fury it bounced across the floor splattering me and the big woman.

"Godamnit! You tell that bitch warden she don't give me my arm back, one of her guards won't be pleased." She kicked the cup at her feet which skittered across the floor until it crashed into a table leg. "You!" She pointed with an arm that ended about ten centimetres after her elbow at the woman who had spoken to me that morning. "Go tell her." She stopped in mid-pace, glaring at everyone who loosely surrounded her. "What you gawping at?"They suddenly all found everything else but her interesting.

"You'll have to come back—" the big woman began.

"When'd I die and leave you in charge?" The black woman glared at her. "You thought my offer through?" she asked Mrs Randle in a different tone.

"I'm still thinking. This newbie wants to see you."

"I'm Patrice." She was maybe early forties, non-descript except for her shock of hair that stuck out in all directions. She looked as if she had a bird's nest on her head but I wasn't about to point that out. She had an air of absolute authority about her and the appraising look she gave me made me feel she could see far more about me than I was willing to share. "What'll you be - client or sister?"

"I, I just wanted to know if it's possible to get some medicine to my brother. He's in Milton Keynes, he's eleven and he's dying." I forced myself past the word.

"The doctor's won't give him none?"

"That's how I ended up in here, I tried to steal some."

Patrice perched on a corner of the table, one hand on her knee, her other arm dangling. "Prescription medicine?" I nodded. "Price's getting higher. What will you do?"

"If you save him, when I have proof he's alive and out of danger, anything."

She stared at me. I struggled to hold her gaze but I wouldn't look away first. I pulled my spine straighter. She suddenly laughed. "You come see me when you get your bracelet, then we'll talk."

"Bracelet?"

She held up her wrist. The first row of numbers, curled up to her elbow, two other rings circled her arm above that. "You only stole, I'm guessing one this time but I like to make sure. You're no good to me if you get three, I need you to get out to be useful."

"But I don't know how long I'm going to be in here."

"I'm a patient woman." she said.

They sounded like the most innocuous of words but somehow they came out like a deadly threat. Even without Mrs Randle's warning, I knew I had to be absolutely sure I wanted to get in her debt. It seemed obvious that nothing good would come from dealing with her, but what choice did I have?

CHAPTER THIRTY-FOUR

I stood in the breakfast line feeling more dirty than missing my morning shower should have made me feel. And there I was again, thinking about my usual routine. How long would it take until I didn't do that? Last night while I waited for sleep it had been almost impossible not to think of home, not to worry about Sebastian. But at least alone in the dark I didn't have to pretend my heart wasn't breaking.

The woman serving looked at my wrist again. "Let's see how important you are to someone out there. Name."

"Maya Flint."

She consulted a list, running her finger down it. I watched it moving up and then down the handwritten columns. "You're not on here."

That couldn't be right. Of course my name was on there. Mum would send me credit. I may have screwed up but I was still her daughter. And there was no way she would abandon me. The list was mistaken. "Are you sure?"

"Of course I'm sure, I do this every day."

"But I've only been here one day. Maybe it's just not come through yet. That's not much time to get things—"

"It's enough. No one's supporting you."

My mind played the words over and over, but still they didn't sound right. How could Mum not be supporting me? Who else did she think I could count on?

Evan's words echoed through my mind again, show no weakness. It had only been two days and I was really struggling. I turned to walk away.

"Hey, we're not that barbaric." the serving woman called. "You get to have your pills and milk."

It felt as though everyone watched me as I took the pills and forced my legs to take me towards the door. I tried to push my shoulders back, to not appear as though I wanted to sink into the floor, to lie down and howl.

I stumbled against the bench, dropping onto it right on the very edge, as far away from everyone else as I could get. I tried to concentrate on the pills, a flat pink one, filling my mind with them, a red oval, anything to block out those words, a brown one, 'No one is supporting you', a small yellow one.

It didn't matter. I couldn't have eaten anything anyway and that would just have been a waste of Mum's points. I took one of the pills, swallowing hard against the lump filling my throat. Someone walked up to me and sat down opposite.

"Is everything okay, Maya?" Mrs Randle asked. I nodded. "You want some toast?"

"I'm not hungry."

"I don't suppose you are but you should eat. Take it, go on. One piece is fine for me."

"No, I have these." I opened my palm.

"Your mum's probably in shock but she'll come round. It's early yet."

But what if she didn't? What if she stayed mad at me? I struggled to swallow the rest of the pills and drain the milk. A line of women was forming at the door.

"What happens now?" I asked.

"Now we're given our tasks for the day, at least that's what's happened every other morning so far."

I waited for Mrs Randle to return her tray to the serving racks and followed her into the line.

"You," the guard pointed her nightstick at me. "Make a new line."

I glanced at Mrs Randle and did as I was told. My second day, I must be going to get my prison tattoo. My heart did a funny double thump and my stomach lurched. There was no getting away from it, this would be the end of my life as I knew it. I took a step forward as if I was going to follow through on the desire to push past the guard and run and run until I was back home.

"Get back." The guard was all angles of hostility and in her eyes I could see she wouldn't be nice in the way she stopped me. I forced myself to take a step backwards.

Dragging in a straggly breath, I bullied my mind to focus only on that moment, the here and now. Living in the immediate present, no thoughts of the past, none of the future, was a kind of meditative state, an anaesthetic to help me cope. In the present I was just standing in a line, waiting. That wasn't so scary. Just in a queue and like every English person, I was good at queuing.

Jackson, the woman who arrived with me yesterday who had no family outside was told to stand behind me. Others drifted in behind her. When the longer line containing Mrs Randle marched off, the room fell eerily silent, as if it were waiting for something, but not in a good way.

Two male guards arrived and the older of the two addressed us.

"For the benefit of the newbies, none of you have credit from outside so you want to eat, you get to do the worst, most dangerous jobs."

"Excuse me, but what if we get credit late?" The question burst out of me before I realised I was going to ask it. But I didn't want Mum's credit to go elsewhere. Because it had to be an oversight.

"Sorry to burst your bubble, honey," a voice came out

of the line behind me. "but they won't. The only chance you have to win someone's sympathy is for them to be paying for you at the start, then they feel too guilty to stop. 'Less of course that someone goes and dies on you, like my old man. Now I got to take my chances. Working like this at my age, it's a disgrace." She tossed her last comment at the guard.

"No one's making you work harder than anybody else." he said. "That's your choice."

"I work harder or I don't eat, you see a choice in that?"

"Stop your squawking, it's how it is. You newbies, you're with me."

We left the main line, followed the guard. The knot in my stomach was working itself out. There was nothing I could do to change anything. I concentrated on the back of the guard's head as he led us down to the lower level. Just walking, I could do that.

He stopped at a door marked 'Danger, no unauthorised access' in big red letters. "You need to listen carefully to the instructions I'll give you in there." he said. "You screw up, you don't get a second chance."

CHAPTER THIRTY-FIVE

The door led into a room made claustrophobic by the amount of machinery crammed into it, spattered with signs warning of 'danger of death' from high voltage numbers with unlikely amounts of zeroes after them. A skinny run of windows about five feet up, which probably equated to ground level outside, might have allowed a little natural light to shine obliquely in if the day had been bright. The air smelt stuffy, second-hand, as if it had already been breathed.

The guard flapped his hand at the machinery that ran the width of the room. "Emergency generators need servicing."

"Don't know nothing about no generators." Jackson said.

"Then you learn." He retrieved a dog-eared manual from the top of the first one and threw it to her. "Best do it fast, you only have a few hours. I'll be watching. Everything you need should be there." He gestured to a table pushed up against the wall beneath the windows on which a basic tool kit had been thrown. "Obviously you're not changing the oil, but you can do everything else."

He opened the door and a small posse of guards

almost fell into the room.

"All sorted in here, deal 'em up." the first guard said.

"But we've got to—"

"All taken care of." He dropped his voice but I could still hear him. "Got the newbies on it, they don't know no better."

"What if She finds out?" one of the others whispered.

"How? You gonna tell her? What would you rather? We can sweat our arses off in here all day or we can get a few hands in. No contest, right?"

Murmurs of approval from the others persuaded the dissenter.

"We watching them in here though?" he asked.

"Only thing I'm watching is my cards beating yours." one said, a little too loudly.

"We can't have anyone surprise us in here with them, outside the door we get a little more warning." The first guard addressed us. "You don't do a good enough job, you don't eat, got it?"

I nodded, I guessed the other woman did too because they left us, locking the door behind them. I looked at her. "It can't be that hard if they're supposed to do it."

She smiled.

We soon got into a routine, cleaning and lubricating the moving parts, tightening nuts, checking wiring. The only sound interrupting the buzz of the fluorescent lights were the occasional muted shouts from the card game in the corridor. At every raised voice I jumped, cursing the guards when I was checking the wiring connections on the switch that flicked the generators on when the mains power failed. I was sure that the danger signs must be for something else, but it was a theory I didn't want to test.

With no watch, no clocks and constant grey pressing up against the windows, it felt as if we were working in a vacuum. Hours must be passing but my stomach hadn't asked for anything, probably just as well. I stood on the table to open the windows but each rectangle of glass was a sealed unit. The stuffiness of the closed space made it feel as if the walls and ceiling were closing in. I might well be claustrophobic by the time we finished.

When the first guard came in some time later, he handed us both a cup of milk. It was tepid and tasted tangy again, revolting. They'd be better off just giving out water. It couldn't be easy getting hold of fresh ingredients so far removed from the supply line. He took the empty cups back and left without a word. Maybe he was losing. A squall of rain smacked against the windows as he locked the door on us, as if the weather was on our side, underlining how unwelcome he was.

A while later Jackson stopped. "I need the loo, you?"

"I'm good, thanks."

When she knocked at the door, the guard opened it, accepted her request and she disappeared into the corridor. I heard the key turn in the lock again. Being alone brought a kind of relief. I could feel myself almost relaxing. I looked at the row of generators we'd finished. Would the guards check them? I bet they wouldn't. Everything here seemed corrupt and everyone only out for what they could get. The soldiers, the warden, the members of the gang, the guards. Letting us work on one of the most sensitive pieces of equipment so they could play cards. It was laughable really.

I walked back to the beginning of the row. If I sabotaged the generators would I be caught? Taking out the sump plug would be too obvious, a puddle of oil beneath each one too easy to spot. But something less noticeable, maybe I'd get away with that?

I flicked all the switches on the first generator the opposite way. Then on the second, third, fourth. If they all pointed the same way, it shouldn't stand out as being wrong. If anyone did notice it, I could always plead stupidity. The guards were hardly likely to tell anyone else about my incompetence when they were supposed to have done the job.

I heard the key turning in the lock and picked up the manual, looking, I hoped, not as guilty or transparent as I felt.

"I found a step we missed," I explained my fiddling with the serviced generators when the guard left us alone again. My co-worker barely acknowledged my excuse. We worked in silence as before, me going behind to sabotage each one.

If I was lucky it would overload them so they would shut down, leaving the prison in darkness. And that had to be useful for something. I could barter with it. Everything had a price in here and this opportunity at least gave me something to trade.

CHAPTER THIRTY-SIX

Just as I realised there hadn't been any rauccus shouts from the corridor for a while, so the door burst open and the guard rushed in. "How've you done?"

"Almost finished. I can do the last one." I said. Too quickly, I was going to give myself away.

"Leave it, let's go." The guard practically pushed us into the deserted corridor. "Follow me."

He marched us through a series of locked doors, hammering at keypads, wrenching keys in locks I had to stretch my strides to their limit to keep up. The other woman was virtually trotting. And then we were outside.

If I hadn't known it was July, I'd have thought I'd woken up in November. I slipped my tracksuit jacket on.

"Wait round the corner." The guard pushed us out into the rain.

What was he doing? He'd been in such a hurry to get us out here but now we had to wait? For what? Where was he going?

The water, when it hit me, was so unexpected and so cold I couldn't work out where it was coming from, what it was. I gasped and spluttered and tried to twist away from my soaked clothes.

"That should do," the guard approved, an empty bucket swinging from his hands. "If anyone asks, you were outside, clearing out the gutters, got it?"

He marched us back inside. In the warmth of the restricted space exhaustion hit me so hard I struggled to stop myself lying down right there on the concrete floor. Maybe I could transfer the food credit I'd earned today to a medical one for an iron tablet. This anaemia was making me feel awful.

The guard opened an unlocked door and gestured us into a room stripped down to its bare minimum, with what looked like a dentist's chair in the middle. Metal cupboards bristling with padlocks adorned the walls. Rummaging in a drawer was a small man, compensating for losing the fight to hang onto his hair with a long thin ponytail down his back. Tattoos covered his arms, snaked out of the top of his T-shirt up his neck.

"Newbies for you, Berlin." the guard said.

"Busy this week, must be the weather, all that heat, driving them crazy out there." Berlin grinned. His smile could have used a lot of work.

I stared at him, at the chair, at a selection of metal implements on a tray, but my mind couldn't figure out what I was doing there.

"In the chair." The guard pushed me forward.

When had I last been to the dentist? It couldn't have been that long ago but even if it had been years I wasn't going to let that man at my mouth. I sat in the chair, pressing my lips together.

He cackled, a strangely high pitched laugh. "It's not your teeth I'm after. Take your top off."

I stared at him. Had he really said that?

"Take your top off." He said it slower, each syllable punctuated by a broader grin.

"You want to do it or should I get Berlin to do it for you?" the guard asked. "He only wants you to take off your jacket."

I peeled off my sopping tracksuit top, glaring at the guard for making me so wet. He seemed not to notice. My jacket slapped onto the floor.

"Better." Berlin sat down so heavily on a wheeled stool, it shot across the room. He grabbed at my chair, rocking it, leaning close to me. I sat back as far away from him as the seat would let me.

"You know the warden's speech, about how you belong to her? I'm about to underline that, gonna give you your prison tat."

I grabbed my wrist.

"When I'm finished with you, you'll belong to a whole other order of things. You know how it works, right? Each time someone passes through here, they get a bit of my handiwork. Usually one band is one time through, two, two and if they get three, let's just say no one on the outside ever sees that. Unless you've done something the Government really don't like then they might give you three straight off. You think that's you?"

I shook my head, trying not to remember how often the info-casts reinforced that the Government really didn't like stealing.

"When you get out, your tat'll remind you of your time here – what job you'll get will be way different than if you'd never met me. Your points ration'll be lighter, your accommodation won't work out so good." Berlin was smiling at me as though he was giving me good news. "First thing people look at when they meet someone new, their wrist. Puts a lot of people off. You won't ever leave this place behind."

"Cut the melodramatics and get on with it, I'm due to go off shift soon." the guard snapped.

Berlin scanned his paperwork. "All 3s and 5s, lucky you, it's a nice number, very rounded, makes me get all creative."

"And skip the creative. Just the bog standard, I want to get off on time today."

143

Berlin did something with a long silver instrument that looked and, when he started it up, sounded, like a dentist's drill. How could I stop this? Could I grab the tray of instruments? I could hit him with it. But what about the guard? And if I even made it out of the room, I'd be caught at the next locked door. The present moment, it was a high pitched scream inside my head. In the present I was just sitting in a chair. And didn't I need the tattoo? Then I could go and strike a deal with Patrice to get Coralone to Sebastian. The time to kick up was if Berlin tried to tattoo me three times.

The guard hit the arm of the chair with his nightstick. "I have to use this on you? Arm out now."

For Sebastian, I shouted in my mind, and managed to let go of my wrist. For Sebastian, I got my elbow on the armrest. For Sebastian, I lowered my arm halfway towards where it needed to be. For Sebastian, for Sebastian, for Sebastian. I blocked out the 'don't do it' my mind was screaming with the desperate chorus of Sebastian's name. Then my arm lay open and vulnerable to Berlin's needle.

"I could tell you this won't hurt a bit," he grinned, "but I'd be lying. Hold still now."

He grasped my wrist, the high pitched whining of the needle started again and he lowered it onto my skin.

CHAPTER THIRTY-SEVEN

Berlin's tattooing needle bit at me with a surprising ferociousness. People used to choose to have this done? But it seemed right it hurt, he was in effect branding me.

There was a kind of snap and the room plunged into darkness.

"What the f—"

"It's only a power cut. Nobody move." The guard's order interrupted Berlin. "I so much as feel a hair stand on end, you get my nightstick wherever I happen to hit. And it won't be gentle."

Berlin released my wrist and I hugged it to me. A frantic tapping sounded like a demented woodpecker had found its way inside. "Pack it in, Berlin, that thing won't work without electric. The generators'll kick in any second."

My eyesight hadn't even had time to adjust to the sudden darkness than the lights flickered back on. The needle buzzed back into action.

"We're on."

"That's your lot for today. You'll have to finish these tomorrow." the guard said.

Tomorrow? No, I needed my tattoo now otherwise

Patrice wouldn't deal with me. Tomorrow, that would mean Sebastian had been without his medicine for . . . seven days. A whole week.

"Why not today?" My question sounded small.

"You want it now? I can oblige you." Berlin grinned.

"No, you won't."the guard snapped. "You know as well as me we go to lockdown on generator power. On your feet, Flint, back to your cell."

He marched us through the zebra crossing lit corridors. They reminded me of the hospital a hundred years ago. He tapped a code into a keypad and the lights snapped off again.

"Goddamnit! Don't move, either of you."

A dim light flickered to life in the middle of the corridor span, barely holding back the darkness.

"What did you do?" the guard spoke through gritted teeth. "The emergency lights only kick in if the generators fail."

No! The generators had failed already. How was that possible?I should have been able to do something more sophisticated to them that I could control. The storm shouldn't have happened already.

"What did you do?"

"Nothing, except what the manual told us to." Jackson argued with him.

That was it. Now I was going to Patrice empty-handed. I clenched my fists against my sides. How could I make a deal now?

"You'd better hope I don't find anything," the guard snapped. "I can be very inventive with punishments."

"You'd better hope the warden doesn't find out you made us work on them while you played cards." I retorted.

Even in the dim-light, the guard looked like I'd physically slapped him.

"That was your allotted assignment," he blustered.

"So why the soaking? Why tell us to lie and say we'd been clearing out gutters?"

146

His hand came up so quickly I heard the slap of his palm across my cheek and felt the sting before I realised he was going to hit me.

"You don't dare threaten me," he ground out.

"That works both ways." I spat back.

He gestured down the corridor. "Move."

He marched us to the lower level of the prison again where no emergency lights worked. His torchlight cut through the darkness on the floor at his feet. Was he going to get us to work on the generators again? Was he going to check them? There was no way he couldn't not notice what I'd done if he knew the remotest thing about them but he stopped outside a door unadorned by danger signs.

"In." He unlocked the door, pointed his torch at me and then inside the tiny room. "Solitary might cool you down."

Seeing only orange flashes in front of my eyes, I stepped forward into the deep darkness. The solitary confinement cells I'd read about in stories were damp stone places that the occupants shared with rats. This one appeared to be the complete opposite. It was hot, the air so dry and stuffy that I could almost imagine myself in a desert.

I stood one step in, waiting for my night vision to wake up. The door slammed behind me and he locked me in. Already I was beginning to hate that sound. Slowly the darkness morphed into the solid shape of a bed. I baby-stepped along its length, patting it with the lightest touch. Nothing and no one else on it, no bedding either. Maybe it was just as well I couldn't see the mattress.

As I reached the bottom wall of the tiny cell, my foot kicked something that sounded like a bucket. Nineteenth century plumbing, wonderful. A faint smell of chemical pine wafted up at me. I backed away from it, trying to stifle the hiccup of memory it dislodged.

I strained to hear anything but even the storm had lost its voice down here. The silence was so complete it felt like when it snowed and muffled the world. I stood until I felt ready to fall down but still heard no scratching or scurrying noises. A rat free zone, hopefully.

The back of my throat ached for a drink but my tracksuit jacket wasn't wet enough now to wring out. Its dampness would keep me cool for a while though. I folded it into a pillow shape and lay down on the thin mattress, curling up on my side.

Now my stomach let me know I was hungry. Perfect timing. If I could ignore that, solitary wasn't so bad. I didn't have to worry about the right thing to do or say here. But in the profound silence and deep darkness, it was more difficult to keep my thoughts in the tiny corridor of safety. Maybe it didn't matter. No one could hear me cry down here.

The door slammed open, waking me instantly. That I'd managed to sleep despite everything confused me. A torch almost blinded me.

"On your feet, Flint." A woman's voice, not the guard who'd put me in here, thank God. "The warden wants to see you."

CHAPTER THIRTY-EIGHT

Oh God, the guard had told on me, hadn't he? And now the warden was going to add years to my sentence. 'You should be really scared if I ask to see you' she'd said. And I was.

"Why?" I managed.

"What'm I, your private secretary? All I know is that she wants to so that's what'll happen. Let's go."

I followed her back upstairs and through the prison squinting at the knife-like intrusion of daylight. It was like when I'd followed Evan out of the hospital to the waiting army truck, my mind yelling at me to do something, anything other than just follow numbly behind but my body doing it anyway. We eventually stopped outside a proper wooden door with no visible bars on it.

The guard knocked. "Pearson escorting Maya Flint as per your request, ma'am."

The muffled instruction I didn't catch must have told Pearson to take me in. I squared my shoulders, pulled my spine straighter and followed her into the room.

The warden was sitting behind her desk exactly as she had been when I first saw her, adjusting her pen in the same way. She wore a crisp white shirt beneath her suit today. The carpet was really soft beneath my feet, the air untainted. I could hear the odd shout through the open window. The whole atmosphere was less institutionalised here. Frighteningly it already felt different.

"Flint," the warden looked at me. "You're a surprise. Who do you know in high places?" The question was so unexpected, I stared stupidly at her. "I asked you a question."

"I'm sorry, I don't know what you mean."

"Don't play coy. Who do you know?"

I shook my head. Why was she talking in riddles? I didn't understand what she meant. I couldn't say the wrong thing but if I didn't say anything she was likely to start adding days to my sentence.

"She didn't get her tattoo?" The warden addressed Pearson.

"No, ma'am."

"She's been taking her tablets, drinking her milk?"

"Yes, ma'am."

The warden looked back at me. "You're telling me you don't know how you went from not having any credit to this?"

I wanted to shout at the woman, talk plain English! "I'm sorry I don't understand."

The warden stared at me for the longest time. I fielded her gaze. Show no weakness, show no weakness.

Finally she spoke. "Apparently you're free to go."

What? I actually felt my mouth drop open. "Is that all the time I had to serve?"

"Nothing carries a penalty of three days. Someone rescinded your sentence."

CHAPTER THIRTY-NINE

My mind scrabbled to play catch-up. Sentence rescinded? I could go home? I could go home and see Sebastian. I could see Jace. I could go home. My legs felt all wobbly but for all the right reasons this time.

"Of course if I let you go now, I'm seriously out of pocket." I stared stupidly at the warden, not sure I understood what she was saying.

"I worked yesterday but didn't have any food—"

"You had a bed, didn't you, in solitary and that costs extra. You wore that tracksuit and T-shirt, those trainers, didn't you? Then there's the matter of the extra day I added, I need recompense for that."

I had no clue what to say. She knew as well as I did that until I was given career decision, I had no access to points or money in my own right. Mum hadn't apparently been willing to support me in prison to keep me alive, how could I persuade her to pay to get me out?

The warden held up my pendant hanging from its gold chain. "Now this looks expensive."

It wasn't expensive, it was priceless. I remembered Dad giving it to me for Christmas when I was seven. I'd been fascinated by the story of how the development he was working on had to be stopped when Roman ruins were found. He took me to see it one day, and I remembered holding his hand while we followed the line of people snail-pacing their way past the two huge windows through which we could watch an actual archaeological dig in progress, while experts sifted through the fragments compacted into the soil.

I remembered when he gave me the Roman pendant, I was so excited that I was holding something older than anything else around me. I hadn't let him put it away to keep it safe for more than an hour, while I sat on his lap and tried to guess to whom it had belonged. I'd been surprised that Mum had brought it with us from York when she'd given it to me to keep for good on my thirteenth birthday.

But more than the pendant was precious because of its age, it and the chain represented the only thing I had of my father. And the warden wanted to take it from me for freedom I already had.

She checked her watch. "You don't have anything else of interest. So this'll have to do. Or you can stay here and work off the debt."

And how long would that take? She could add however many extra days to my sentence whenever she felt like it to keep me here for as long as she wanted. Right then, giving away my most precious possession seemed a small price to pay to get out. "You can keep it." I forced myself to say the words.

The warden nodded. "A wise choice. Pearson, process her out."

CHAPTER FORTY

In the central cell where I'd been processed into the prison, I pulled on my own jeans. Even in the growing heat, I was grateful for the feel of the tight denim around my legs because they were mine. My trainers felt so much better than the prison canvas ones. But even as I slipped my T-shirt over my head, I felt one hundred per cent different from the girl who'd walked in here in these same clothes only two days ago.

Had the warden taken just my chain and pendant? I checked my jacket, the bulky torch was easy to feel through the fabric. In the other pocket my hand closed around the mirror Jace had given me. I didn't pull it out to check. I didn't want anyone to see me in case they got the idea they should take it away because it was special

How much longer would this take? I didn't completely trust that they were letting me go and the longer I waited here, the more likely it seemed they wouldn't. Please don't let this be a hoax. I couldn't bear it.

I forced myself to stop pacing, perching instead on the hard wooden bench.

I stared at the green dot on my wrist. It wasn't entirely obvious it was the beginning of a tattoo, I could maybe pass it off as a birthmark or a mole. I brushed it lightly, surprised to see my finger trembling. Thank God for the power cut – a few minutes later and my life would have been transformed forever. As it was now I had the chance to forget about the last couple of days, start again, and no one on the outside would know. Except I wouldn't ever forget the snapshot images of Mum's face in the hospital corridor, the woman shot on the motorway, Mrs Randle's sore tattooed wrist.

Pearson opened the door and led me to a small office. She pointed at a wooden chair beside an overloaded desk. "Sit, you need to sign some papers."

I scanned the forms she handed me, torn by the need to get up and run out of the prison and the desire to check I wasn't being tricked. No mention of why I was being released, but I didn't dare question it. I scrawled my name at each X as instructed. Pearson took the forms back. "That's it, you're free to go."

"What about my ID?"

She shrugged. "Never had a case like this before. When you came in your ID would have been sent back to London with the soldiers who brought you to be marked with your prison number, same as everyone else's. They're returned to us before an inmate's released. No one saw this coming, your ID's probably still in the system."

"But you know I can't go anywhere, do anything without it."

"Not my problem."

I noticed a pile of the Government friendly pink paper in the trays half-buried on the desk. "Could you just issue me something on Government paper to explain why I don't have it?"

"And what am I going to put on it?" Pearson pushed the paper against the back rest of the tray. "That I said it was okay for you not to have it? Like I'm so important – you should ask whoever's springing you."

Pink paper, the exact Government shade, I

remembered seeing it at Toby's once. He'd moved it when he saw me notice it but to get hold of it he clearly had connections. But why would he have done this amazing thing for me?

"You want to go or you gonna sit there all day?" Pearson asked.

I couldn't get off the chair fast enough.

Pearson unlocked the last doors and then I was outside, in the prison gateway. The air smelt wonderful, the sun never so welcome on my unprotected skin. She unlocked the personnel door in the main exit gate. There was nothing on the other side, no transport, no people.

"How am I supposed to get home?" I asked.

"Where's that?"

"Milton Keynes."

"South's that way." She flapped a hand directly away from the prison. "What are you waiting for?"

"Isn't this a no-go zone? How can I get through that?"

Pearson laughed. "You think the Government would send transport for you? I were you, I'd start running."

She stepped back through the door and slammed it shut, locking me outside its safety.

CHAPTER FORTY-ONE

"The dogs'll get her." The soldier's comment when he shot the woman on the way up ping ponged around my mind. Evan's concern about stopping in a no-go zone even holding a big gun frazzled my nerves even more. But I couldn't stand here – they might decide to drag me back in. I forced my feet to move.

I had absolutely no idea where I was. North was all I knew so as long as I went south I should find Milton Keynes. The prison had to be near a station for its supplies. I could follow the railway tracks because MK was on the main north/south line. And I might be lucky enough that a passing train would pick me up. But how to find the station?

Everywhere I looked nature was reclaiming what mankind had tried to take from her. Tangled greenery scrabbled over every man-made surface until it looked like it had all been covered with a living cloth. I guessed the roads to the station would be the most travelled, the greenery not as able to keep its hold on them.

I stopped at a junction, left or right or straight on? Nature told me left. I switched my jacket to my other hand and followed my hunch. My stomach growled, it felt as though it was turning in on itself. I hadn't eaten properly since the day before yesterday. But last night's storm should have left pockets of water I could drink so with a bit of luck at least I wouldn't dehydrate. I had to trust that would be enough to get me home.

The sky felt huge above me as I walked, an enormous expanse of blue stitched together by feathery clouds. What was that? I stopped walking, shielded my eyes against the sun's glare. I had to put my head back so far to keep it in sight I was in danger of falling over. High, high, high above me a sleek shape crossed the sky. Was it a plane? I couldn't hear anything. I stared at it so hard my eyes began to run. A plane. What else could it be? I strained to watch it until it passed beyond my tiny patch of the world.

What did it mean? That at least one country was rich enough to still be flying. The plane had to be going somewhere so at least two had escaped the pandemic or had recovered enough that they were operating mostly normally.

I felt a strange bubble of emotion building up in me. Hope, if others could get back to normal, so could we. Isolation, that others had done it but were leaving us behind, alone, still quarantined.

My neck ached from staring up at the empty sky. Whatever the plane – it had been a plane, hadn't it? – meant didn't matter right now. It couldn't get me home.

I rolled my head to each side stretching out the muscles and carried on walking. Roads of abandoned houses led me into a city that might once have been uncertain about a prison being tangled up in its boundary. I tried the front door of the first house but even after so many years, the locks held. Empty as it was, it still felt wrong to break a window. There probably wouldn't be any food worth salvaging anyway and the water would be long gone.

I peered in through the bay window, cupping my hands against the glass to cut out the sun's glare.

Something stared back at me. Oh God! I jumped backwards, fell over something. The fully-clothed skeleton sitting watching me didn't move. But still I scrabbled away from it, away from whatever had tripped me up, clambered to my feet and bolted up the street. Only the silence and eerie nothingness of the area followed me. Stop, stop, stop! I could be wandering the streets in a huge circle until I keeled over if I wasn't careful. I pulled up and lent my hands on my knees, sucking in deep breaths, peering down the road where the skeleton kept its vigil.

I'd been too young to understand everything that happened after the pandemic. It wasn't talked about much and I'd never really thought about it before. That the Government would have left the dead in their homes seemed incredible. What about the risk of disease? I remembered when they used to take bodies away. Soldiers in scary masks that gave me nightmares. When they came to take Charlie, I'd heard Auntie Carol screaming.

Ignoring Mum's threat that I shouldn't go outside, I'd opened the front door to see what was wrong. An army ambulance was parked outside their house. Bradley, my best friend, was standing in the doorway, his face as white as the painted wood around him, silent tears streaming down his face. A red cross had been slashed on their front door, a call to the Army.

Auntie Carol was hanging onto a blanket covering a stretcher held by two soldiers. A third was prising her off. In the tussle the blanket slipped. Charlie was on the stretcher wearing his blue teddy pyjamas. His blond hair looked darker than usual. How could he be sleeping through the noise his mother was making? The rocking of the stretcher should have woken him up.

"My baby, my baby, my baby." It was horrible to hear her.

Mum grasped me by the shoulders and steered me back to our front door. "Wait here, Maya."

She stepped over the tiny fence that separated our

gardens. "Carol, it's all right, it's Anarosa. You have to let him go now."

The third soldier pulled the gun that was slung over his shoulder up into a firing position and pointing it at Auntie Carol, barked a command that I couldn't catch, muffled as it was through his mask. They looked so scary with those big black things strapped to their heads with the wobbly straps like giant insects.

"That's not necessary," Mum had shouted. "Show some compassion for God's sake, she just lost her husband and now her youngest child." I knew Mum would sort it out. "Carol, it's okay, you can let go now. Charlie's gone, but Bradley still needs you." Mum gently pulled Auntie Carol's hands from the cover. "Give him a kiss, then let him go."

She did as Mum said, kissing Charlie on the cheek and smoothing his hair. Her lips moved but I couldn't hear what she was saying. I looked at Bradley who was still crying by the door twisting Charlie's favourite teddy in his hands.

"Mummy, mummy!" I hoped she would hear, I didn't want to go near the scary soldiers. "Charlie's forgotten Moppy. He'll want Moppy." I pointed at Bradley who held up the battered toy.

"You're right, sweetie. He will." Mum took Moppy from Bradley, cupping his chin and whispering something to him, before she tucked Moppy between Charlie's arm and his side. And all the while he lay stiller than when we played sleeping lions.

The soldiers put Charlie and Moppy in the ambulance. Mum had put her arm around Auntie Carol and turned her away, to take her indoors.

Their neighbour on the other side came out, with a face mask pressed over her nose and mouth.

"Come to gloat?" Mum shouted at her. "You could have given her time to say goodbye before you drew the cross, you heartless cow."

I put my hand over my mouth to stifle a giggle. I'd never heard Mum call anyone a name before. You heartless cow. I wasn't sure what it meant, but I'd have to remember it. It sounded so grown up.

I dragged myself back to the here and now, pulling my breathing under control, walking on. It was getting hot. Maybe I should take my jeans off. It wasn't as if anyone would see me and if I could cool myself down, I'd save a lot of body fluids by not sweating. And my legs didn't usually burn.

I glanced around me even though I was the only living thing here. The skeleton sitting in the driver's seat of the car in front of me would hardly care what I was doing. The door closest to what had been the kerb was partially open, the driver eternally waiting for his passenger.

I felt the hairs on the back of my neck pull to attention as if I was being watched. I tightened my grip on my jacket. The houses could hide anything, anyone. Skeletons might be the least of my worries. And what was camouflaged in the window-high forest of grasses and weeds, the evolution of neat cottage front gardens?

A growl that made me want to hide filled the silence, a dare that the dog, wherever it was, could get me before I reached safety.

CHAPTER FORTY-TWO

The dog growled again, a longer and more menacing challenge this time. Should I try and force my way into one of the houses? I'd have to find an open door, if I broke a window the dog would be right behind me. But I could hide from it in another room and, unless feral dogs had learned how to turn door handles, I'd be safe enough. Until I needed food or water or sleep. And I'd be disturbing what amounted to a grave. The houses beckoned me with all the appeal of something out of a horror story. Maybe better that I stayed on the move outside.

"They're unsure of humans now." Evan's words from that awful night on the way to the prison didn't give me much comfort.

With a growl that let me know it had just been clearing its throat earlier, a shaggy dog burst out of its hiding place in a garden ahead of me on the opposite side of the road. My heart hammered so hard at my ribs it felt as though it was going to find a way out. It took everything I had not to break into a terrified run. Reason and logic kept me pinned to the spot, I couldn't outrun it so I'd have to outsmart it.

I thrust my hand into my jacket pocket and pulled out my mirror. Not helpful. I slipped it into my jeans, trying the opposite pocket to get my torch. It wasn't anything of a weapon and I didn't expect to be capable of hitting the dog, but it made me feel better to have something heavy in my hand.

It growled again, a long note of warning, punctuated by a coughing fit of barking. Its teeth seemed ridiculously huge and sharp. It drooled like a mad thing. I caught the dog's gaze and stared at him. I could cite any number of scientific papers, but I knew nearly nothing about animals. I could be infuriating him but I had no idea what else to do. Hold his gaze. Stare him down. Make him see I wasn't afraid of him. And therefore not his prey.

I puffed my chest out, drew myself up to my full height, held my arms slightly away from my sides, making myself look as big as possible, too big for him to bring down.

The dog growled again. This time I heard an answering bark somewhere behind me. Two of them, and there were obviously more, kept here by the food waste from the prison. Inside one of the houses was probably my only chance.

The dog turned into a blur, reaching for me in a frenzied temper. I threw my jacket at it, my sweat-slicked hand accidentally launching my torch as well, turned and ran. I charged up the front garden of the nearest house and threw myself at the front door but the lock held. What was it with home security here? I scanned the overgrown garden for something to break the front window.

But then another sound that didn't belong impaled my attention. An engine? It really was, an engine. I raced out of the garden, shot a glance at the pile of jacket-entangled dog and bolted down the road. I lengthened my strides as far as I could, trying to ignore the likelihood my feet would tangle themselves up and I'd fall over.

I launched myself around the corner, following the

sound. It was an army truck but it was too far away for me to reach. It seemed to be heading the way I'd come, towards the prison.

I couldn't hope to catch it. Ragged breaths tore at the back of my throat. I waved my arms over my head but couldn't croak out more than a squeak for help. As I dropped my arms, my hands brushed my pocket - my mirror . . . I could have kissed it. I angled it towards the driver, reflecting a patch of molten sunshine at his wing mirror. Please see it, please see it.

The dog renewed its barking. It was getting closer. I heard it turn the corner behind me, a strange dragging noise, one of his legs tangled in my jacket. I raced towards the truck, trying to keep the blinding light from my mirror where the driver could see it.

Red lights at the back of the truck, then a white one and it was reversing towards me.

I staggered towards it, realising too late as the distance between us shortened, that I could be running into way more trouble than that of facing a feral dog.

CHAPTER FORTY-THREE

The army truck closed the distance between us quicker than I could have dared hope. It stopped a couple of metres from me and a soldier jumped out in a blur of camouflage.

"Get in the cab." he yelled, running round me, his shout almost lost in the gunshot that made me jump every bit as much as the one that had ended the life of the woman who'd bargained for her escape. I pushed the memory away, I couldn't deal with the guilt I felt for that yet. When it all caught up with me, I knew I'd be in for a rough time. Karma could be a bitch.

I almost gasped as the word popped into my head, but the soldier could hardly know what I was thinking, could he? I clambered up into the cab to get away from the dog, distance myself from my rogue thoughts. I slammed the door, willing my thudding heartbeat to calm down before I had a heart attack.

The driver's door opened and the soldier climbed in.

"It's you."

"Evan?" We said together.

He checked the paperwork clipped to the dashboard. "What's your name?"

"Maya Flint."

"What're you doing out here? You know about the no-go zone?"

"Much more than I want to but I couldn't stand outside the prison forever. They might have changed their minds about letting me go."

"The warden was supposed to release you into my custody. She's a real bitch, that woman."

I nodded. I remembered her checking her watch, hurrying to get me released before Evan arrived.

"You okay?" His eyes were a striking blue. I hadn't noticed that in the darkness. And he seemed sincere in his concern.

"I'm fine. The dog?"

"The shot frightened it enough so it ran off. Couldn't get your jacket back though."

"It doesn't matter."

He revved the engine. "I've got orders to take you to your home in Milton Keynes but you'll have to direct me when we get into the city." He turned the truck around. "Why did they release you?"

"I've no idea."

"Seriously?"

"Seriously."

"There's water in there." He gestured at the rucksack in the footwell by my feet. "And rolls, I figured you'd be hungry."

"What'll it cost?"

"God, they brainwashed you fast. No charge, I won't expect favours for them. I'm not like some of the other soldiers. I just figured . . ."

I didn't want him to think I thought that about him. "Thanks, you figured right."

The rolls were a bit hard, yesterday's freshness dried out of them but they tasted better than anything I'd ever eaten.

Apart from cooking a little in the hot cab, the journey

was one hundred per cent better than the last one. Even the noise of the engine wasn't as bad. And Evan was nice company, not prying into what had happened over the last few days.

"So what're you looking forward to most, about being home?" he asked.

"Seeing my brother, my best friend, my mum. Having a shower, I probably don't smell very nice."

"Driving up and back in one go, I'm probably not so good myself." He grimaced. "Not great considering it's not ever I get to ride with a pretty girl."

"What's it like, being in the military?" I steered the conversation away from me.

"Well you saw some of the prize idiots I get to work with. I guess it's like any career, some really want to do it, at least some of the older guys, the ones who were in before the Government began to decide who would join up. Some just like the power trip, then it's hard . . ." His voice tailed away.

He changed the subject and we chatted easily all the way back to MK.

"Here's fine." I said when we reached the turn off to my estate from the grid road.

"You're sure? My orders were to take you to your house."

I hesitated but what did it matter? I'd never see him again. "Ordinarily that'd be great but my mum and me didn't part on the best of terms. I'd rather not announce my homecoming to the street by arriving back in an army truck. She wouldn't like it and I don't want to upset her any more."

"If you're sure."

I nodded, nerves suddenly drying out my mouth. I didn't know what I'd find at home, but whatever it was, I wanted to discover it on my own.

"It won't be that bad, you know." Evan said. I hoped he was right.

"Thanks for the lift, for saving me."

"My pleasure."

"Thanks, too, for what you said to me, about showing no weakness. It really helped."

"I'm glad." As I grabbed the door handle he spoke all in a rush. "If I'm ever back here, can I come see you?"

"That'd be nice. Take care, Evan."

He patted his sidearm. "Always."

I smiled and got down from the cab. He beeped the horn making me jump, smiled and waved at me when I looked round. For a soldier, he was really nice.

My road looked the same as I walked up it. Why shouldn't it? It was me who felt different. I glanced at Jace's house, I'd go see him when he was back from school.

I slipped through the back gate, careful not to slam it. The corn was nearly ready. The lettuces looked wilted and bright red globes that should already have been picked pulled down the branches of the tomato plants. My bike leant against the fence as though it were a normal day. Jace must have collected it from the hospital.

I straightened my spine and pulled in a deep breath against what I might find inside. I opened the back door. The house was quiet but it didn't feel empty. I crept through the kitchen and peered into the lounge. Sebastian was propped up on the sofa, reading.

"Hey you." I croaked.

"Maya!"

I rushed up to him, hiding my face in his hair as I hugged him until I could trust myself not to bawl. I perched on the edge of the sofa, felt his forehead, the back of his neck, checking him over everywhere else visually. "How're you? Has Mum got you more Coralone?"

"I'm okay."

"Have you been sick?" I remembered poor Jasmine and Donna.

He shook his head. "Got a cough, but that's all.

167

Where've you been, Maya?"

"Mum didn't tell you?"

"She said you'd gone away but she didn't say where. I missed you, Auntie Esther, she sat with me but it's not the same as you."

I patted his leg. "Well, I'm back now so it'll be me from now on."

"Mum said you weren't coming back."

I felt an arrow poison my bubble of happiness. Why would she say that? "Grown ups aren't always right. See, I'm back and I'm not going anywhere, promise."

He grinned. "I got new books from the library. Look, a comic book."

"Wow, it's so great to see you reading. Did Mum take you to hospital? Did they give you more Coralone?"

"No."

"Do you have a new medicine?"

"Maya!"

"Mum." I was off the sofa and halfway across the room before I realised her expression wasn't a welcome home. My arms dropped to my side as though they were suddenly too heavy to hold up.

She marched into the kitchen. "What're you doing here?"

What did she mean? "I live here."

"No, Maya. You don't."

CHAPTER FORTY-FOUR

I stared at Mum, not quite able to understand what she was saying. "Of course I live here."

"No, Maya, you live where the Government tell you and that's in a prison." She hissed the word as though to utter it might make her end up there too. "You have to go back, before you get us into trouble. If they take me away, there'll be no one left to look after Sebastian."

"What're you talking about? They let me go, it was all a mistake. They even arranged transport for me How else could I have had a lift from a soldier?" I tried to take the injured tone out of my voice. "I haven't escaped, if that's what you're thinking."

"I don't see any soldiers here, I haven't heard any army trucks."

"I asked him to drop me off at the grid road because I didn't want to upset you."

"Wait there." She walked out of the house.

"Where are you going?" I called after her but she didn't answer.

Show no weakness. The thought itself almost made me cry – I never dreamt I would have to use it here at home, where I was supposed to feel safe.

I took the stairs two at a time, I might be able to see where she was going from upstairs. But all thoughts of craning out the window disappeared when I saw my bedroom. Mum's duvet was on my bed, her things on my chest of drawers and shelves – where had she put my books? I opened the wardrobe, Mum's clothes. I could have expected that. It was logical really, I could have been away for years. And no mother with half a gram of maternal instinct would opt to sleep in the converted garage downstairs when there was an empty bedroom right next to her sick child. I got that. But this—?

I went into Sebastian's room and sat on his bed. I'd been gone only three days and Mum had removed all trace of me. She hadn't had enough points to send me anything to eat but she'd found enough to buy paint to obliterate me from her life. All the designs I'd drawn and doodled on the walls since I was eight, the legacy of my childhood, were gone, painted over. With bare walls my room looked all wrong.

"Maya, come down here." Mum was back, her tone no less stony than before. I swallowed hard, I would not let her see me cry.

Esther was standing in the hallway. "Maya, dear, how lovely you're home."

I nodded, trying to dredge up a suitable return smile.

"I won't be long, Esther." Mum's tone was noticeably warmer to her.

"Take your time, Sebastian has a new comic book to show me."

"I can sit with him," I said, ignoring the wobble in my voice.

"Esther's here because you're coming with me."

"I want to stay here, with Sebastian."

"You'll do as you're told." Mum held the front door open.

Much as I wanted to, I knew it would just make things worse arguing with her. I stepped outside and let her lead the way.

We stopped outside number fifty-nine.

"Wait here."

I watched her knock on the door and talk to the woman who answered as if she knew her. The woman looked at me enough times that I began to feel defensive, began to wish I'd stood behind a parked car, stayed at home. I realised I was fidgeting from foot to foot and had to make a conscious effort to stand still.

Mum waited, her back to me, while the woman went inside and came out and handed her a piece of paper.

After a little more conversation, the woman shut her front door. Mum turned the paper around in her hand and set off down the road. I guessed I was supposed to follow her.

After her normal conversation with the woman, I thought Mum might have softened towards me, but no. She marched up the road, her feet snapping at the pavement, her shoulders and neck clenched, a bundle of fury. Even with my longer legs, I found it hard to keep up with her.

It wasn't until we turned into his road that I realised we were going to Toby's. Now I really didn't understand – why would she bring me here?

CHAPTER FORTY-FIVE

Mum marched straight up the steps of Toby's house and knocked.

A young guy I'd seen a couple of times here before opened the door. He looked at us both but thankfully didn't show if he remembered me. Mum handed him her piece of paper. He read it, looked his question at her.

"Is that all right?" She sounded nervous, she'd tensed up so much she looked like she'd forgotten to take her blouse off the coat-hanger before putting it on.

The guy waved us in and gestured at the lounge door. "You can wait in there."

No, no, no. If Jessica saw me, she'd give me her usual brilliant welcome and I'd be in more trouble with Mum than now.

But the lounge was empty.

"Why're we here?" I asked when the guy left us on our own. Mum's face was completely closed. "I said, why are we here?"

"I heard you."

"Oh, so you're ignoring me. Real mature." Maybe she wouldn't talk about anything to do with me, but perhaps she'd talk about Sebastian. "Why didn't you take Sebastian to hospital?" Something I didn't recognise flickered over her face. "Did you get him new medicine? He seems a little better."

"Better? He's not better, you've seen him for five minutes, he's only worse."

"So why haven't you taken him to hospital?"

When it became clear she wouldn't answer me, I felt something inside snap. "Look, you blame me for Sebastian being so sick, I get that, but why don't you do something about it?"

"Stop yelling, they'll hear you."

"So? Answer me!"

"I was doing something about it until you messed everything up. Did you not wonder how I happened to be at the Dispensary right when you were arrested? I'd gone there to take the Coralone myself." She adjusted her hands so I couldn't see the stump on her left hand. "But you getting caught tipped Fred off that I needed it so he had my pharmacy privileges revoked." She looked away from me. "You sabotaged the only way left to get the Coralone."

Oh God, I'd done it again. I was so tired of trying to do the right thing and having it all explode in my face. I realised my mouth was hanging open but what could I say to that?

I was becoming the world's biggest fuck-up merchant. The censored word hardly made me blanche. There was no other way to describe it. I was like a modern King Midas except everything I touched turned to crap.

"What about getting Sebastian admitted?" My question was very small, about as big as I felt.

"There's no point, there's no Coralone at the hospital now so there's nothing they can do to help him. Sebastian's better off at home."

She looked away from me again but I caught the shadow of desperation and fear that crossed her face. I hesitated. I wasn't sure if I could really bear to hear the answer to my next question but I couldn't just pretend it hadn't happened. And surely I'd heard the worst of everything now? "Why wouldn't you support me in prison?"

She appeared to have been struck deaf again.

"Mum, I'm talking to you."

She looked at me with that horrible closed face but the door opened and a man I didn't know broke the moment. He was tall and wiry, his skin almost the same light gold as mine. He had a prison tattoo on his wrist that curled up his arm. Another row of numbers circled the top edge of the gang marque.

"You need a question answering?"

He draped himself over the arm of the chair opposite her.

"I'm sorry to bother you. Thank you for seeing me. I just, my daughter was taken to prison three days ago. She just turned up at home telling me they let her go."

"What'd she do?"

Mum tucked her right hand over her left. "Stole."

I felt his gaze on me, scrutinising. I held my hands up so he could see all my fingers, my bare wrists. He looked back at Mum. "What's your question with all that?"

"What do I do if she's escaped? I have a sick son, he needs me, I can't be involved . . ."

She couldn't be involved with her daughter? I felt as though she'd trampled over what remained of our relationship. I knew I'd done wrong to steal the Coralone, but I'd only done it for my brother's sake. I'd been trying to save her child, didn't that count for anything?

"How d'you get out?" The guy rapid-fired questions at me.

"They let me go."

"How'd you get back?"

"A soldier brought me, in an army truck."

"Which prison?"

"I don't know, up north somewhere."

"Who paid for your food on day one?"

"The warden."

He turned to Mum. "She tells the truth. She ain't got a tat – you get that second day, always. They let her go. Ain't no way no one's gonna be escaping on they own from any of the prisons. They tell you why they let you go?"

I shook my head.

"They must have told you, Maya."

"Guess that's something else not to believe me about, isn't it." I shouted at her, stormed out of the room, down the hallway, fumbled at the front door and ran down the steps, straight into Toby.

"Hey, steady, girl. Where you off in such a rush?"

"Nowhere. Toby, I wanted to thank you."

He flashed his gold-edged smile. "For what?"

"Getting me out."

"Outta where?"

"Prison."

"You think I have that kind of influence? Wish I did, wouldn't have to bust my," he lowered his voice and leant a little closer, "arse, working so damn hard if I did."

"But you're the only person I know who could pull off something like that."

"Appreciate you thinking so highly of me, but it wasn't me."

If not him, who then?

"Did you manage to get any Coralone, the medicine my brother needs?"

"Nah, still nothing doing."

"Okay, thanks." It wasn't okay at all but I didn't want Mum to see that I knew Toby.

"Maya." Mum caught me up at the bottom of the road.

She still hadn't answered my question about not supporting me in prison and I just couldn't let it go.

"You told me when we first moved here that unless you'd walked in a person's shoes you couldn't judge them, but that's what you're doing to me, Mum. I had to do something to save Sebastian because you weren't."

"Yes, I was, but I could hardly broadcast it, could I? And once that was taken away, thanks to you, there was, is, absolutely nothing I can do for him."

"So you're mad at me for trying to do what you were going to do?"

"I'm beyond mad, Maya. I don't blame you for breaking Sebastian's medicine, that was an accident. But for doing what I specifically told you not to, I blame you for that because your actions have killed your brother's chances."

She really felt like that? Her honesty was brutal. Deep down I'd convinced myself that it had been an error that I'd had no credit, that Mum would never let me down like that. But there had been no mistake.

My feet had stopped moving. I couldn't think what to say because she was right. She might just as well have said I'd killed my brother.

And when I looked at her, I could see that recrimination shouting at me from every line on her face. I didn't know how I could ever live with seeing that every day because she was right.

CHAPTER FORTY-SIX

The laughter and shouts of kids on their way home from school intruded into the tiny copse where I'd been hiding after running away from Mum. I was such a coward and it was so stupid. What was I going to do, never look at her again? Even if I stumbled across a bottle of Coralone in the next five minutes and Sebastian was okay, the hurt of what she'd said to me would always be there. And if the worst happened . . .

I'd battled those thoughts to no avail all while I'd waited until I could go and see Jace. Now I could at least try and take my mind off them. Who was I kidding? At least I could see someone who would be pleased to see me.

I knocked on his front door and waited. I didn't normally use the front door but surely he'd have answered it by now if he was there. Maybe he wasn't in. Maybe he didn't want to see me either. Maybe the hideous welcome home Mum had given me would be universal. No one liked criminals, went out of their way to shun them, but I never figured he'd do that to me.

I had nowhere else to go. I'd have to go home. At least I'd be back before Mum went to work as ordered and as painful as that would be, I would have to bear it because this was my new norm. But then I heard the lock being turned, Jace's door opened and I'd hardly registered the shock on his face before I was inside, he'd slammed the door and pulled me close.

"I probably don't smell so great." I mumbled.

"Don't care." Jace pulled me tighter against him.

This was what I needed, the simple human contact of one person holding another. No awkward questions, no terrible suspicions, just him being pleased that I was home. I knew Mum was worried about Sebastian and blaming me for everything was fair enough. But it hurt so much that she hadn't seemed the slightest bit pleased or relieved to see me back home safe. That she'd wanted to send me back. I pulled my thoughts up. How would a pity party make things better? I didn't want Jace to see me cry. And things were what they were. Somehow I would have to get used to it.

The longest time passed while Jace held me, until I relaxed against him, not needing to feel embarrassed at how I might be smelling, at our close proximity, until I could just enjoy the feeling of being so close to someone. Within his arms the solidity of him made me feel safe. The relief that he was so pleased to see me made my knees feel weak.

"I thought I'd never see you again." His voice sounded deeper than usual.

I didn't know how to answer him. Anything that came to me was too glib to say out loud. Finally he let me go and stepped backwards only enough that he could look at me. "When d'you get home?"

I shrugged. I'd totally lost track of time while I'd been hiding. "A while ago. Mum dragged me to Toby's, she doesn't believe they let me go, she thinks I escaped. She's—" Hadn't I just decided to stop my pity party?

"You need to go home?"

"Not right now."

"You hungry?"

Evan's bread rolls felt like a long time ago. "I guess I should be, I haven't really eaten for a couple of days."

Jace gave me such a look of understanding and empathy that I had to look away. He stepped closer again, putting his arms around me. "You don't have to talk about any of it, if you don't want to. But I'm here if you do." I nodded. "I'll make us some food. You go shower."

My thanks were interrupted by a knock at the door. I recognised the shape of the caller even made blurry by the frosted glass. "It's my mum," I whispered.

"You want to see her?"

I shook my head. "I can't, not right now."

"Upstairs, I'll deal with her."

I fled up the stairs and hesitated, the mirror image of his house throwing me slightly as it always did. I shut and locked the bathroom door gently and sat on the floor with my hands over my ears and my eyes shut. See no evil, hear no evil or certainly nothing that would hurt me any more for a little while at least.

CHAPTER FORTY-SEVEN

I had never seen Sebastian like this. It sounded as though he was trying to cough up a lung. I held him while it racked his body, while he spat out the gunk.

"When did this start?" I asked when he flopped back on his pillow.

"The day you went away."

I gnawed the inside of my lip. This was the longest he'd been without Coralone since he'd been diagnosed. It couldn't be a co-incidence, the withdrawal of his medicine and now he was getting way worse, just like Mum said.

I sat with him until he fell asleep. Even with his bedroom window wide open, I was sweating while I was just sitting. After a quick shower, I sat on the back step. The sprinkling of stars over the night sky brightened the more I stared at it. It was mesmerising. Strange to think that people had once dreamt of exploring them, had sent robotic spacecraft to the other planets in the solar system, journeys over such distances it was mind-blowing. Strange to think people had once travelled all around this planet, strange to think they'd travelled the length and breadth of this country. How small our lives had become.

I went to check on Sebastian. He was somehow

sleeping through his intermittent cough. I refilled his glass of water, felt his forehead. Minding him was such a huge part of my life the balm of my old routine soothed the nightmare of the last few days. I wouldn't spoil the moment by wondering at how Mum would be when she came home. I knew I'd taken the coward's way out by hiding at Jace's until she'd gone to work but putting up with her anger in the morning would be better than seeing the way she looked at me now.

At around one I laid the sofa cushions on Sebastian's floor, curled up beside him, listening to the horrible rattling sound of his breathing, waiting for the next laboured breath to reassure me he was still alive.

It was like I was back at the start. I couldn't steal Coralone, I couldn't borrow it, I couldn't get an advance on another bottle. Did that leave any other options?

The night dragged on while I kept half an eye on the growing lightness through the curtains, half an ear out to make sure Sebastian didn't miss a breath. And in that peculiar dream-like state an idea shocked me to consciousness.

I stared up at the ceiling, the idea charging around my mind. It made total sense, it was the last logical step, the only thing left I could try. But going to London, could I really do that?

London was a big place, I'd find it easily enough. Down the old M1 and I'd be right there but what if the entrance to the city was patrolled? Even if I had my ID, anyone checking it would arrest me because it listed Milton Keynes as my home, but to be stopped without any . . .? And then there was the bit between the two cities – was that another no-go zone? I shivered. But this time I'd be on my bike, which would surely give me a reasonable chance. Actually once I got there, London being so vast would be my biggest problem – how would I know where to go?

Maybe Toby could help me out, with a bit of luck his

network extended that far.

It was such a radical idea, travelling so far, there would be so many opportunities to be caught, arrested, sent right back to jail. But I couldn't not try. I was the one who broke the Coralone, I was the one responsible for Mum not being able to get any. Not trying wasn't an option, even if I failed, the guilt might be easier to live with. Who was I kidding?

All while I ate breakfast, made myself sandwiches and packed a backpack, I wrestled with what to leave in a note for Mum. In the end I settled on, 'I'll be back in two days' and made myself sign it 'love Maya'.

Fifteen minutes before she was due back from work, I bent over Sebastian and watched him, tracing the outline of his face with my gaze until my back ached. I kissed the top of his head as gently as I could so as not to wake him.

"Love you, kiddo." I breathed. "I'm going to get you Coralone okay, you hang on till I get back, you hear?"

I clock-watched for another five minutes. My timing was everything. I propped the note up on the stairs, somewhere Mum would find it when she came in and went to check on Sebastian.

I unlocked the back door, grabbed my bike and put it outside the gate. In the kitchen I waited, listening to the silence which meant Sebastian didn't need me. As soon as I heard Mum's key in the lock, I slipped out, pulling the back door closed, running down the garden, out the gate into the alley. So intent was I on getting away before she noticed what I was doing, I had no idea anyone was behind me until I felt a hand grab my shoulder.

CHAPTER FORTY-EIGHT

I ducked away from the hand, spinning round, hitting out with my backpack. "Jace! You nearly gave me heart failure."

"You nearly broke my ribs." He rubbed at his side.

I shook the backpack. "I think you broke my sandwiches."

"Where're you going in such a hurry?"

I looked at my house. "I'll tell you but not here, meet you at the grid road entrance."

He ducked into his garden to grab his bike, I got on mine, bending low over the handlebars, trying to make myself invisible.

He caught me up before I reached the edge of the estate. "You can't be going to school this early."

I shook my head. "I don't even know if I can go back. I'm going to London. I left Mum a note, I doubt she'll ask you but if she does, tell her you don't know anything."

"That won't be far from the truth, seeing as I don't. You want to share?"

"I'm going to the factory that makes Coralone." He stared at me as if I were sprouting horns. "Nothing you say will make me change my mind." I hoped he wouldn't try. "It's the only way I can think of to get some."

"Do you even know where this factory is?"

"Not exactly, but I know someone who will."

"How can you know someone in London?"

"Not me, Toby." And now he would be disappointed in me, like he always was when I mentioned Toby. "I know what you're thinking—"

"I don't think you do."

"I'll be back tomorrow night at the latest. Can you tell your gran I'm sorry that Mum'll ask her to mind Sebastian again. It'll be the last time."

"Go see Toby, Maya. I'll get sorted and wait at the big roundabout at the bottom of the H8 for you." I stared at him, what he said was so totally the opposite of what I'd expected, it was like he'd started speaking another language. "You're not to go without me." he added.

"No way, Jace. You have school, you can't mess up so close to career decision. One screw up between us is enough."

"You don't get it, do you?"

"Get what?"

He smiled at me, completely unexpectedly. "Let's just say I already figured out going to the factory that makes it was the next thing to do."

A gaggle of kids walked past, laughing and chattering, a normal let's get together early before school day for them. I bet they didn't realise how lucky they were.

"Jace, I—Thanks, thanks so much. But seriously, I can do this by myself."

"I'm coming with you, if you don't wait for me, I'll just catch you up anyway. But if you don't wait, I'll never speak to you again."

"You wouldn't."

"You want to put it to the test?"

Of course I didn't. Without his friendship I'd have nothing. "I'll wait."

As it turned out, I didn't have the chance to see if I

would be tempted to save Jace from himself – by the time I'd collected a scribbled note from Toby asking his cousin to help me out and got back to our rendezvous point, Jace was already there, with a backpack, lying in the grass, waiting.

"You know where we're going?" He got to his feet.

"Pretty much. Toby has a cousin who can help us, he lives just a little way from the bottom of the M1." I was gabbling, rushing past the explanation so Jace didn't ask me what I'd had to trade for the map. And I really didn't want to think about owing Toby an unnamed favour. The price of doing business with him scared me. Something else to squeeze into the part of my brain where I was currently ignoring all the other things I couldn't think about. It was getting pretty crowded in there. "You ready?"

"Yep.' Jace shouldered his backpack.

"I really appreciate this. You're such a good friend to me, I don't ever seem to be able to give enough back to you."

"I don't want much."

"I hope you know I don't ever take you or your friendship for granted."

He gave me a crooked smile. "Let's hit the road."

CHAPTER FORTY-NINE

Jace and I been riding for hours when the sky began shrugging itself into an overcoat of grey clouds. I watched them knitting together in the middle, blocking out the blue to take my mind off how tired I felt. How every revolution of the pedals was becoming more and more of an effort. I struggled behind him for what felt forever but I knew even my stubbornness wouldn't keep me going.

We laid our bikes down on the verge and I dropped into the long grass, too tired to care what might be underneath me.

"You okay?" he asked.

"Will be. Just need a minute. The only good thing that came out of going to prison was seeing the doctor. Apparently I'm anaemic."

"How can you be? That's what the vitamin tablets are supposed to stop, stuff like that."

I struggled with myself for just a second before telling him. "I've been trading mine with Toby."

"Shit, Maya."

"Jace!"

He looked at the empty expanse surrounding us filled only with vegetation and the rotting hulks of cars and trucks and silence. "Who exactly's going to hear me out here? So how do you get cured?"

I shrugged. "I had an iron tablet but I only got one because Mum didn't give them any credit for me. I guess I need more."

"Credit?" I told him about how Mum hadn't supported me. Even in the telling, it hurt.

"Shit, Maya."

I wished he'd stop looking at me like that. "Shit, Jace, will you stop saying that?"

We looked at each other and laughed. It felt really good.

"Here." He handed me a sandwich. "If you're anaemic you probably need to eat."

"Thanks."

I forced myself to take a bite. The sandwich tasted perfect.

Getting back on my bike was the last thing I wanted to do but after a few more minutes we rode on. London was a real long way on a bike. I concentrated on pushing the pedals around, again, again. I forgot about keeping an ear out for any growling or barking, about looking for patrols in the distance. My whole world was pushing those pedals around. I would speak to Toby about getting hold of some iron pills, it was getting so I could barely function. How did Sebastian do it, how did he cope with some days not being able to even get out of bed? The thought of him made me push a bit harder.

"What's that, there?" I could see something up ahead. "It's not Army, is it?"

"I can't hear any engines but maybe we should get off the road."

Into the thickly wooded verges on either side that could hide any number of feral animals? I didn't think so.

As we got closer it became obvious it wasn't anything to do with the Government. The something morphed into a someone, lying in the road, someone small, a little girl, around ten or so. She didn't seem to be moving. I jumped off my bike and felt her wrist.

"She's got a good pulse."

Jace put his jacket and backpack next to mine on the tarmac. "I can't see bleeding anywhere."

"If you hold her head still, we can roll her, see where she's hurt."

As we gently rolled her over, the girl's eyes snapped open and she sprang up, jabbing at us with an evil-looking knife.

CHAPTER FIFTY

"Do as I say and no one gets hurt." The girl punctuated her words with gestures with the knife.

Jace stood up, he looked a fearsome target for a ten-year-old. "I don't think so."

I followed his lead, but I was only halfway to standing when I saw a group of teenagers coming out of the bushes behind him. It was hard to give them an exact age but any height or strength advantage we might have had dissolved beneath their superior numbers. I had no doubt they could prove more dangerous than the dog I'd got away from yesterday. Binoculars around the neck of the skinniest kid were the least innocuous thing they carried. Rocks, knives, a golf club, a catapult told me it could all end badly.

"We're gonna take the pack. You're gonna let us." The girl we'd stopped to help thrust her knife at both of us, before scooping up Jace's rucksack, shouldering it and merging with the ring of kids gathering round us.

"No you're not." Jace made a grab at her, at his pack.

The kid next to him swung his golf club up over his shoulder. "You really wanna do that?"

Jace backed away, rejoining me in the middle of the

circle.

"Your parents know you're out threatening people? What if I'm a GI?" I demanded.

The tallest, presumably the leader, spat on the ground. "That's for GIs. You wanna report me, go ahead. I've got all these witnesses that say I wasn't even here. You've got bullshit." A couple of the kids giggled but I could hear their stretched nerves. "You passing through a no-go, no one's gonna care what happens to you. You're not supposed to be here." The leader was trying to galvanise his troops.

I pulled myself up to my full height hoping to intimidate him. "How do you think we're here? Our army patrol isn't far behind. You'd better return our property and get going while you still can."

"You're bluffing." The leader spoke convincingly enough but he looked unsure. A couple of the kids glanced at each other and began shuffling away from us, breaking the solidity of the circle.

I shrugged, trying to look nonchalant. "Your funeral."

The ones shuffling broke into a run, bolting for the trees, the girl who'd taken Jace's pack among them. I grabbed for my own backpack, grasping one of the straps at the same time as a scrawny kid who was stronger than he looked.

Jace grabbed hold of my strap to help me win the tug-of-war, but before he could wrench it off the kid, something flew through the air and he folded to the ground onto his jacket.

"Jace." My grip loosened, torn between wanting to check him and wanting to hang onto my backpack. I felt the crack as something else hit him on the head. The kid with the catapult! I charged at him. He ducked away, running in the opposite direction to his mates, across the motorway. He'd better run, using Jace as target practice. I followed the kid over the crash barrier in the middle but he skidded underneath the trailer of a lorry skewed across the lane where its driver had abandoned it. Great. There was no way I could get him now. If I went after him from this side, he'd shoot out the other and vice versa. But if I did catch him, what was I going to do with him? I didn't want to hand him over to the authorities.

I turned back to Jace to see our bikes disappearing into the tangle of greenery from which the kids had first appeared. I jumped the crash barrier and ran back across the carriageway. Too slow. The kids and our bikes had been swallowed whole by the foliage by the time I got there.

Jace caught hold of my arm. "Let it go, Maya."

"But they've got our stuff. They'll be slow pushing our bikes through that lot, we can catch them."

"But they know the area. They know where to hide." He was slightly stooped, holding his side.

"Are you okay?" I asked.

"I will be when we get out of here. They could be rounding up adult reinforcements."

"But—"

"No, Maya, we're not risking it. Our capture would make any GI's year. We're leaving. Now." He winced as he picked up his jacket and headed off down the motorway towards London. It didn't help that I knew he was right. I glared at the verge and followed him.

CHAPTER FIFTY-ONE

I had no trouble keeping up with Jace while my anger lasted. But, as it faded, every single muscle reminded me that I shouldn't be stressing my body so much until I'd replaced the iron I was lacking. Finally I had to ask him to stop. He laid his jacket out on the tarmac for us to sit on.

I plonked down beside him. "How's it feel, where they hit you?"

"Fine, just got the wind knocked out of me." He rubbed his head. "Have a bit of an egg. Lucky shots. Little bastards."

"They took everything. I've got nothing to trade with Lawrence now."

"Lawrence?"

"Toby's cousin."

"They took the directions?"

"No, they're in my pocket." I'd learnt that lesson from throwing my torch away at the dog. I picked at a weed snaking its way out of the tarmac. "I'm sorry about your bike."

He gave his half-shrug. "Hey, you're okay, I'm okay. It could have been worse."

"If I weren't so dumb and easily suckered—"

"You wouldn't be my best friend. I love that you wanted to stop and help her. Who knew she was a conniving—"

"Someone might be listening." I warned him.

"I almost don't care." He tucked my hair behind my ear.

"But I do, you're in enough trouble because of me. And now you're without a bike. I'll make it right—"

"Maya, stop. It's not a big deal. Once we get the Coralone we'll figure something out to get home."

But now a hard journey had become nigh on impossible. I had nothing to trade for the factory address, we had no food or water and having left our designated shops for buying food in Milton Keynes, no way to get more, even if we'd had money.

Jace was checking out where he'd been hit, a raised and angry weal on his stomach.

"That looks sore." I ran my fingers lightly around the edge.

"I'm a hero, no biggie. Let's get going."

"Don't want to make you big-headed or anything, but yeah, you are. I'm so lucky to have you." My hand stopped making circles around his welt.

"You know that works both ways."

Somehow the distance between us had evaporated and I was looking into his eyes. They were such a pale blue, all at odds with his hair, his tanned body. I couldn't tell who leaned in first but the jolt that made my insides somersault when our lips met rocked me so strongly that, if I'd been standing up, I'd have fallen over.

Wow, who knew he could kiss like that? I wanted it to go on forever. I felt his arm around my shoulders, making me feel safe again, reinforcing that I could do anything with him by my side.

But this was Jace, my best friend. What if these other feelings didn't last? What if they were just a visceral reaction to the danger we'd been in, just like when we'd hidden on the roundabout? What if they wrecked our friendship?

I pulled away from him. "I can't, I'm sorry."

He looked so surprised I wanted to bite my tongue off. "You can't kiss me like that and then tell me you don't feel this, this thing between us."

"But we're friends, we shouldn't be doing anything to jeopardise that."

"Far as I can tell, that'd only enhance our friendship. I know it's scary—"

"It's not that. I'm only *not* scared when I'm with you."

"So what's the problem then?" His gaze was too direct, too honest.

I pulled at the weed again. "I just can't. I couldn't bear the thought of losing you."

"I'd never let that happen."

I could tell how much he meant it, how the thought upset him as much as it did me. So he should be able to understand that I couldn't risk him. I didn't even know how to begin to explain it. "I thought my parents would always be there for me, right until they died. Maybe they did too. But now . . . "

"I'm not like them, you know that."

"I know that while we're friends, when other . . . feelings get involved, who knows how that'll change things? I tore at the grass until I scraped my fingertips.

"It won't for me, Maya. Nothing will ever change how I feel about you."

"I can't risk it. You're too special to me to lose."

He stared at the grass I was shredding. Then suddenly in a flurry of movement he was pulling away from me, standing up, telling me 'let's go', drowning out my whispered apology.

CHAPTER FIFTY-TWO

The end of the motorway dipped down towards London as though in deference to what, as far as I understood things, was once one of the great cities of the world. I'd gone through a phase of wanting to know about the bigger world when I was roughly Sebastian's age, but apparently that was an area the Government had decided we didn't need to know about now and the sections in the libraries on other countries and our joint histories were basically empty shelves. Of course that made me want to know even more but no one ever seemed interested in talking about the past, how things used to be, the places they'd visited. It was like the world began and ended with us now.

As we got closer to this city, its outer boundary was as deserted as the rest of the way, no patrols, no checkpoints. Thank God.

"Where does this guy live?" Jace asked, like he was an expert on London streets.

"Off the main road into Wembley, Toby said." I pointed at his scribble, "up that way."

"And he can be trusted?"

"He's Toby's cousin. He won't let us down."

He got that same look he always did whenever I

mentioned Toby. But this time I was just grateful he was saying anything. We'd walked for ages in silence, not the usual one we were happy to share, because we were totally comfortable with each other, but an absence of talking and closeness. Irony had a bizarre sense of humour, if I lost Jace's friendship because I didn't want to take it to the next level, in case we fell out and ruined our friendship . . . I was too tired to argue it out in my head. My hips hurt, my legs were stiffening up. I wanted to lie down and go to sleep on the pavement.

A huge concrete flyover reared up above our heads. Weeds had snaked up the supports discarding slivers of concrete as they squirmed their way into cracks and crannies. As we crunched over the cement confetti I wondered how long it would be until the supports became useless and the sections above our heads crashed down. I stepped out from under the behemoth's shadow, walking instead past the forecourt of a boarded-up petrol station. Ridiculous really, it wasn't as if it was going to fall down right now, it could probably bear a few more years of neglect first.

The top of the rise levelled out into what had been a wide road, not disimilar to the grid roads in Milton Keynes. Houses huddled together on either side. I could see a few trees up on the right circling what could be a school. But there was none of the explosion of greenery like at home.

This time last week I hadn't been out of Milton Keynes since the day the Army moved us in. Now I'd been up north somewhere and down to London. And I hadn't dropped dead of infection like the info-casts warned would happen if people started moving around the country again. The warning about feral dogs was more justified and maybe they should mention terrorist kids. But that hardly fitted in with the Government's crime-less society. Where spying under the guise of looking out for each other, was being a good citizen. Crime pushed to the fringes where people didn't look so the Government could claim their policies of tight population control worked. Except the prison I'd been in seemed to have been full enough.

I checked off another dirty road sign against my scribbled instructions. We turned right at an intersection into a street that looked exactly the same as the one we'd just left. How did they find their way round here?

People milled about, a handful of children threw a ball at each other, all watching as we approached and walked by them. Each time we passed through a pocket of food-scented air, I had to force my feet to keep walking on. My stomach felt like it was digesting itself. Jace probably felt it more than me though, at least I'd begun to get used to not eating enough.

"This is it." I rechecked the map. "Number forty-seven, should be up there, on the left."

Just as Toby's house didn't look any different on the outside from his neighbours, so Lawrence's looked a twin of the adjoining houses. I knocked at the front door.

I was wondering whether to knock again, when it opened enough that it pulled taut the security chain.

"Hi, is Lawrence there? I'm a friend of his cousin, Toby, from Milton Keynes."

The door didn't move. The person behind it didn't say anything. I waved my scribbled instructions into the gap and a hand snatched them.

"How d'you know Toby?" The man had the deepest voice I'd ever heard.

"I tutor his daughter, Jessica, he gets me things, from time to time."

"What d'you want now?"

I could feel the gaze of invisible hundreds on my back, spying on me, a hundred reports being written out and sent to the machine that was the Government for processing and following up. A hundred Mrs Randles being arrested and held without being able to contact their families. "Can we come in? We're a little exposed out here."

The sentry thought about it then closed the door. That wasn't what I expected him to do.

"Now what?" Jace asked.

"We wait, he's probably gone to check with Lawrence." I sounded as though I was trying to convince myself as much as Jace.

"What do we do if he won't let us in?"

"He will." But whatever they were doing was taking so long. What if he didn't? I didn't know where else to go, what else to do. The chain rattled, stifling my panic and the door opened. The sentry gestured us in.

The house smelt of something spicy, a lingering aftertaste of food more exotic than anything I'd ever eaten. Lawrence was clearly well-connected and rich if he could get hold of spices like that.

Our guide waved us into a room on the right. The vacant armchair and sofa begged me to sink into them but the look from the skinny man sitting in the other chair told me not to.

"So you know Toby ?" He flapped my note at me. "Why's he need you to tutor his daughter?"

There was virtually no family resemblance between them. Lawrence looked to be about a head taller than me, lean and wiry. If people still played sport competitively he would have been a good basketball player. There was a centre of calm about him but I didn't doubt that he was dangerous, I could see it behind the gaze he fixed on me.

"Do you have kids?" I asked. He inclined his head so slightly I almost wasn't sure if it was a yes or a no. I decided to go with yes. "Then you know about the school tiering system, about how not so bright kids aren't likely to make it through to career decision. Toby doesn't think his daughter is a waste of resources, she just needs a little one-on-one help to boost her up. He doesn't want her to be military, no one wants to be military unless they can be the one giving the orders."

"She's not so old."

"The system makes its mind up from the minute we start school. They get funny if anyone gets clever or starts failing. No one wants to be making the system pay attention to them. I'm keeping her the right side of average." I hoped Jace knew I was just playing myself up for Lawrence's benefit. He knew me, he couldn't seriously think I was as big-headed as that made me sound.

"You can do that, all the way through school?"

"I'm playing the system myself." He certainly didn't need to know where it had got me.

"And him?" Lawrence gave the same slight nod in Jace's direction.

"He's my best friend."

"You're risking a lot, out of your home town."

Like I didn't know that. "I'm looking for the factory that manufactures Coralone to get some medicine for my brother."

"No one's gonna do nothing without payment." The sentry shifted his position in the doorway as if to underline what Lawrence was saying.

"I know, I'll sort something out. Toby thought you'd know where it's made, I hoped you'd be able to give me the address."

"Like I said, no one gonna do nothing without payment. How you paying me?"

The question I'd been dreading. Hopefully he was a reasonable man. What difference could it really make to him if he gave us an address or not? "We were mugged on the way down here and lost everything. All I can offer you is what I can do for you, I'm smart, I know a lot about healthcare—"

"Don't need a teacher or nursemaid. You got nothing to trade, I'm not interested. You know where the door is."

CHAPTER FIFTY-THREE

Lawrence looked back down at the sheets of paper on his lap.

This couldn't not work. It really was a last ditch attempt. If I couldn't get Coralone from here . . .

"Please, my brother's dying."

"Not my problem."

"Isn't there anything I could do for you? Or could you give me the name of someone else who knows where the factory is?"

Lawrence fixed me with a hard stare that made me feel about a hundred times more uncomfortable than Sebastian's ever had. "I'm not a charity."

"I know that, and I know what I'm asking's unusual but please, wouldn't you do anything if you were in my position?"

Jace took hold of my arm. "Come on, Maya, let's go. We'll have to think of something else."

I shook him off. "There is nothing else. Look, Lawrence, I'll do whatever you want and all I want in return is the address of where they make the Coralone."

"Maya!"

I held Lawrence's gaze, trying to ignore the looks Jace

was shooting me. "You got a clean record?" Lawrence asked finally.

"Yes. No. I don't know."

"Which is it?"

"I was arrested and sent to prison but I was let go, a mistake apparently."

"Thought they didn't make mistakes."

I held out my wrists. "No bracelet."

"I see that, but if you don't know your record's still clean, that's no good to me."

I wanted to fall at his feet and beg him to help me. An address, that's all I wanted. What was wrong with everyone, why couldn't we just help each other out without always wanting something first? Not everything demanded that a price be paid.

"My record's clean." Jace spoke quietly. "I can do whatever it is you want done."

"No, Jace." I grabbed his arm but he was ignoring me as well as I had him.

Lawrence addressed his minder. "Get the package for Walsh." He turned back to his papers.

"Jace, I can't let you." I half-whispered. "You've no idea what he wants."

Jace gave his half-shrug. "It's the price. You can't pay it, I can."

"What if I don't want you to?"

He looked at me. I could see a world of emotion reflected in his eyes. Was he pitying me? I didn't want pity, especially not from him. But then I realised it wasn't pity, empathy rather and pain and the deep bond we shared. I'd never been able to read him so clearly.

"I want to." he whispered back, unhooking my fingers from his bicep, squeezing my hand.

I wanted to throw my arms around him but the minder came back into the room and handed him a battered cardboard package.

"You need to deliver this to a man named Walsh."

Lawrence said. "You don't know London?"

We shook our heads. Lawrence sighed, shuffled his papers until he found a blank one and drew a sketch on it. He scribbled something at the bottom, flipped it over and added something else on the back. He held it out to Jace. "Name, address, how to get there. 'Cause of your connection to Toby, I signed it so Walsh will give you what you want. Get it there tonight, soon as. Don't open it, don't let anyone else open it, don't get it wet, treat it like it's your firstborn. Should take maybe a couple of hours. Factory's not far from his place." He looked pointedly at me. "You see any patrols, you best disappear."

He waved us towards the door, then added "You come back here, I never saw you before. I'll shop you soon as look at you."

CHAPTER FIFTY-FOUR

Outside the light felt all wrong. Clouds bulged against each other, pregnant with nature's fury bringing a weird dusk to the capital. 'Don't get it wet', one of Lawrence's warnings rolled around my head. Was there a chance the rain wouldn't start before we delivered the package?

"Jace, you know you can back out of this. I can take it."

"And you know I won't." He studied the map.

"It's asking so much of you, to break the law like this." I whispered even though the street was virtually empty.

"Far as I know I'm not breaking the law, I'm just being a postman."

Why then had Lawrence insisted on a clean record if we weren't breaking the law?

"I just don't want you to jeopardise more than you already have. Skipping school is a lot less serious than being sent to prison."

"Try telling Miss Pattershall that." I smiled at his joke. His expression changed and I couldn't read him at all any more. "I know life hasn't dealt you a very fair hand, I know you've been let down by your mum, but you know I won't ever do that. I'm here till the end for you."

Wow. I felt a ridiculous urge to cry. "That means more than you know." It didn't come close to what I wanted to say really but after what happened on the motorway I could hardly tell him now that I loved him, could I? That would just be cruel but I reached out to hug him and that seemed to surprise him even more. The package between us made it a little less awkward. "So where do we have to go?" I tried to be all business-like when we pulled apart.

Jace tucked Lawrence's note in his jacket pocket. "Hammersmith. Apparently we go back to the main road and keep going."

The keep going went on for what felt like hours. The sky became more threatening, the premature dusk thickened, becoming our ally as people hurried past, not paying us any attention, concentrating only on getting home before the storm broke. Lights began appearing in windows. As we got closer to where a squiggly line on Lawrence's map depicted the Thames, a sudden burst of light around a corner surprised me. "They have working street lights here."

It was almost a shock, seeing the pool of light brightening the pavement around the lamp post. I could see another orange glow made fainter by distance at the end of my field of vision.

I remembered playing games with my shadow in York in the dark when I was little. I used to run to the next lamp post, watching my shadow recede until I stepped on it and then laughing to see it magically reborn as I passed beneath the light. I hadn't ever seen a working streetlight in MK.

"It makes reading a whole lot easier." Jace pointed towards the other glow. "Down there and left at the end."

We wove our way through the streets of the capital. None of the closely packed mish mash of building styles and types seemed to fit together. Glass and steel constructions in strange designs squeezed around the peculiar shaped older buildings from London's distant past.

As we got closer to the river, even the sparse weeds or grasses colonising the roads at the edges of the city, hadn't been able to take root here. Too many pairs of feet, bikes, pedicabs must pass over them each day for nature to regain her footing. This must be how cities used to look before cars stopped using the roads and the authorities stopped repairing them.

Jace led us round the corner and we both stopped at the sight of an army jeep coming up the road. Now the streetlight wasn't so friendly. It broadcast our guilty faces, the contraband package, our illegal status.

"Keep walking." Jace slipped the package under his arm instead of holding it out in front of him like it might bite him.

"Do you think that's wise?" I hissed. "It might need to be kept horizontal."

"That wasn't in Lawrence's list of instructions. Don't open it, don't let anyone else open it, don't get it wet, treat it like your firstborn. I'm still holding it gently, only like this doesn't draw attention. If we look as if we know where we're going, they won't mind us."

Carrying the package past the patrol was enough for him at that moment, I wouldn't add to his burden by reminding him that I had no ID or that his would get him arrested. He was probably every bit as aware of that as I was. I blinked at the headlights, bright in the gathering gloom. Tried to empty my mind of everything, willing my face to look nonchalant, sure I must look guilty as hell.

I thought of Sebastian, conjured up his face as I forced my legs to keep taking steps, to walk head-on towards the on-coming army jeep. Just a regular patrol, nothing to worry about.

The jeep rolled to a stop, the passenger door opened and a soldier got out. Sebastian, this was all for him. This would be worth it when we got the Coralone for him, when it cured the terrible death rattle in his chest, when he lived to see his twelfth birthday.

The soldier walked towards us. Was he corrupted or was he like Evan? I could feel a bead of sweat running down my back. I felt exactly as I had when the soldier gunned down the woman on the way to prison. My hunger had dissolved away into a million butterflies that churned my stomach, made me feel clammy with the urge to throw up. My back and shoulders tensed against the gunfire the soldier could unleash.

"You see a patrol, you'd better disappear.' Lawrence's warning played so loudly in my mind I was amazed the soldiers couldn't hear it. My steps stuttered to nothing.

"It's okay." Jace took hold of my hand and pulled me forward. "Breathe slower, keep walking. I won't let anything happen to you, promise." His solid presence bled into me, calming me, helping me to walk on.

We drew level with the soldier, I concentrated on the feel of Jace's hand in mine. Just walking down the road with my friend, I could do that. The soldier walked straight past us, his arms swinging freely, his weapon holstered.

"Easy," Jace whispered as we passed the jeep.

Something hit me on the head. I reached up, fingertips padding at my hair, seeing what had got me when something else hit my hand. Fat drops splattered onto the pavement all around. It was raining.

CHAPTER FIFTY-FIVE

"Run!" Jace yelled.

The soldiers shouldn't suspect us for trying to get out of the rain. We ran to the bottom of the road and turned into a street filled with squat square pre-fab units, their windows mostly dark, closed for the night.

"Let's try that one." I ran onto the first hard-standing, ducked down the side of the building.

There wasn't much in the way of shelter round the back but a small roof jutting out over the rear entrance mimicked a porch. That would have to do. We could run up and down the street and not find anything better.

We ran under the cover, panting. I could feel my heart doing a double-take, the palpitations the prison doctor had asked about. That was okay, as long as I didn't pass out here. Jace had enough to think about.

He put the package under his jacket and wrestled with the zip. "You'd be better off wearing this, at least it'd zip up all the way on you."

"I'm wet already. It makes no sense us both getting drenched."

"But you might keep the package dry better."

I pulled the fronts of his jacket together and tugged

on the zip until I got it most of the way up. "You're good, see."

It was pouring so heavily now that everywhere was one giant puddle and the continued smack of rain made it look like the water was boiling.

"How much longer do you think, till we get there?" I asked.

Jace shook out the map. "Hard to say."

"What's the time?"

"Just gone six thirty. It'll be okay. We'll get the Coralone soon. Then we'll go straight home. We'll be back before morning."

"The factory's probably closed now." I couldn't help my pessimism.

"They may have a night shift running. He'll be fine, Maya. I thought he was looking better, yesterday."

I pressed my lips together. Jace hadn't heard the terrible death rattle in Sebastian's chest.

We watched what felt like more rain than fell in MK in the entire year waterfall over the tiny roof that sheltered us, cascade over the building opposite, flood the tiny hardstanding.

I was beginning to wonder what we'd do if we were stuck there all night when the storm force dropped a few notches.

"We should probably try to deliver it now." we said together.

We splashed out into the rain which had streamlined into more vicious drops like pine needles. The wind threw them at us first from one direction, then another. At least the streets were almost deserted. It was as if a curfew had been sounded by a silent siren.

By the time Jace pointed out a low rise building ahead of us, I was soaked through. "That's it, number 132."

Number 132 was set back from the road slightly, behind a hardstanding that would once have housed residents' cars. A couple of bikes leant against the front of the building. Light filtered out into the premature night around the edges of badly-drawn curtains on the ground floor. As we walked up to the entrance, it snapped off.

Jace pressed the button labelled 'Walsh' on the front door panel. We waited so long for an answer, he was lifting his hand to ring again when a voice crackled over the intercom. "What?"

"I have a package for Walsh," Jace checked the soggy instructions, "from his uncle."

"Which one?"

"His favourite."

"Push the door, top floor." An angry buzzing almost drowned out the voice.

Inside the building the darkness felt more solid. I let the banister guide me up the stairs behind Jace. A man was waiting in the lighter gloom of an open door. Even in the quasi-dark I could see it wouldn't be easy for him to pass himself off as Lawrence's nephew, he was as white as Jace, a little shorter than me and not as wiry as Lawrence.

"Walsh?" Jace asked.

"Yeah."

"There you go." Jace handed over the package

Walsh peered at it. "Thanks." He turned to go back into his flat.

"We need our payment." I said quickly. "Your 'uncle' wants you to give us some information."

"What kind of information?" Walsh spoke with a strange accent I couldn't place.

"We need to know the address of the plant that manufactures Coralone, it's a medicine. Lawrence said—"

"No names! Don't you know anything?"

"Sorry."

"Not sure I can help you."

"We have a note from your uncle." Jace held out the paper Lawrence had given us, which looked decidedly the worse for its soaking.

Walsh took it and disappeared back into his flat,

closing the door behind him. Another door shut on us. I reached out to knock when Walsh was suddenly in front of me holding a lit candle. I guessed he was in his mid-thirties. Untidy dark hair touched the round neck of his T-shirt, his face, neck and arms showed that he'd spent a while in the sun without sun cream.

"What's your business with the plant?" he asked.

"My brother's Coralone got ruined, I haven't been able to get him any more. I hoped the manufacturer could help. He's really sick—" I stopped myself. It probably wasn't a good plan to burst into tears.

"This could have been written by anyone." He flapped the paper.

"But it's signed right there." Jace jabbed at it.

"At best it's a clumsy attempt at forgery." Walsh pointed with the candle at where the rain had made Lawrence's signature run down the page as though it was about to slide off. It wasn't very legible.

"But we brought the package so you know we came from him." I couldn't believe he was being difficult.

He shrugged. "Guess so, but now I have it I don't need to give you anything for it."

"Human decency should make you want to." I retorted.

He laughed. "That's over-rated."

"It's only an address for God's sake, what difference does it make to you if we have it or not? We've come all the way from Milton Keynes—"

"You think lying's gonna make me feel bad?"

"It's not a lie." I said flatly.

"See?" Jace held out his ID. Walsh moved the candle, close enough to read it. He looked at Jace sharply.

"I'm not leaving here until you give us the address." I said.

"Suit yourself. You should know the Army's stepping up patrols, because of the storm. I wouldn't want to be caught out where I shouldn't be tonight in a whole other city. But it's your call."

Walsh went back into his flat and closed the door behind him with a quiet but final click.

CHAPTER FIFTY-SIX

I stared at the closed door. Surely what I thought just happened couldn't be what had actually happened? Why would Walsh refuse to help us? What did he care if we knew where the plant was? What was wrong with everyone? Didn't they realise the simple truth that all any of us had in the messed-up world we lived in was each other, and so it was up to each of us to help the other out. What was wrong with people? I didn't know how I wasn't screaming.

I could almost feel the expression of pain on Jace's face. I looked back at the door, it was easier to handle. My brain floundered, I couldn't even think of any scenarios to weigh up. We'd had the lead we needed and now it had turned into a dead end. Dead. The word hiccupped in my mind.

I banged on the door. "Walsh! We had a deal. Do the honourable thing." I banged again and again until I could feel bruises forming on my hands. But all Walsh was doing at that moment was ignoring me.

"Hey, you, what business do you have here?" A woman's shrill voice cut through my assault on Walsh's door. She was standing outside the flat on the other side of the stairs. "You don't live here, what do you want?"

I felt Jace put his arm around me. "Come on, Maya. Let's go."

"No." I raised my voice so the woman, and I hoped Walsh, could hear. "My friend's in there and can't hear me knocking."

"If there's a problem, he's the only one in the block with a radio."

"Maybe if we all bang on his door, we might be able to rouse him. Could you come and help?"

"Well," she searched for an excuse.

"I'm sure it's nothing serious," I added. "He's not sick or anything."

"Why else wouldn't he come to the door?"

"He probably doesn't even realise it's closed, you know what he's like."

My five second summation of Walsh was instantly accepted by the woman. "He is private, that one."

She joined us and we all banged on the door. There was no way he couldn't not hear us. How the people downstairs weren't complaining I didn't know. Finally, when I thought I couldn't slam my hand into the wood even once more, Walsh opened it. "What d'you—"

"Your neighbour was kind enough to help us." I interrupted him. "If you buzz us in, you need to keep your door open so we don't end up disturbing your neighbours who might call the authorities when there's really no need." I hoped he understood my meaning.

"Thanks so much, for your help." I jumped in to fill the silence and dismiss his neighbour at the same time. "Again, we're really sorry to have disturbed you." The woman walked slowly back to her flat, probably wondering why we were still standing in the hallway.

"What're you playing at?" Walsh's tone could have frozen metal.

"You give us the address, we go away, you never see us again. You don't, I'm going to find the nearest patrol and tell them you just received a package from a black marketeer." It wasn't much of a deterrent but it was all I had.

"They won't care."

"Probably not, but they'd confiscate it for their own use. You want to see if I'm right?"

"You're bluffing. Your ID will get you into trouble before you can get a patrol anywhere near here."

"Didn't you hear me before? My brother's dying. I don't care what happens to me as long as he gets his medicine."

Walsh must have recognised the truth in my words. "Wait, I'll get changed and take you there myself."

When he went back into his flat, I slid down the wall and sat on the floor. Jace sat next to me. "Okay, so who are you and what've you done with Maya?"

"Guess you can't see how much I'm shaking. But it is true I'm desperate."

"Sebastian's lucky, to have someone like you fighting for him."

"You're forgetting I'm the one who broke his medicine in the first place." There wasn't much he could say to that.

Walsh bundled out into the corridor a few minutes later, pulled his front door shut and deadlocked it. "Let's go."

Outside the expanse of angry sky actually helped sharpen my night vision. Walsh was as prepared for the storm as I wasn't. Waterproofs covered every inch of him, down to what appeared to be thick-soled army boots. He wore a rucksack tight against his back that made him look like a hunchback.

Rain smacked against him as though loving the challenge of trying to find a way past his protection. It pummelled my clothes with no resistance. It didn't take many minutes until I could feel it trickling through my already soaked layers and reaching my skin underneath.

"Jace, what are you doing?" I realised he was unzipping his jacket.

"You'll catch your death."

I put my hands on his to stop him. "Please, keep it on, it's senseless us both being drenched. Besides it's obviously just more Government scaremongering. Despite what they say, a chill won't kill me."

"Keep up." Walsh ordered.

Keeping up with him wasn't so easy. He marched us in what I thought was pretty much a straight line, heading due east as though feral dogs were after us. Jace reached for my hand. He was warm where I was freezing. He'd reached out to me. Thank God, did that mean he was over what had happened on the motorway? I squeezed his hand and was answered by one in return that made me feel much warmer on the inside.

As we route marched through the practically deserted city, the buildings began to change, becoming older and more ornate. Lawrence had said the factory wasn't that far from Walsh's – his definition of not far was a lot different to mine. I was about to ask Walsh how much longer when he stopped in front of a building non-descript only because it was mirrored so perfectly by those on either side of it. It didn't look anything like a place where manufacturing happened.

There were no signs proclaiming what went on behind the smart brick interior. The sash windows were mirrored, reflecting only darkness back at us. The fronts of all the buildings were cleaner than anything else I'd seen so far. Maybe these had been the last renovations before such things were relegated to peoples' memories.

"This is it, a manufacturing plant?" Jace voiced my doubts.

"Building façades mean nothing. Nothing's ever quite what it seems, or haven't you worked that out yet in the sticks?"

"Milton Keynes isn't the sticks." Walsh seemed to

have a real knack of saying the exact thing to annoy. I wondered what career the Government had given him. Something not dealing with people would be favourite.

"It's all locked up here, we'll need to go round the back." he said.

"You know this place well."

"It's my city, of course I do."

He led us past the row of sextuplet buildings, around the block into the back alley that led onto the rear entrances. The gate to the one in the middle opened under his touch. The factory was still open? I felt hope surge through me. I had to hold myself back so I didn't push him out of the way.

He pulled the rear door open, shone his torch briefly into the building to show us the layout and gestured for me to lead the way in. I stopped in the darkness a few steps in, waiting for his direction.

Footsteps, heavy, booted, coming down stairs somewhere ahead of me. Like dawn when the sun gets high enough above the horizon to nudge aside the darkness, so everything lightened around us as a storm lamp preceded a soldier into the corridor.

"You," he pointed at Jace and Walsh and then at a door on their left, "can wait in there."

"You," he looked directly at me. "Come with me."

CHAPTER FIFTY-SEVEN

"What did you do, Walsh? Where are we? Why's there a soldier here?" My questions tangled themselves up into one.

"Let's go." The soldier reached out for me.

I pushed him away, launching myself at Walsh but Jace grabbed me before I could land a slap or a scratch or a kick on him. "I won't let anything happen to you, Maya. Look at me, you're safe."

"I don't care about me. He lied. This isn't the plant, there's no Coralone here. He's wasted our time, he wasted Sebastian's time." I pushed against Jace. The soldier grabbed me again. "Get off me." I yanked my arm so hard trying to free myself I felt a muscle pull in my shoulder.

"Let go of her." Jace reached out for the soldier's hand, trying to prise him off.

The soldier held the lamp up to my face. "You don't stop, I'll smash it on her. See how much you like her when she's scarred and blinded. What d'you think?" Jace let go. "Better. Now up the stairs." the soldier bellowed.

"You coward, Walsh." I screamed even as the soldier dragged me away. "I hope your G.I. treachery reward is worth the death of my brother. People like you need

217

shooting."

The soldier's lamp lit up a bare stubby corridor on the first floor. He steered me to an open door on the right and shoved me inside. I turned round to ask what was going on but I was alone.

The room felt stuffy and close. A storm lamp behind a metal grille lit up a table and two chairs, nothing too scary. There were no windows, no other way out than through the closed door. Except there was no handle on my side.

Khaki-coloured walls were scored so badly in places it looked as though someone had been playing drunken noughts and crosses.

I sat down and pulled my chair in. It didn't budge. Screwed to the floor? What kind of place was this? The table was carved up more badly than the walls with layers of initials. Defacing property, didn't people in London know the penalty for that was more community time than swearing, spitting, drinking alcohol? Actually, probably not the drinking. Everyone knew people did it but it was further underground than the Channel Tunnel that used to join England and France.

Did the initials belong to the 'disappeareds'? Was that what was going to happen to me? Even though I was now in the warm and dry, I wished I was back out in the storm. At least out there I had a better chance of dealing with whatever came along. In here . . .? I looked around the room. Probably best not to think about that. I'd seen too much corruption in the regime to be able to convince myself now that everything would always be okay.

I banged on the door but the noise I made seemed to be swallowed by the air. The room was sound proofed? I scrabbled at the door but unless I sprouted 10cm long nails as strong as metal, there was no way I could get out by opening it from the inside. I needed to get them to open it for me. I pulled and pushed at the mesh of the metal grille housing the storm lamp. They'd obviously planned that desperate people might try to set fire to the furniture – the mesh was too tightly spaced for me to get any purchase on it. The grille was screwed shut.

Godamnit! I slapped the mesh, it fit so well in its frame it barely reverberated.

I paced for a while then realised I could at least use this time to sort myself out a bit.

I pulled my jumper over my head and wrung it out, splashing water onto the floor. Shaking it out, I laid it over the back of my chair. Did I have time to wring out my T-shirt too before anyone came in? I was almost past caring. Just to feel halfway dry would be worth flashing someone.

The door opened to let two soldiers in. One was non-descript, his camouflage doing its job, but the other made me feel short and his bulk would have made Jace look weedy. A man in civilian clothes followed. He sat down opposite, opening a file on the table with a neat flourish, hooking his glasses behind his ears in an elaborate gesture that made him look like a great storyteller. Something about him convinced me that I didn't want to hear even his best tale. Even the trim ribbon of hair that hugged the back and sides of his head that should have made him look grandfatherly just made him cadaverous.

Show no weakness, Evan's warning reminded me. It was scary how many times I'd needed to call on it outside the prison.

"I'm going to ask you a few questions." The civilian said. "You can choose not to answer me, but you ought to know that's what the soldiers are for."

CHAPTER FIFTY-EIGHT

"You're probably too young to remember the Bill of Human Rights?" The civilian seemed to be expecting an answer. I wasn't sure what to tell him. I'd read of it, a law that seemed to fit an ideal but which in practice had led to criminals being set free or paid extortionate amounts of compensation while the people they'd made victims ended up losing more than their ability to sleep at night. I shrugged slightly, hoping that wasn't the wrong answer. He could interpret that as he wished, a 'yes', a 'no', an 'I don't know what you're talking about', an 'I'm your typical teenager who couldn't care less' gesture.

"Just so we're clear, it no longer exists in this country. So I ask the questions and you answer them, and if you don't like it, they'll" he nodded at the soldiers, "sort it out for you, clear enough?"

I nodded. My feet squelched in my shoes. Rain water still dripped from the hem of my T-shirt, onto my sodden jeans. I wished I'd wrung it out first.

"Name?"

Oh no. The next question would be for my ID and then what would happen? If I lied it would probably make things worse, but if I told the truth, would my transgressions be taken out on Mum, Sebastian? What about Jace? What were they doing to him? Walsh had better make sure I never saw him again.

"Maybe you don't understand me?" The civilian stared at me. The lenses of his glasses made his eyes bulge. "I'm not in the habit of repeating myself. Soldier!"

Before I realised the soldier behind me had crossed the room, he'd pulled my arm up behind my back. Agony tore through my shoulder and I couldn't hold back a sharp cry of pain.

The civilian nodded and the soldier let go and returned to the wall. I rubbed at my shoulder, he would pick the sore one.

"Name." The civilian acted like nothing untoward had happened.

"Maya Flint."

"ID."

I tried to swallow but my mouth had dried up totally. I heard the boots coming towards me this time.

"I don't have it." I croaked. "I was just released from prison, they said they'd get it back to me, but I don't have it yet."

"Wrists." the civilian barked.

I held my arms out, palms uppermost, flipping them over.

"Where's your prison tattoo?"

I pointed at the green dot. "They started to do it, but the power went out so they couldn't finish. I was released the next day."

"No one gets out of prison without a tattoo."

"There was some kind of mistake."

"There is never a mistake in this regime, people exist to make sure of it, I'm one of them and I'm very particular about my record. No mistakes, ever." He nodded again to the soldier. I looked up at him, badly timing it so that his slap connected with my face. The world shifted sideways a little before snapping back to where it had been before. I held my hand over my smarting skin, shook my head.

"The truth now." the man said.

"I'm telling you the truth. What would I gain by lying to you? I don't want you to keep hurting me." I looked at the soldier, hoping to ignite a shred of humanity in him, but he was staring at the wall.

I tried the civilian. "If you're a Government man, aren't you supposed to care about us? About me? I haven't done anything wrong. You should be protecting me, not hurting me."

I might as well have not said anything.

"Why did you come here?"

"The man I was with in all the rain gear, he said he could get me some Coralone."

"What do you want with Coralone?"

"My brother's sick."

"How sick is he?"

"He's dying, he needs his medicine."

"New shipments just went out, why do you need more?"

I sensed an edge to his voice. This was going nowhere. I stood up and leant across the table, right into the odious man's personal space. In a far off part of my mind I couldn't believe what I was doing but I didn't want to stop myself. "I haven't done anything wrong. It's your system's fault I don't have my ID, so if you want to charge anyone about that, that's you."

I leant in closer. "Let me and my friend go and we won't say anything about your rat down there. I guess Government Informants don't work as well if everyone knows who they are."

He looked up at me, blinking mole-like behind his glasses. "I don't think you're in any position to make demands of anything." he blustered. "I have the might of the Government on my side."

He nodded sharply and suddenly I was lying on the floor, pain exploding down the left hand side of my face.

Blood trickled out from my mouth onto the floor. I stared at the pattern the splashes made on the concrete. That would be why they didn't have carpet in here.

I looked up at the horrible man, scratching away with his pen. "You may have might behind you, but you don't have right." I couldn't seem to stop myself pushing it further. "Why don't you get your hands dirty, why don't you beat up the sixteen-year-old girl, instead of letting your trained monkeys do it?"

At a nod from the man, the soldier bent down and hoisted me up, holding me by my T-shirt off the ground. The fabric bunched up around my neck acting like a noose, trapping blood in my head. I could feel myself getting light-headed. I grasped at the soldier's hands, digging my nails into his skin but it was like trying to claw at a statue. I thrashed about with my legs, kicking against him, flailing. I connected with the immoveable chair, the shock juddering through my right leg.

I pulled my head back and rammed it forward as hard as I could, but I wasn't close enough to connect with the soldier. All I was doing was speeding up the approach of darkness.

The world was starting to move away from me. A clanging sound filled the air around me. A shout. A voice I thought I might have recognised. "What's going on here? Leave her alone."

The grip on me vanished. I dropped to the floor. Coughing, choking, holding my neck, I looked up. Straight into the eyes of my father.

CHAPTER FIFTY-NINE

I was staring at my father. My dad. My mind hiccupped over the word. I lay on the floor where the soldier had dropped me, one hand cradling my neck gawking at the tall man in the doorway. After so long I couldn't remember his face in my mind when I thought about him, I was only able to conjure up the frozen images of him I knew by heart from old photos. But there he was, right in front of me. I could only stare at him stupidly, waiting for my brain to catch up.

"Get out." His command to the civilian was so authoritative that I found myself pushing myself up from the floor, trying to obey him. He threw the man's file into the corridor, the oversized confetti of papers falling to the floor almost as one.

The civilian stood up, the aura of danger that had surrounded him popped, a school bully put in his place. "Mr Bessick, sir—"

Bessick? That was wrong, his name was Flint, Jeremy Flint. Why was that man calling him Mr Bessick?

My father looked at the soldier who'd been strangling me. "Take him downstairs." He jerked his head at the civilian man. "I'll debrief him. You," he addressed the other solider who still acted like door furniture. "No one comes in here."

He waited until the room had emptied and the soldier took up his post in the corridor before he closed the door and put a hand out to help me up. We were exactly the same height. His hair was peppered with grey now and more lines fanned out from the corners of his eyes but it was him.

I wanted him to hold me, tell me everything was going to be all right, that I didn't have to carry the burden of trying to save my brother anymore. That he could do what I couldn't, that he could save Sebastian using the resources of the Government. I wanted him to tell me that he loved me, that he would never leave me again, that it had all been a big mistake, that now he'd found me, we'd be a family again.

But he didn't say any of that. Instead he pointed at his mouth, then held out a pristine white handkerchief. "You're bleeding."

I dabbed at my lips, they felt swollen.

He sat down and gestured at the chair opposite him. The storm lantern he placed on the table made the room feel positively daylit.

"You really are my dad, aren't you? Jeremy Flint?"

He nodded so slightly I could almost have imagined it. "What are you doing here? You're supposed to be in Milton Keynes."

So he knew where we lived. He'd answered one of my million questions. "If you know where we are, why did you never come and see us?"

"It's complicated."

"We're your family, what's complicated about that?"

He looked at his hands and back at me. A faint smile tugged at the corners of his lips. "You were always forthright, always said what you felt. I see you haven't changed."

"Yes, I have." I hesitated. What should I call this

man, this stranger? Even in my thoughts the word 'dad' felt odd, like something I'd learnt in another language and mostly forgotten. "Of course I've changed, I was seven when you left. I'm sixteen now. I've grown up."

He nodded. "Yes, you have."

"Why did that soldier call you Mr Bessick? Your name's Flint, like mine."

An expression I didn't recognise crossed his face. I'd never realised that Sebastian looked so much like him, until now, seeing him so close, it almost hurt to look at him. From the minute the auto-immune disease that was slowly nibbling away at Sebastian started to overshadow our lives, there had been an unspoken question that was too painful to think about. Would he reach his teenage years? What about his twenties? His thirties were something far away like a planet that humankind knew was there but could never hope to explore because the distances involved were just too great to be reached in a lifetime.

Seeing our father in his forties, looking so fit and well, so alive, somehow reinforced the fact that Sebastian would never grow into himself.

"Is that complicated too?" I asked so softly I wasn't even sure he could hear me.

"It's a Government thing. I chose the name Simon Bessick when I took up my post. You know about the anonymity of the people who serve?"

"They do have schools in Milton Keynes."

He nodded. "And you're very smart, aren't you, Maya." It wasn't a question. "Would you like to go to Science Academy, I know you're not on a career path for it but I can make it happen for you."

Could he read my mind? "What're you talking about? I don't want to go to Science Academy."

"Really?"

"You don't know the first thing about me, so don't pretend to."

"I know enough, Maya. Who do you think got you out of prison?"

CHAPTER SIXTY

I felt my jaw drop open. My father had got me out of prison? I remembered the warden asking who I knew who was so powerful they could get me released. The last person I would have guessed was him.

"Who do you think got your record expunged so you'll be treated like a normal citizen for the rest of your life instead of an outcast with opportunities always denied you?" he said. "I've been keeping an eye on you since you were eight. I've seen your school records, seen how carefully you've been hiding your intelligence."

"You don't know anything."

"Maya," his voice was softer, the expression on his face melted into something a daughter should see from her father. "I was with you for the first seven years of your life. You don't just suddenly get intelligent when you start school, it was there from the minute I first held you. In your eyes, I could see it."

I blinked hard and swallowed. I wasn't going to let this man make me cry. He owed me the tears I could feel filling my eyes, closing my throat. I shook my head.

"You don't wear the gold chain I gave you?" He filled the silence. "I always imagined you would, I thought you liked it."

"I do, I did, I used to wear it every day. The warden took it off me to pay for my prison uniform."

His face tightened but he only changed the subject. "Why're you in London? You've had a taster of how much trouble you can get yourself into and you're travelling without permission?"

"How do you know I don't have permission?" I challenged him.

"No one has permission to travel anymore."

"Why not?"

"It's complicated." He seemed to like that phrase. But it all seemed pretty clear cut to me. The Government wanted us to stay where they'd put us for their own reasons. "Why are you here?"

"It's Sebastian. I broke his Coralone and I haven't been able to get any more from his clinic or anywhere else. I figured if I went to the factory that produces it, they could give me some."

"Maya." I noticed that he used my name nearly every time he spoke. Was he reassuring himself I was really there, or was it just that it felt weird to him to say it, as strange as the word 'dad' did to me? "Nothing is as simple as that."

"You're telling me they won't give me any either?"

He crossed and uncrossed his legs, bumping into my feet, crossed in exactly the same way as his. He stared at his hands, cupped together on the acne-ed table. "How is he, Sebastian?"

"Don't you know?"

"How's your mother?"

I almost told him that anyone else would know better than me, but whatever had happened between us in the last few days, Mum was the one who had stood by our family unit. "She's fine."

It didn't seem a very loyal thing to say. How much did he know about us? He couldn't know sometimes I heard her crying because she was terrified of losing her son? That I had no freedom because he'd left. That I wanted to be normal, I wanted a boyfriend, I wanted to hang out with other girls so the kids at school wouldn't always think I was a freaky nerd. Most of all I didn't want to have to lie awake at night, worrying about what would happen to us if the terrible treadmill Mum was on killed her.

I didn't know how to say any of that to the man sitting opposite. It would be too disloyal to Mum to hint at the smallest imperfection in our lives. And I owed him nothing.

"She's good." I managed a little more conviction.

"Has she met anyone else?"

"Why would she want to? She's waiting for you to come home."

He ran one of his hands over the back of the other. His face lost any expression that I could read. "Maya, you need to go home, back to Milton Keynes. I may not be able to protect you again if you're caught."

"If you've been keeping an eye on us, you must know Sebastian's really sick. He hasn't had any Coralone for over a week, he's desperate for it. You're part of the Government, surely they'll give you some? Then I can go home. You could arrange for me to get back, Jace and me, we were mugged on the way here, we lost our supplies, our bikes, everything. Even if we started home now, there's a chance that Sebastian might. . ." I swallowed again. I couldn't afford to get emotional now. I swiped at my eyes, wishing I hadn't, the left side of my face was killing me. "I need to get home fast, with the Coralone. You need to help me. Please."

He folded himself back into his chair, legs underneath, in his own space. "I can't."

"Yes, you can, you're part of the Government, you can do what you like."

He gave a short sharp sound that could have been a

laugh or a cough and stood up. "I'm glad I had a chance to see you, but you have to leave."

I stood too. "You're my father, you're Sebastian's father, you can't not help us."

"Maya, nothing is as black and white as you think. This world of ours operates only in shades of grey. I'm sorry but I can't."

I must be hearing things, that blow to my head had damaged my hearing. That was the only rational explanation for what he was saying. How could he not help us? Why was he not already ordering someone to bring him Coralone?

But he just stood there, looking at me.

"You have no idea how hard it is, having to lie to Sebastian, telling him everything's going to be all right when he knows better than you it's not. He's my brother, but sometimes he feels more like my child, and I'm scared stiff that when he dies he'll be taking half of me with him. You don't know how that feels."

My voice had risen dangerously high, I checked myself so that he could still understand me.

He turned to go but I grabbed his arm. "Please, I'm begging you. I'll do anything. Please, help your son, before it's too late. You owe him that much."

He prised my fingers off his arm and his voice was altogether harder, much more like the Governmental tone of authority he'd used when he first burst into the room. "You can't judge me, Maya, you don't know the first thing about me."

"And whose fault is that? You're the one who left, we would have followed you anywhere, Mum would have followed you to the Moon, you only had to call for us."

"Leave the city immediately, get back on the road to Milton Keynes while the soldiers are still busy with the storm. There's nothing I can do for you."

He snatched the lantern up from the table, rapped at the door and when it opened, stormed out of the room. I grabbed my jumper and ran after him. My leg still felt wrong from where I'd kicked the chair, making me limp. Down the stairs trying to stay close to the retreating light of his lantern I stumbled, grabbing onto the banister to stop myself falling headlong behind him. The light disappeared abruptly ahead and I heard the sound of boots coming to attention.

"Mr Bessick, I can explain—"

The civilian man's voice didn't sound so cocksure now. I pressed myself back onto the wall of the stairwell.

"I'm not interested in your explanations." my father said. "You will forget what happened here this evening. This is a matter of national security that is way above your clearance. You will forget the name Maya Flint. You will not try and investigate any anomalies you think you might have found. If I find you don't comply with my instructions, you'll be incarcerated at my pleasure. Am I making myself clear enough for you?"

"Yes, sir, might I just add—"

"No caveats, that's it. If I even hear anyone else breathing that name, I'll assume it came from you and you'll suffer for it."

My father whirled out into the corridor, the lantern lighting up a small circle around him. His face was set in angry lines. He marched straight out of the building. His fury-fuelled strides ate up the distance in half the time of mine as I limped behind him. I burst through the door, out into the night and the rain. A gust of wind held me back, whipped away my call. A large black car was parked in the alleyway behind the building. They had cars here too?

One of the rear doors opened. An interior light lit up an elegant-looking woman and a little girl who jumped up and down on the seat beside her. Long dark hair, skin not entirely white, she could have been me.

The wind paused and in the sudden stillness between howls I heard her high shriek of pleasure when she saw my father. "Daddy!"

CHAPTER SIXTY-ONE

I'd forgotten how to do everything. I'd forgotten how to run up to him and demand to know why she was calling him Daddy. I'd forgotten how to jump into the car to get the answers to the million questions I still had for him. I'd forgotten why I came to London, forgotten the rain was soaking me.

I could only stand and watch the car accelerate away.

"Maya." I was vaguely aware of something on my shoulders. "I found you a jacket." Jace's voice spoke near my ear. He pulled a hood up over my head. "What's wrong? What happened? Did they hurt you?"

I didn't know what to say.

He grabbed me by the shoulders. "Maya, are you okay?"

I was shivering so violently I couldn't answer him.

"I think you're going into shock. I need to get you out of this weather." He took my jumper out of my hand, helped feed my arms through the jacket sleeves and zipped it up. "We need to get away from here. Then you can tell me."

He grasped my hand and led me away. I had no idea how long we walked for, I just followed.

"This seems as good a place as any to wait out the storm." He had to shout above the wind. Even as we stood opposite a disused multi-storey car park, so it buffeted us like a bully, a quick blow to the left, then the right, retreating before we could brace ourselves to counteract the next icy blast.

The wind toyed with a large yellow sign hanging down from its housing at a crazy angle. The main vehicle entrance was blocked off but enough breeze blocks were missing from the bricked up pedestrian doorway that we could twist and turn through the awkward gap. Jace handed me a rucksack I hadn't even noticed he'd been wearing while he climbed through after me.

"Let's find somewhere a bit more hidden." He shouldered the rucksack and took my hand again. He was warm, the feel of his skin against mine reassuring, intimate, healing.

Producing a torch from somewhere, he shone the beam at our feet so we could avoid the rubbish and broken bottles littering the ground.

"Where did you get that?" I asked.

"Courtesy of our military. I did a bit of snooping around, picked up a few supplies. Let's go up a couple of levels, we'll be safer then."

We picked our way through the obstacle course until we found a ramp that had once let vehicles climb to the next parking area.

"Hey!" The darkness in a corner as we rounded the next level solidified into something tangible, coming at us with surprising speed. "You don't belong here."

The man's voice was gruff, as though he hadn't used it for a long time. A rush of stale body odour overlaid with something acrid and strong floated around him. "This is my place, my domain. My word is law. You don't belong here."

"We don't want any trouble. We're just looking for a place to ride out the storm." Jace said.

"ID." The man barked the syllable we'd both been dreading.

I opened my mouth to lie, but the words log-jammed together. Had we escaped the military only to be brought down by someone undercover in a bricked-in car park?

"We don't have any. At least she doesn't, here," Jace let go of my hand and withdrew his ID from his jeans pocket. "This is mine," he shone the torch beam on it, pointing to his address. "You can see it's useless here, I shouldn't be here, I should be home in Milton Keynes. It's a long story, I can bore you if you like?"

The man studied the ID in the light of Jace's torch. His face was weathered, like an old shoe that had been left out in the rain too many times, the story of a hard life etched right down to his bones. A straggly beard peppered his chin. I couldn't tell how old he was at all. But I couldn't believe he was military. Maybe that was the point, he could get into places normal soldiers couldn't.

"You got payment?" he asked.

"Just gonna get it out the rucksack, okay?" Jace waited for the guy to nod then squatted and wrestled something small and shiny out of the front pocket. He held his torch-light on it so the man could see the pen knife. "That enough for a few hours?"

The man took it from him with his thumb and forefinger, the only fingers he still had on his left hand. As used as I was to seeing mum's disfigurement, I couldn't stop looking at the level of punishment he'd suffered. He pulled at the secrets hidden inside. Shiny protuberances and blades popped out at all angles. "Can't be too careful who we let in here. You can stay, just for the storm, mind. But not here, this is my level. Most are taken, you can probably fit in somewhere at the top. Just for the storm. You still here after, you'll be going out the quick way, straight down."

"Thanks." Jace's voice echoed around the structure. He followed the sound with his torch beam picking up a strange entanglement of wood and cardboard, something that would have made the best den when we were kids. The man's home presumably.

We trudged up the concrete ramps, climbing the floors. Small fires held back the darkness in places, two sometimes three on a level, reflecting back surprise on the faces huddled around them. But no one questioned us being there.

Another lie told by the Government, that every person mattered, that everyone was cared for. What were the stories behind each cardboard and wooden structure? I couldn't imagine any of the people camping out in them would prefer living like that to somewhere with a roof and proper heating.

Okay, sometimes in the winter things weren't that great when the power cuts came one after another and there was no way to heat the houses. I remembered Mum getting all upset in the first winter after we'd been rehoused. I remembered her screaming at the gas fire, pulling at it, trying to wrench it from its home in the fireplace.

"It's fake, Maya, this fire, the chimney, none of it works." Mum had shouted so loudly it had even upset Sebastian who was upstairs in his bedroom, shivering under all our bedding. "I can't make a fire. What am I going to do?"

And in my eight-year-old wisdom I thought it was obvious. I'd seen the people over the road cutting down trees from the verges on the nearest grid road to burn in their living room. We could do the same. It'd be like camping, something the children in the book I was reading did lots. It sounded like real fun, we could pretend we were camping too. Maybe then Mum would stop shouting all the time.

But then she did something completely unexpected. She stopped her assault on the fire and drew me onto her lap.

"Maya, sweetheart, the people over the road made a big mistake. They needed a chimney to burn a fire because burning things makes a gas. They couldn't see the gas but it made them go to sleep, and they died."

"Did they have the flu?"

"No, they didn't. It's not just the flu that can kill you."

That was news to me. "Will it kill me?"

"You don't have the flu."

"No, the other thing that can kill me."

Mum had folded me in a big hug. "You don't have to worry about that. I won't let anything happen to you."

"Maya." Jace tugged gently on my hand. "Come on, let's go up again."

I let him pull me away from the fire that had rekindled the childhood memory, up another ramp. This level was dark, uninviting and apparently empty. The keening wind threw the occasional smatter of voices at us from below.

"This'll do." We stopped in the middle where the rain couldn't reach us.

I was still shivering in waves that went right down to my fingertips and toes.

"You cold?"

"Bit, not as bad as before."

Jace pulled me towards him, rubbing his hands up and down my back to warm me. I could have stood there all night enjoying the feeling of safety he gave me.

"I had no idea." I whispered eventually. "That my dad was even alive, I mean."

"Your dad?"

I gave him an abbreviated version of what had happened. "Why do you think he did it? Left us, started again with a new family? D'you think it was something we did, Mum or Sebastian or me?"

Jace held me tighter. "It has nothing to do with you, Maya, or anything that you did or didn't do. It's all down to your dad, the kind of person he is. I know he's your father and probably I shouldn't say anything bad against him, but he's selfish and cruel. I can't think of anything to justify anyone abandoning their family. It's cowardly and—"

"God, Jace, don't sugar coat it, say what you really think."

A bubble of hysteria exploded out of me, thankfully in a laugh not tears. Jace laughed too. It felt good to let go, just like we had on the motorway but the line between laughter and tears had never felt so thin.

"Are you hungry? Jace asked when I finally stopped.

I couldn't tell because my stomach ached so much. "I guess so, you have stuff to eat in that magic sack of yours?"

Jace grinned. "I just might."

We ate until we could barely move.

"Here." He held out a bottle.

"What's that?"

"Something to keep out the cold."

I took a sip, expecting it to be water. Not expecting it to be strong and bitter and to burn its way down my throat. "What is that?" I choked.

"Some kind of homebrew." He took a sip. "Whoa, that's strong. More?"

I took a careful swallow, letting the liquid glide down my throat. My nose crinkled up and I shivered.

The smell of it was familiar, tickling at the edges of memory, prodding another childhood scene into replay. The man in charge, that was the smell around him. It had been at home I'd first smelt it, around Mum, a miasma. I let my favourite word roll around my mouth, my mind, settle in the memory. Mum, secretive in her bedroom, passive and calm. A glass of water beside her. Except when I tried to take a sip she snatched it off me and the liquid had slopped all over my hand. The calm peace had crumbled and she'd screamed at me, gathering me in a hug when I burst into tears. That was the last time I remembered that strange smell on her.

"Is there anything you didn't take?" I took the homebrew from Jace again.

"Chairs, tables, anything nailed down."

I held the bottle up to him in a toast, like I'd read about. "To you, Jace, for all you've done for me, for all you mean to me."

The words were out before I could stop them or censor them, my usual caution landing on the floor along with the splash that flew out of the top of the bottle as I gestured with it. Another gulp made me cough again. Jace took it from me, slapping me on the back.

"Right back at you." He drank and before I could stop myself, I found I'd laid my head on his shoulder. The tiny circle of our world lit by his torchlight didn't feel right at that angle. I lifted my head again, looking at him. He was very close, his face right in front of mine. I moved closer, my lips mere millimetres from his. He stayed where he was, still watching me. Earlier, it was because of earlier.

"I'm sorry, about before, on the motorway, I was stupid—"

His kiss stopped my apology. Tender and soft, gentle enough that it almost tickled. But the electricity between us was so strong I was surprised we weren't lighting up the whole car park. The awfulness of the day drifted away. Jace's closeness and his caring made me realise that the pain of my father's betrayal could only touch me if I let it. He was only my father by an act of biology, his choices meant I didn't have to think of him that way. He'd decided to be Simon Bessick, not Jeremy Flint. A man in the Government who had helped me out because of an echo from the past, a guilty conscience maybe. Thinking of him as Jeremy Flint, as my father, gave him a power he didn't deserve. The man I'd met, Simon Bessick, was a stranger.

Jace pulled me into a hug. "Are you okay?" His voice was a little husky.

"For the first time today I think so."

"You're not worried about our friendship?"

"No, this just feels right."

He traced the outline of my face with his finger. I winced when his gentle touch skirted my left jaw. "Did they hurt you?"

"It's not important."

We kissed again, differently this time, deeper, more searching, more passionate. I sensed there were depths to him that I'd had no idea existed. And he was the person I knew best in the world.

"Who did you learn to kiss like that with?" I was breathless and giddy and grinning.

Jace grinned back. "Not something you don't know, Maya Flint?"

"You're not going to tell me?"

"A gentleman never kisses and tells."

"Do you think a gentleman can help me find something to burn, I'm still freezing."

He shone the torch around the parking level but the distance swallowed up the light before it could penetrate the more solid darkness in the corners. He kissed me and got to his feet, holding out his hand to help me up.

The closest corners didn't hide much. The 'residents' had long stripped out anything useful. We walked up to the opposite end of the level, Jace's torchlight dissecting the blackness, marking out a path. The darkness suddenly became liquid, reacting to our intrusion, erupting in a flurry of screeches and screams.

A woman had jumped up from where we'd disturbed her. A whole wardrobe of clothes swirled and flapped around her in a ragged rainbow. Jace's beam found her face and she shrieked at us, spitting out words that should have had her locked up. I held my hands out, showing her we were no threat.

"Sorry, we didn't know you were there. We don't want any trouble. We'll go, find another level."

The woman's screeching tailed off into hysterical laughter. With the speed of the insane, she lunged at me. I stumbled backwards, caught my balance.

Jace looked as if he was prepared to stand and reason with her. But her strange mumbling freaked me out. I grabbed his hand. "Jace, let's go."

We ran back along the line of his jiggling beam of light. Over the rustle of our jackets, my panicked breathing, the slamming of our footsteps on the concrete, I couldn't tell if she was chasing us.

When we reached our belongings she'd vanished as though we'd imagined her. Between us we grabbed everything we'd left on the ground, shoving it in pockets, under our arms.

"Here." Jace gave me the torch so he could swing his rucksack up on his shoulders. "Shine the light on me a minute."

He held up his hand and the beam picked up blood smeared over his palm.

"How did you cut yourself?" I shot a quick glance into the darkness behind us even though it was as silent and still as if the woman had never appeared.

Jace pressed at his bloodied skin. "It's not me."

I looked at my own hand. A cut as clean and slick as if a surgeon had made it bisected the palm of my right hand. The skin, still red and barely mended from when I'd cut it when I dropped Sebastian's Coralone, was covered in blood.

CHAPTER SIXTY-TWO

"Shit, Maya, that looks deep." Jace held the side of my hand and peered at the cut.

"Watch what you're saying, you've no idea who else is up here."

"You're kidding right, after everything that woman said? She used words I've never heard before. I've probably got something in here I can bandage you up with."

"Maybe we should get off this level before you do your Florence Nightingale bit?"

We crept down the ramp to the one below. Ambient light from the residents' fires on each side was probably enough to give us some warning if anyone else wanted to attack us. I sat on the concrete with my back against one of the pillars that held everything above our heads in place.

Jace dug around in his rucksack until he found a small bundle. He spread the meagre first aid supplies out with total concentration.

"This is gonna sting like hell." He held my wrist and tipped some of the homebrew over my palm. He was a master of understatement. I had to bite my lip to stop myself from screaming.

He shone his torch at my wound while I was still

inhaling. "You need to get it looked at."

"You have Steri-strips?"

"Only plasters."

He stuck them vertically over the cut, pulling the edges together. When he'd finished bandaging my hand, I held it up in the air, trying to help my body heal itself.

"You need stitches." Just from the look on his face I knew I wouldn't win an argument. Right about then I wouldn't have won an argument with a drawing of him.

Another hospital for the same injury I'd had only a week ago. It was so unlikely it was almost funny. But another hospital meant another supply of Coralone. My heart did a little tap dance. What was I thinking? I wouldn't be rescued from prison this time. That had been a one-off thing.

I shouldn't care about that. I owed Sebastian. Him living was more important, wasn't it? And hadn't I already screwed things up for myself?

'Who do you think got your record expunged so you'd be treated normally?' My father's words. Did that mean he'd salvaged my career decision? Did I really want to risk throwing away my second chance? But how could I live with myself if I didn't?

"What?" Jace was asking.

"You're right, I need to get to a hospital."

He looked surprised I'd given in so easily. "Okay, let's get going then." He shoved everything back into his rucksack. "Are you okay to walk out there in that?" He nodded at the outside. The wind caterwauled around the car park, howling like a beast gone mad.

"My legs are fine. Besides it'll be in our favour." Not many other people would be stupid enough to be out in it.

I stumbled as the ramp's slope jumped up to meet me. My feet seemed to be obeying someone else's instructions. Jace's grip around my good hand tightened. "Probably should have gone a bit easier on the homebrew." he said.

"Are you kidding? Now the sting has gone, my hand doesn't hurt at all."

We'd scarcely stepped onto the first level than the man who appointed himself sentry, called out. "Storm's not over."

"We need a hospital." Jace said. "Someone up there cut my girlfriend."

I smiled. My girlfriend, it sounded nice.

"You weren't on the top." The man's tone was even but it couldn't hide the accusation that it was our fault.

We approached him as though he were a wild animal that might spring up and attack us at any moment.

"We thought we were." Jace said. "We had no idea anyone was hiding near us."

The man nodded. "Dolores, she's not had her pills for a while. Strange things are happening, she said. She's all right as long as she gets her pills, the sweetest thing."

I had a hard time reconciling the madwoman who had thrown herself at us as anything remotely resembling a sweetest anything. "Where's the nearest hospital?"

"You don't have any ID, his is useless. The only thing going to a hospital will get you is trouble. You know you can't get treatment without it."

"She's bleeding," Jace put his arm around me, "We've got to try."

The man shrugged. "You only paid rent to stay a while, information costs more."

"How much more?"

"What do you have?" The man's tone changed.

"Food, that's about it."

"I'm not hungry."

"Forget it then. We'll find it on our own."

"Not before the Army get you. You sure you don't have just one other little knife, something you're holding onto for yourself?" he wheedled.

"I'm not. Last offer, army ration pack."

Even in the torchlight I caught the calculated gleam

that lit up his eyes. But when he spoke his voice was all at odds with his expression. "I suppose I could make an exception, be charitable, in view of the girl's injuries." He held out his hands. Jace handed over a small square cardboard box. The man snatched it and hunching away from us, rifled through the contents.

"Right out of the entrance," he spoke over his shoulder. "Follow the road past where the cars used to come in here to the end. Go left, right at the three-way junction and you'll pick up signs for the hospital. It's no more than a mile or so."

The no more than a mile or so began to feel like we were walking back to Milton Keynes. The rain came at us horizontally, turned into freezing needles by the spiteful wind. We'd let go of each other's hands, shoved them in pockets, trying to minimise what the weather could pummel. Occasionally the wind paused to gather its strength making everything feel bearable for a few seconds but then threw the weather at us all the harder. This was more than a storm, probably one of the hurricanes from across the Atlantic, arrived in such a hurry it hadn't had time to wear itself out before reaching us.

I screwed my eyes up against the rain, searching for the sign the man had told us about. He had no specific reason to help us. He could have told us anything. His cultured accent, hinting at a better past than mine, didn't mean anything now.

We were almost underneath it when I saw the big H sign. Thank God. I didn't think I could have handled another deception. The battle I was fighting with myself that every minute now was a minute less likely that Sebastian was still breathing was enough to cope with. Everything was taking too long. We should have been back in Milton Keynes already. Things had seemed so black and white in the plan I'd hatched last night. Hang on, hang on, I rapped out the command to my brother with every step.

And then we were there. The hospital, a huge brick building, reared up in front of us. Most of the windows were blacked out but some showed storm lamp light, others wavering torches.

The medicine Sebastian needed was in there, the treatment I needed was in there but I couldn't get close to any of it because I didn't have the right piece of paper.

CHAPTER SIXTY-THREE

Frustrated wasn't the word. How were we going to get into the hospital? No ID, no ID, no ID, it rapped through my brain to the same rhythm with which Fred had hit the man in MK General.

"Maya, we're going to be suspicious just stood here." I felt rather than heard Jace shout at me.

No ID, no ID, no ID.

There was no way to get round that. The irony was that my ID was probably on a desk somewhere in this vast city being processed along with the IDs of those who'd died and those who had just been born. Died, that was perfect.

"I know how to get in." I yelled, steering Jace back in the direction we'd just come, down the side road that bordered the hospital, onto the road that ran parallel to the entrance. In comparison to the front, the back was as deserted as if a curfew was in effect. Just as I'd hoped. We slipped around the barrier that used to keep out vehicles, sticking to the sides of the hotch-potch of buildings, where shadows embraced us as friends.

Then I saw it, the entrance I wanted. No one should be around there who'd care enough to ask for ID. I couldn't even see any obvious cameras.

I put my good hand against the door to the mortuary and pushed.

Closing the door behind us muffled the howl of the wind so much I felt as though I'd suddenly been struck deaf. It was so good to be out of the rain. Standing still in the darkness I strained with every available sense but I couldn't hear anything or feel the presence of anyone.

I put down my hood and whispered. "I think we're alone down here, we could probably get away with some light."

Jace switched his torch on dim, further containing the beam through cupped fingers. We were alone in a long corridor. "I have an idea how I could get my hand stitched without ID."

I opened the nearest door a couple of centimetres, checking that only darkness greeted me. A quick swing of Jace's torch told me whether the room was any good. The third co-operated.

"This one," I whispered.

Jace followed me in, his torchlight ricocheting off the hard surfaces of a wall of industrial washing machines and driers. "Finding the laundry is part of your plan?"

"Are you kidding, this is better than I'd hoped."

He set the beam to bright and held it over the nearest laundry bin while I rummaged through it. I pulled out green and blue and pink scrubs in all sizes with as many different stains and smells. The first couple showed the last wearer had been standing uncomfortably close to an arterial injury. The next was folded in on itself, the smell emanating from it made me drop it immediately. I found a top which only had something around the hem and a pair of trousers with something spilt down the leg. Hopefully just an accident in the canteen.

I stripped off my jacket, my jumper and pulled the top on over my T-shirt. I peeled off my wet jeans, trying to ignore the fact that I could feel Jace's gaze on me. My legs had taken on the blue tint of the wet denim. Pulling on the bottoms I was amazed at how much warmer I felt just to be in dry clothes. My warmth began unlocking the body odour of the previous wearer and I caught wafts of them every now and again. It felt surreal.

On the worktop I found a couple of pencils. I scrunched my hair round into a bun of sorts and stuck them in it to hold it up. Thanks to the hood of my army jacket, my hair had almost dried but at least with it out of the way I wouldn't look as much like a refugee as I felt.

"Impressive, but don't you still need an ID, hospital pass or something?"

He was right. There was only one thing that would help me. I took a deep breath. It wouldn't be for long. I pulled the only slightly soiled scrubs top over my head and picked up the one I'd dropped. The smell of old sick nearly made me heave.

"You're kidding, right, you're not going to wear that?" Jace sounded totally freaked out. I couldn't blame him, I was too.

"Trust me, if I didn't have to I wouldn't. But who will want to question me if I smell this bad." I coughed, held my breath, steeling myself to pull the top on.

"Maya, you're one kind of courageous."

I turned away from him, took my T-shirt off and pulled on the most offensive thing I'd ever smelt. I coughed again, trying not to give into the urge to throw up.

"It's probably best if you wait here. I'll be as quick as I can." God, it smelt horrendous. It'd do perfectly.

"Okay, I'd hug you but. . ."

I grinned at him with forced confidence. "You can make it up to me when I get back. If you put my jacket on, a quick glance may make people think you're Army."

"Brains and brawn, what a team. Here, take the torch, I have a spare. Be careful and hurry back."

CHAPTER SIXTY-FOUR

Conversations, shouted orders, the slamming of doors, crashing of equipment, the sounds of a busy hospital reached me before I was halfway up the stairs. Storm lamps scattered everywhere gave enough light that I could put my torch in my pocket.

As I passed through a door, a soldier coming the other way grinned at me until he smelt me.

"Jesus." He stepped back quickly.

"Perks of the job." I ducked through and marched up the corridor as if I knew where I was going. It was working better than I'd hoped.

I knew I'd reached A & E before I entered the department. I could hear children crying, people moaning, coughing, an argument between an outraged woman and a man with a quiet conciliatory voice. A scream made me jump, followed by hysterical wailing that wouldn't have been out of place at a funeral. Perhaps it was the precursor to one.

The dispensary would be somewhere through the treatment area probably, but there didn't seem to be the neat and tidy segregation of Milton Keynes General. Here it was just one mass of seething humanity.

"Hey, you!"

I looked in the direction of the shouted command before I stopped myself. A harried woman in blue scrubs was looking directly at me. I pulled myself up to my full height, pretending I wasn't sixteen, pretending I didn't feel ridiculously like a little girl playing dressing up.

I teetered on the brink of running off down the maze of corridors or blundering past her back to Jace. But either would draw too much attention, make me too memorable. Better to see what she wanted as though I really should be here.

"Christ, you stink." She said as I got closer.

"I know, I need clean scrubs." At least I was mostly becoming immune to the wonderful eau de stomach contents I was wearing.

"Need you in here first. Kid with CIDP."

The same as Sebastian.

"The kid's too far gone now but we need to put on a good show for the parents." The woman was business-like and efficient.

"He's had Coralone?" The question was out before I realised I was going to ask it, a knee-jerk reaction.

She looked at me as if I'd asked if he was dying. "He'll code—"

"Doctor!" A nurse whose red hair clashed vividly with her pink scrubs interrupted.

"Right about now. Showtime, people, make it good." the doctor murmured.

The kid turned out to be a boy, not much younger than Sebastian. If I had thought his cough was a death rattle, I didn't doubt now how healthy he'd seemed. Every breath this poor kid struggled for sounded as if his lungs couldn't possibly cope with the effort of another.

I couldn't move. My mind battled to make sense of what I was seeing and in confusion, shock, worry, loss of blood, because of my anaemia, whatever, the boy's face kept changing to that of my brother. Sebastian on his death bed, Sebastian in Milton Keynes trying to keep breathing, death hovering so close the healthy people in the room could smell him.

"You," the doctor nodded at me, "CPR. The parents are watching." she whispered.

I cupped my hands on the boy's tiny chest, pressing in the rhythm Mum had taught me as soon as I was old enough to remember it. One, two, pain shot through the palm of my cut hand. I ignored it, willing the plasters to hold.

The boy's mother let out a cry that was so heartfelt, so bereft I wanted to cover my ears so I wouldn't hear her if she did it again. The nurse walked over to the mother's side and put her arm around her shoulders, giving her the scant comfort of the close presence of someone else. Comfort her husband at that moment couldn't give.

I recognised the hard stare he directed at me and the doctor. I knew the bargaining that was going on in his mind, the frantic exchange. If only he lives, I'll never do such and such again, if he lives, I'll be this way now, if he lives I'll do the hardest thing for me, I'll do anything. I'll take his place, he just has to live.

"Aren't you going to defibrillate?" I asked.

The doctor looked at me in that strange way again. "A show, remember." she mumbled.

A show? We owed it to the kid, to his parents, to try everything. What if it had been Sebastian?

I tilted the boy's head back and breathed into his mouth. One, two, three, four. Quick little breaths to reinflate his lungs. Back to his chest, one, ignore the pain in my hand, three, four. The doctor had taken the hint and was attempting artificial respiration. I concentrated on the CPR. Breathe, breathe, breathe. Come on. He was so young and fragile. Come on, don't give up. Your parents need you. Come back.

As I leant on his chest, willing my movements to reach his heart, to pass some of my life force into him, I felt his ribs crack like the bones on a chicken carcass when I broke it up to fit the saucepan to make stock. Oh my God! I yanked my hands away from him as if he had burnt me.

"I'm calling it. Time of death," the doctor consulted her watch, "12:18am. Thank you everybody." She turned to face the parents. "I'm sorry for your loss."

"Can we have a moment with our son?" The boy's father seemed beaten, utterly defeated, as if his spirit had evaporated right along with his son's last breath.

"Of course." The doctor gestured to me and the nurse to leave the cubicle. She pulled the curtains around the grieving parents. "Give them five minutes, then take the body down to the mortuary. And you," she looked at me, "get clean scrubs."

Dismissed as we were, I expected the nurse to go off and do whatever nurses did. Instead she looked at me and said "You'd better come with me."

CHAPTER SIXTY-FIVE

I stared at the nurse. I might have expected to be caught for not wearing a hospital ID by a porter or a security guard, but by a nurse?

"You're bleeding." She gestured at my hand. Blood had seeped right through the bandage. "Let me take a look at it."

Nightmare feelings of handcuffs and leg-irons receded. I followed her into the next cubicle, where she inspected my cut. "This is nasty, how did it happen?"

"It's on the site of a recent injury. It looks worse than it is."

"Have you checked for nerve damage?"

I hadn't thought of that but my fingers seemed to be working okay. Actually right then sensation was working all too well. "It's fine."

"How did you do it?" The nurse opened and closed cupboards laying out what she needed.

"Someone took exception to me." I hoped that was suitably vague.

"The way some of the patients are you'd never think that they'd come asking for our help and that we're only trying to give it. You report it?"

"Any news on the storm?" I tried to deflect her questions away from me.

"The Barrier's holding, as far as we know."

The Barrier? "Good." I mumbled, hoping it was the right response.

"But this has to be the big storm they keep warning us about so who knows?" she went on. "There's probably a storm surge building right now."

A sob of raw anguish and heartbreaking grief from the other side of the curtain made us both look up. In his brief life it was clear the boy had been really loved.

"I've been a nurse a long time, through the flu and everything, but this is the hardest thing." She suddenly seemed older, more worldly-worn, her hair even a paler echo of the sunset reddy-orange that had blazed at me while she supported the grieving mother.

"Seeing a child die?" I asked stupidly.

"Not being able to use proper measures to save them, just letting them die. I'm sure the Government know what they're doing but . . ." her voice trailed away, the caution that ruled our lives reasserting itself before she said something to a stranger that might be construed as criticism.

Why were they letting children die?

I felt the floor spinning up to meet me, the sounds of A & E were drowned by the sudden rushing in my ears. My eyes were open but I could see nothing except a darkness that blinded me from within. No. Not now. I couldn't pass out here. From a long way away I heard the nurse saying "You're done." But I couldn't move.

While she cleared up I tried to stay centred on the here, the now. I flexed my calf muscles, twisted my ankles, tried to get the blood flowing round my body again. Why now? Was my anaemia getting worse? I flexed my muscles harder. The sounds of A & E gradually came back to how they should be.

"I've got to clear the space, get the boy down to the

mortuary." The nurse had become all efficient again.

"I'll take him." I offered.

"You should wait for the porters really."

"I know but I don't mind, I need to get cleaned up anyway." I gestured vaguely at my top. "It's better for the parents if we take him now, rather than wait for the porters. Like cauterising a wound." I didn't know where the rubbish I was spouting was coming from, but it sounded like I knew what I was talking about. If it had been Sebastian in that boy's place, if it were me and Mum grieving I'd want to never have him taken away from us.

I watched while the nurse shooed the parents on their way, while she pointed them in the direction of the hospital chapel, while she reiterated over-used condolences. I wanted to ask if there was somewhere his parents could sit with him for longer but that might make her pay all kinds of attention to me.

"I'll be right back with the paperwork." she said.

Left alone with the child, I smoothed his hair back behind his ear. He was warm, he could have just been sleeping.

"I'm sorry we couldn't save you," I whispered. "So sorry."

Strands of his brown hair laced themselves through my fingers, coming away in my hand when I withdrew it. I patted them back onto his sheet. His brown hair overlaid black in my memory. Just like Jasmine he must have felt too sick to have his hair washed and brushed in ages. Oh, poor Mrs Fook, did that mean Jasmine had died too?

The nurse bundled back into the cubicle, manoeuvring a gurney. She copied the child's name from his admission records onto something on her clipboard which turned out to be a tag that she tied to one of his toes. She pulled the sheet up over his face and untucked the one on which he lay.

"Ready?" I stared at her blankly. "To move him onto the gurney. On three."

We lifted him off the bed using the sheet he'd been lying on like a sling.

"You know what to do with his paperwork, you know, on a Coralone case?"

The nurse took my confused silence as acquiescence, patted the file of notes she laid on the child's legs and disappeared through the curtains.

On a Coralone case — what on earth did that mean? Why should it be different from any other? Looking at the sheet-covered bundle, my mind couldn't quite accept that the kid wouldn't mind the sheet over his face, wouldn't care that I was using him as part of my disguise.

"I'm sorry." I whispered.

I released the gurney brake and manhandled it out of the cubicle. About four steps into the corridor a guy with floppy blond hair in a blue uniform stopped me.

"You need help?" He pinched his nose. "What is that smell?"

He was a few inches shorter than me so much closer to the horrible stain on my top.

"That would be me. Pressie from the little guy before he died." Sorry again. While he was right there I felt wrong lying about him even though he was beyond knowing or caring.

"It's not contagious, is it? I mean there've been so many of them recently, what with their hair falling cut and everything. It has to be the start of another epidemic, right?" There was real fear in his blue eyes. Poor guy, that paranoid about illness and given a career in a hospital.

"He had an auto-immune disease. Not contagious. Not an epidemic. But you don't have to worry, I'll take him to the mortuary. That way you'll be doubly safe, safe from the smell of me and from the little guy's germs."

"Germs! But you said—"

"We all carry germs, most of them are harmless, some not so nice, like the ones that give us colds or stomach upsets but they're not all lethal."

"Oh,"I could almost see him physically relax. "That's okay then, I can help you. You know you're supposed to wait for us to do things like that anyway."

"We're all so busy and I need to get cleaned up."

"I'll take him."

"No, really, it's fine,"I tried to make my grimace appear like a smile. "I promised the parents."

"The lifts aren't working."

"I know."

"So you'll need to use the stairs. I'll carry him down. You can hardly do it, can you? You'll get him covered in that." He gestured at my front.

Damn, I'd backed myself into a corner that I couldn't see any way out from. Better to go with it for now. "You're right, thanks."

He took the gurney from me. "Let me, for some of them you need a certain knack."

When we reached the stairs, he parked it against the wall, and took a storm lamp from the tiny collection on a shelf. "You want to get this?"

He held it out to me and passed me the file of notes. When he lifted the kid's body up, the child's arm swung out from beneath the sheet. I tucked it back underneath.

"I haven't seen you round here before, you new?" the guy was saying.

"Not really." I didn't know if they had locum doctors and nurses here. Probably they had to but I didn't want to raise his suspicions. Vague and non-committal seemed the best way to go.

"You're really young to be a doctor. You one of those bright kids who jumped a few years in school?"

"No, just good genes."

"I'd agree with that. So when you get off shift, you want to go grab a coffee or something?"

I tripped on the next stair. Was he asking me out? What should I say? No, adults socialised by having coffee or tea together all the time. That was all it was, friendly contact in an unfriendly world.

"I'm on for ages yet." I murmured.

"Me too, the storm and everything, everyone's on all night I reckon. I'll come find you after."

Oh great, this staying completely non-memorable was going really well. As we reached the lower ground floor the lamp showed a gurney neatly lined up against the wall. I could have kissed it.

"If you just put him on there, I've got it the rest of the way. Got the paperwork to sort out. Thanks for your help."

"You're really dedicated, aren't you? Not like some of the other docs, up themselves, they are. I'm looking forward to our date. Later." He winked and ran back up the stairs.

I held the lamp up. The laundry was the second door on the right. The mortuary had to be past the corridor offshoot where Jace and I had come in. I balanced the lamp on the end of the gurney and walked down the corridor.

It was where I'd thought it must be. 'Mortuary'. Just the word on the sign above the double doors was enough to make me shiver. Seeing a skeleton up close and personal was totally different to seeing a body. A body would be recognisable as a person. And didn't they smell really bad? And what about the germs they carried?

My hands tightened around the gurney I'd been pushing. A gurney with a body on it. Too many years of info-cast conditioning had a lot to answer for. I pulled in a deep breath. However I felt about going in there, I couldn't leave this poor boy lying in the corridor.

CHAPTER SIXTY-SIX

I latched back one of the doors and risked a peek inside. A large cold empty space. Four tables, presumably used for post mortems, lined up across the middle of the room, all thankfully empty and so scrubbed they almost gleamed. I latched back the other door and pushed the gurney through.

The warm light from the storm lamp bounced off a wall of stainless steel doors, suddenly cold and too harsh because I knew what would be behind them. There was another set of double doors opposite where I'd come in but there didn't seem to be anyone through there either, no movement, no dark shapes reflected through the frosted half-glazed doors, no light shining back at me.

Behind those doors was a storage area unlike anything I'd ever seen. Racks lined the walls, holding bodies shrouded in sheets, as if the people who worked there had all felt tired at the same time and gone for a nap together. I half expected one of them to sit up and demand to know what I was doing there with no ID.

My light caught the toe tag of one of the bodies. It had the same red cross the nurse had drawn on the child's tag. Did they all have one? Is that what made them

Coralone cases? I put the lamp down near the door and pulled my torch out of my pocket. Thumbing it on, I read Joshua Dawkins, l/d 16:56 July 15th. Yesterday.

I shivered a protest against the frigid air being circulated around the storage room. The toe tag on the body beneath Joshua Dawkins bore the same red cross. Stella Crick, l/d 11:22 14th July. I looked at each one of the toe tags. They all had a red cross and the peculiar code l/d.

Back out in the main room of the mortuary, I checked the toe tag of the boy I'd brought down. Niall Everly, l/d 15:54. I looked at his admittance notes. He'd been brought in at seven thirty that night, struggling to breathe, barely conscious. The notes spelt out a detailed medical history, most of which I didn't understand. His parents had given him his last dose of Coralone just before four. l/d 15:54, l/d = last dose. The hospital were recording when he'd taken his last dose. When all the patients with red crosses on their toe tags had taken the last doses of their medicine.

I looked at the bank of stainless steel mini doors that hid other secrets. I didn't need to look in there. What else could I possibly hope to discover? I pushed Niall up to one of the tables, picked up the storm lamp and unlatched the exit doors. But what if looking in there could tell me something?

I pulled in a deep breath that chilled me still further. Just the first one. That was all I needed to check. I grasped the handle, closed my eyes and pulled. It opened easily. Empty.

The next one wasn't quite as innocuous. A shrouded figure filled the bulk of the interior space. I grasped the handle attached to whatever the body was lying on and pulled. It slid out surprisingly easily, the bulk of the huge man not impeding its progress at all.

I really didn't want to look at the head end. I didn't want whomever this had been to intrude on my nightmares. I tucked the sheet back enough to find the toe tag. Trying not to look at the man's feet, I pulled the tag up with my fingertips and read it by torchlight. No red cross, no keeping tabs on the last dose he had taken of anything.

I really needed to check one more, just to be sure. Just one more then I was out of here. I pulled out a slighter body this time and forced myself to lift the sheet. No red cross on the toe tag.

It seemed none of the bodies housed behind the chrome doors had red crosses. All of them in the add-on area did. The Coralone cases. What did that mean?

I had to let it go for now. I had a date with the dispensary.

CHAPTER SIXTY-SEVEN

I dithered outside the laundry room. I wanted to let Jace know I was okay but he couldn't see my expertly dressed hand because I didn't want him to know what I was about to do. I pressed my fingertips against the door then marched up the stairs back into the main hospital, before I could let dreamed up hopes for my future stop me.

Thoughts of what it would be like to be Jace's girlfriend, to not have to put up with the pitying looks from the popular girls, parading around with their latest accessory boyfriend, to not have to listen to the taunts that I must be gay or frigid or a freak because I never did anything that would define me as a normal girl. And that was without thinking about feeling special because someone cared for me. And later on to do the things most people wanted, to be together, to have a family, even if right now the thought of that was as alien as the thought of taking a flight somewhere.

Head down, purposeful strides, I ignored the knocking noise my heart was making as it thudded against my ribs. Quickly through A & E, I found the dispensary. And, of course, someone was on duty there.

"What do you need?" The woman looked and

sounded completely bored. She held out a hand with at least one ring on every finger for something I didn't have. She'd performed this routine so many times her skin had settled into a pattern of cracks and crevices that framed her words, going through the motions until the Government told her she didn't have to do it anymore.

"Coralone please." I hoped my request didn't sound as desperate to her as it did to me. "They asked me to get it now, emergency, the paperwork'll follow."

"Is that you? That godawful smell?"

"Like I said, it's an emergency. I need to get back, with the Coralone."

"You all know the rules, there can't be any exceptions." The woman's face settled into a new pattern. "But I can save you the trouble, can't give you any Coralone anyway, we're out. What do you need?" She held out a bejewelled hand to the pink-scrubbed nurse who'd started a queue behind me.

I had no choice but to walk away, feeling like I was right back at the beginning, when I'd gone to the clinic, when I'd first broken Sebastian's medicine. My hand hurt now like it did then, a whole new layer of déjà-vu.

The factory, going to the source, was really my only option. But where would I find the address? The pharmacy probably wouldn't keep the records on-site with the drugs. I remembered tales of bureaucracy gone mad from Mum, of her moaning that the admin office was now the source of true power. I just needed to find that.

"Never seen you before and now twice in," the porter from earlier held his lantern up to his watch, "half an hour, must be my lucky night. You still haven't changed?"

I shrugged, an 'I'm too busy' gesture I hoped. I'd become mostly immune to the smell now, just catching the odd whiff that grabbed at my throat. "I need to get some information from the admin office."

"Now?"

I nodded. "I know it'll be closed but I made a mistake

in a report and I need to correct it before anyone notices."

"Don't you want to get changed first?"

"Trust me, I'd love to but I just have to do this one thing, then I can." At least that much was the truth.

I wasn't practised at all in the art of using a look or gesture or feminine wile to get my own way. I ought to have been paying attention to the masters of the art in my form group. All I knew how to do was to smile. So I smiled.

"I can get you in," the porter said. "I know the code, but you don't go telling anyone."

"Of course not."

"You can thank me after coffee," he winked again. "This way."

He led me away from the bustle of A & E, his storm lamp parting the darkness in front of him. I was just beginning to wonder where he was taking me when he stopped in front of a door and entered a code on a keypad. I counted five beeps.

"One of the secretaries," he explained away his illicit knowledge. "She wants to go out with me, she's nice enough but you know, not in your league."

What would he think if I told him the truth that I wasn't a doctor but a sixteen-year-old suspended from school, whose ID was in the prison system? He probably wouldn't be so keen to help me then.

"I need to add in the name and address of the place that manufactures Coralone. I don't suppose you have any ideas where to find that?"

"Course."

As easy as that?

He put the storm lantern on top of a metal filing cabinet and pulled open the top drawer.

"Probably here, under 'c', what was it again?"

"Coralone, c-o-r-a—"

"Got it." He pulled out a folder and handed it to me.

"Thanks." I could hardly believe I was holding what I

needed, that something had gone right for a change. Lying the folder open on the nearest desk to the light, I grabbed a pen.

"You want me to get your report out for you? I think I know where that'd be." the porter said.

"My boss has still got it," I ad-libbed. "I just need the address on a scrap of paper."

I winced as the pen pressed against my cut. It was worse than the first one, at least I'd been able to write before.

"Let me, that must be sore." He took the pen from me and coughed, screwing his face up in disgust.

"Sorry, I'll just stand out of your way." I stood a few paces away watching him writing in painstakingly slow longhand. "Where is it again?" I tried to keep my tone light, disinterested even. At least I hoped it came out like that.

"Stratworthy House." He said it as though he were spelling it.

"Is it far from here?"

"Nah, not really. Farmer Street's off Trident Road, you know the big one going north from the river—"

"What're you doing in here?" Another lantern appeared at the door, announcing a security guard by the glint of his epaulette buttons, the reflected shine of his boots.

"Just helping out a colleague," the porter said.

The security guard peered at us. "You," he waved the lamp at the porter, "I know. You," he waved it at me, "I don't. Let me see some ID."

Keep calm, don't panic.

"Sure." I patted my scrubs trousers, looking down when I apparently couldn't feel my badge. I tried both pockets. "That's odd." I made an exaggerated show of looking around as if I must have just dropped it. "I remember putting it on when I came on shift."

"I hope so, for your sake. You know what no ID

means."

"It's got to be here." I dropped to my hands and knees, hoping the desperation in my voice would be mistaken for concern over my missing ID. "Oh, I bet I know where it is. We just had a kid code on us, messy death. In all the confusion it must have got pulled off. I'll go check."

"I'll come with you."

I left the admin office, setting my pace so I stayed a couple of steps ahead of the guard.

"Slow down," he puffed behind me.

"Can't, I'm in the middle of a busy shift."

"In the admin office?" he panted.

I sped up further. I rounded the corner into A & E eyeing the closed curtains of the treatment cubicles. Could I hide in one of those? Would the few seconds he'd be disoriented looking for me be enough that I could get away from him? But he'd probably smell me no matter where I hid.

Non-memorable be damned. I put my head down and ran through the department.

CHAPTER SIXTY-EIGHT

I charged down the stairs two at a time, gripping the handrail with my good hand hard enough to give me a friction burn to stop myself ending up a tangled heap at the bottom. I shot through the laundry room door.

"We've got to get out of here, quickly. A guard's after me."

I pulled the hideous scrub top over my head and sliced the darkness with my torch beam looking for my T-shirt.

"Why? What happened?"

"I got challenged about no ID." I dropped my voice, in case the guard had seen where I'd fled.

"But your hand's stitched up?"

"Yep, it's fine. I got the address of the Coralone plant."

"Is that why you've been ages?"

"Long story." I pulled my T-shirt and jumper on. "I'll fill you in on the way."

Jace had taken off the army jacket and held it out for me. I stuffed my arms in. It was warm from his body. I pulled out the pencils from my hair, shaking it loose. "Jeans?"

"Up there." He pointed with his torch. "No electric means no dryers but it's hot in here, they may be slightly less wet."

The feel of sodden denim was enough to make me want to keep on the scrub trousers but I knew they'd be soaked through within a minute of leaving the hospital and the wind would make them feel non-existent. I wriggled into my jeans, knowing I was taking too long, making too much noise.

Jace held out his hand, helped me up off the floor and pulled me against him. "You okay?" He mumbled against my lips.

"Yes." I breathed.

He kissed me, long and searchingly. He filled my senses, filled my everything, until all I was was the sum of him and he me and I couldn't tell where one ended and the other began.

When we pulled apart I was certain that if he hadn't been holding me, I would have fallen over. My knees seemed to have forgotten what they were supposed to do.

He ran his hand lightly through my hair. "You ready?"

I didn't want to go anywhere. I wanted to stay right there in his arms. It felt so good, so right. How had I never realised how I felt before? We spent practically every day together, shared everything and I'd never thought of him like this. For someone apparently so smart, I'd been amazingly stupid.

"Maya?"

"Sure, yes, I'm ready."

He kissed me again, a quick peck this time. "Let's go then."

I opened the door the tiniest crack and listened. I couldn't hear anything and no matter how hard I stared I couldn't see anything other than uniform darkness. Switching his torch to its dimmest setting, cradling the beam with his fingers, Jace let it play up and down. The

269

corridor was empty. He clicked it off and whispered. "Okay."

We ran to the exit. I pulled the door open and launched myself outside crashing straight into the security guard, who grabbed hold of my hood and hair.

"Thought you'd got one over on me, did you?" He shouted above the keening wind. "Might be able to outrun me but it's up here that counts." He tapped his temple.

I wanted to scream. I couldn't be caught by another guard. I couldn't be stopped from going to the factory now – I was so close!

"Can I have a word?" Jace shouted.

"You got ID?"

"Of course. I need to speak to you in private."

"Have to wait till I've processed her."

"She won't go anywhere, she'll wait right there, won't you?" Jace looked at me. How could he possibly get us out of this? Whatever he wanted to try was worth a go. I nodded.

"Don't know that I can just leave her here, not without securing her the guard said.

I tried to pull away from him – I couldn't deal with handcuffs again.

"That's not necessary. Seriously, she'll stay there. I'm saving you a lot of work." Jace took hold of the guard's arm and practically frog-marched him to the corner of the building before he could object again.

The guard stared at me all while Jace talked to him. My mouth dropped open when I saw Jace pull his ID out and hand it over. What was he doing? Now he'd be arrested too.

I realised I was creeping forwards, taking automatic steps towards Jace to help him when his plan fell apart, which would be right about now, as soon as the guard saw his MK address. The guard even switched on a torch, the better to read the offending location.

Then the wind took a breath and I heard the last

270

words I ever expected to come out of Jace's mouth.

"You can see it right there, that number," he pointed at his ID, "that's my GI number."

CHAPTER SIXTY-NINE

Those words coming from Jace were so wrong, so impossible that I would have bet my life I hadn't heard right, if it hadn't been for his reaction. I'd stopped walking, my feet paralysed beneath the weight of his revelation. How could he be a Government Informant? GIs were the worst in everyone, sneaking, spying, ratting out their friends and family for cash. We all knew they only cultivated relationships in terms of what they could learn about others, how they could twist things to their own ends.

Jace? He did that?

"Maya." He held out a hand to me.

I could no more take it than I could gun the security guard down.

Jace was a GI?

"No." The word breathed out of me like a sigh. My best friend, my *boyfriend* was a Government Informant.

"Maya, it's not what you think. I can explain, let me explain."

The meaning of what he was saying didn't come anywhere close to me, the words were only sounds as clear to me as animal noises. And all I could see was the terrible reaction on his face that I'd heard him.

I whirled away from him, ran away from the hospital. Before I knew what I was doing I was running in my rhythm, controlling my breathing, in, out, in, out, stretching out my strides, arms pumping, wrists held loosely. One, two, one, two. The numbers filled my mind, I tried to fill my soul with them as well.

One, two, one, two. Just keep running. I could outrun him, I'd always been able to beat him. Since we were nine-year-olds together, running the length of the street, I'd always been faster. I manhandled the memory back where it came from, where it would stay from now on.

I wished there was only the one, two, one, two. I tried to concentrate on my ragged breathing, the wind pushing me one way then another, the incessant splattering of rain on my hood, my sleeves, soaking my bandage, the wetness pouring in through the tops of my trainers when the pavement dipped and the never-ending puddle deepened.

Then I wasn't running any more. I turned a slow circle where I'd stopped. No one behind me. No one else anywhere. It was gone 1:00am, probably nearer 2:00, anyone with any sense was at home in bed.

Jace was a GI. He spied on people, on me, ratted us out to the Government. How could he? Why? What on earth had ever possessed him to do that? To be that? Was it the money? He and his gran didn't seem to have enough to throw about, but then she did all her baking and what about her roses? Tiny clues that meant nothing really but all added up to a something. Is that how Mrs Randle had been caught?

What did Esther think about it? She had to know what Jace was, they were really close. But I'd thought he was close to me too and he hadn't told me. Because he knew how I'd react.

I could feel anger and hurt at his betrayal in every place where the jacket touched me. No wonder he'd been able to get supplies for us, he and Walsh had probably had a great time chatting about who they'd sold out, while the soldiers had been beating me up.

I tore off the jacket and threw it on the ground. I wanted to cry and scream. I wanted to hurt something so it hurt like I did. I paced up and down in front of the pile of jacket as if I wanted to wear the pavement out.

I had to get a grip. I didn't have time to fall apart right now. I'd have more time than I would ever want to prod at this hurt when I was back in MK. Each time I saw Jace it would kill me. Right now I had to remember Sebastian was counting on me.

As I calmed down I became aware of the rain pelting my hair again, my mostly dry jumper. The jacket, a darker heap on the darkness of the pavement, accused me.

I was only spiting myself. Jace wouldn't care if I was wearing it or not. Yes he would. He'd want me to stay dry. But it wasn't for him I'd wear it. I stomped over to it and thrust my arms into the sleeves, making my body all awkward angles so it felt uncomfortable, like I used to do when I was younger and Mum got me clothes I hated.

I wiped my face and walked to the next turning looking for a street sign. As far as I could work out I'd been running away from the river so all I needed to do was walk parallel to it and I should hit Trident Road. But which direction to try first?

Everything that could have gone wrong since I left MK had, and more besides. So trying right seemed way too optimistic. I went left. Just as I thought I must have chosen wrong, a narrow side turning ended on Trident Road. I let my feet decide up or down and just went where they led. Every few steps I batted away thoughts of Jace. How long had he been a GI? What had he told about me? About my family? About our neighbours? Did he actually really care about me, or was that just some ploy that the Government had him making? Why? Why had he sold out? Did I really know him at all?

CHAPTER SEVENTY

I nearly missed the Farmer Street turning. I read the name without registering it until I was almost past it. And from the buildings I'd never have guessed I was in the right place. None of them were obviously factories. Some three, some four storeys, all old double, treble or even quadruple fronted Victorian buildings.

Stratworthy House. I found it towards the end of the road. No sign or anything announcing what it was. As closed up as it should have been in the middle of the night. Maybe I'd have more luck around the back where there could be a night watchman who might be open to persuasion. I tried not to think that I had nothing to bargain with.

At the rear, railings topped with razor wire kept watch around the perimeter of the factory's land parcel. Tall double gates were locked together with a chain wider than any bolt cutter's bite. A security panel blinked at me from beside the rear entrance, armed and just waiting to catch me. No nightwatchmen, no obvious cameras but who would be stupid enough to break in there with everything else?

The terrible feeling of being caught at MK General

flooded me, the pronouncement of the security guard that I was going straight to prison, no trial, no possibility of leniency, a vicious déjà-vu. What would be the punishment for breaking in here? Whatever it was, not as high as the price of me not doing it. A vision of Sebastian, lying pale and still in the hospital mortuary, his toe tagged with one of those red-crossed labels, was too strong for me to ignore.

There had to be a way in. I had to find it, that was all. It was like a piece of scientific research, I was at the starting point, I knew where I wanted to end up, I just had to find how to get there. Breaking it down like that cleared my mind, calmed me, helped me concentrate with a clarity I hadn't felt since before I'd broken Sebastian's medicine.

The gates were out, I didn't have the tools to get past the chain. Scaling the railings was no good either, I couldn't get over razor wire. And the alarm panel which had now stopped blinking was clearly unpredictable. I even looked at the roof but that was a really stupid idea.

So much security for a place that produced medicines. There was no way I was going to crack any of it. I'd have to wait until the morning. I just had to trust that Sebastian could hang on for a few more hours.

My body was screaming at me loud enough that I couldn't ignore it anymore. There were more parts of me aching than not. The muscles that straddled my shoulders had pulled themselves taut, straining each fibre of my back. My thighs and hip bones were chafed and sore and my trainers, my comfy live-and-die-in shoes, felt as though they would kill me if I took one more step.

How I felt emotionally – I couldn't even go there. It was only the picture of Sebastian in my mind that was keeping me upright after the betrayals and revelations of the night. It wouldn't take much more to make me lie down and not get up again. I pushed away thoughts of the long lonely walk back to MK. The present moment, that was all I could think about. Just getting out of the rain for a while.

If anything it was coming down harder now. It felt like a Chinese water torture.

I walked towards the building on the right hand side of the factory. The railings surrounding that one were much lower, no ornate toppings of pain on those. If only that was my target. I shone my torch over the back of it. The beam hopscotched past the door. Weird. I played the beam over it again. It was slightly ajar, very slightly, scarcely anything. But it was open, it would give me shelter until the morning.

I placed my hands on either side of one of the ace of spades type decorations that topped the railings and pushed myself up and over. Jesus! I'd forgotten about my hand. The pain was worse than when the woman had cut me. I snatched my hand up and overbalanced, crashing down onto the concrete. I lay there a second in the rainwater, wishing I hadn't done that. I dragged myself upright. At least I'd fallen on the inside of the railings.

My jeans and trainers felt like I'd taken a bath in them. I picked up my torch and checked it. Amazingly it still worked. No blood on my bandage, only rainwater. Thank God, the stitches must be holding but the pain was caught in a loop, undiminishing, making my eyes water. Shouldn't be so easy to forget not to use my hand for anything now. I flexed my legs, everything worked okay but by the time I got home I was going to be a walking bruise.

I looked closely at the open door. As far as I could tell there was nothing around it, nothing that looked like a trip wire, or an alarm cable. Nothing to feed my paranoia. Maybe a careless employee had just not locked it properly, wanting to get home before the storm broke.

Only one way to find out.

I pushed open the door.

CHAPTER SEVENTY-ONE

My torch picked up a maze of boxes stacked two high in some places, three against the walls. No security guards. I stepped inside and pulled my hood down, hearing only silence. No rain pounding me, no howling wind but more importantly no klaxoning alarms, no slamming down of security shutters imprisoning me where I stood.

I left the door ajar, just in case closing it set something off and headed for the small flight of stairs in the back corner of the room. Looking at where I'd come in, something prickled my mind. Something odd. The boxes by the wall looked as though they'd been lined up using a ruler but the rest were spread haphazardly around the room.

So what were the ones by the wall hiding?

Tucking my torch under my arm, I grasped hold of the bottom box and pushed and pulled at each corner in succession, 'walking' it out from between its neighbours. Boxes of air it seemed. Just a smokescreen.

With a final tug, I pulled the box column away from the wall and wormed my way in behind them. My fingers straddled a blip in the plaster – architrave – and beyond that I could feel the smoothness of a door. An interconnecting door between buildings from here into Stratworthy House? Was I finally getting the break I deserved?

Like the external door this one was slightly ajar, held open by a small wedge of battered wood pressed against the frame. So where was whoever had put that there? I snapped off my torch, but I still could only hear my breathing, the rustling of my jacket. The building felt dead.

Excitement shoved aside my exhaustion. The door opened silently, easily. I squatted, peering round the corner at a lower level than any lurking security guard would expect. The room it opened into was completely dark. I breathed quietly, straining to hear the answering echo of anyone else. I heard nothing.

Risking everything I flashed my torch around the room. My senses had been right, no one there. Just filing cabinets. Row upon row with scarcely enough space between them to allow the drawers to open. No Coralone down here I was sure. I'd have to go up into the main body of the building to the processing plant itself.

I could see nothing on the ground floor, the darkness split only by the red eye of a movement sensor glowering at me. I froze. The light blinked silently out of existence.

I risked a quick burst of torchlight along the floor, enough to see three doors off the corridor I was in. One was clearly the front entrance, another was labelled 'stairs'. The third opened up into a space that couldn't have been more surprising. It was about twice as big as our school gym. The whole school could have sat exams in here together.

A few piles of what looked like flat-packed cardboard, waiting to be made into boxes and a broom in a corner were all that troubled my torchlight. At the far end of the room the chrome façade of two lifts glinted back at me. Lifts would be too noisy – stairs were the way to go.

On the first floor, I opened the twin of the door I'd tried downstairs.

Two clinically white runs of silent machinery filled the space. That was more like it. Exhausted as I was, I had to stop myself running to the end where the medicine presumably came out, ready to be packaged up and shipped out. Walking was quieter. At the end of the machine there was nothing. They were producing medicines, after all, things that had to be kept properly stored to protect their active ingredients. It wasn't the machinery that made it I needed, it was the storage room.

Up again to the second floor into a space that mirrored the first exactly. Another two runs of machinery, one of which seemed to be undergoing a refit. Laid out on the floor beside it were lengths of hose and strange shaped pieces of metal.

I didn't expect to find any Coralone here either but I checked anyway. The air didn't smell clinically clean like I might have expected, nor was there any hint of Coralone's distinctive scent.

Up again. The third floor had a totally different layout. This space had been divided up into separate rooms along the front and back of the building, split by a central corridor.I shone my torch through the glazed doors into what appeared to be labs. Even from that small distance I couldn't tell just by peering through the doors whether there was any Coralone in there or not. I needed to get inside. But the door was locked. Of course it was.

The second and the third and all the others defeated me too. So now what? I still had one more floor to try. I'd check that out first and maybe I wouldn't need to break into these labs, if I could figure out how to.

Even standing still for those few seconds, I could feel the exhaustion my adrenaline rush had been keeping at bay drowning me. The last floor. Come on. I dragged myself to the stairwell door. The movement sensor blinked its watchful eye at me. A deafening siren split the air. The alarm, telling the whole street I'd broken in.

CHAPTER SEVENTY-TWO

The shriek of the alarm reverberated through my chest for a couple of seconds and then stopped. Silence rushed in to replace it, pressing against my ears, my body. I hardly dared breathe, watching the sensor. The alarm remained silent.

What did it mean that it had suddenly switched off? Had it called the authorities? They'd be stretched my father had said, so maybe I had time to check the top floor? It was my last remaining chance, I couldn't not.

I opened the door to the stairwell. Footsteps on the stairs. They were here, already? Was there a guard I'd missed who was coming now to arrest me? Hide, hide, hide, but where?

The only place was behind the door but that would hardly work for more than a handful of seconds. As it opened I flicked on my torch, hoping to blind whoever it was enough so I could slip past them. But trying to get a fix on his face, I recognised him. "You!"

"Put your torch down!" Walsh shielded his eyes. "God, you don't give up. What are you doing here?"

"Leaving." I didn't want to give him anything he could use against me with the authorities.

"How d'you get this address?"

"It's not important." I moved past him and reached for the stairwell door.

He shone his own torch at me. "What happened to you?"

I cradled the hurting side of my face. It had been tightening for a while, swelling beneath the damage from the soldier's blows. The bruises must be showing already. "You did."

"What?"

"You handed me over to soldiers. They didn't like what I was telling them."

"Jesus, they were only supposed to question you, keep you overnight. I'm sorry." He peered at me. "So why didn't they?"

"What does it matter?"

"It matters a lot, why didn't they keep you overnight?"

If we were playing twenty questions, I had a few of my own for him. "Why did you turn me in?"

Walsh held my gaze for what felt like ages. "On the level? There's something not right about this whole operation here. I couldn't have you interfering."

"Getting me locked up was your solution?"

Walsh shrugged. "Someone might have realised I've been paying a little too much attention to this place and for all I knew you could have been sent by the Government to test my loyalty. Basically I was covering my own back. I didn't know if I could believe your story about the dying brother."

"Believe it."

"I can't think what else would make you so determined. So how did you get away without being locked up?"

"I'm Simon Bessick's daughter."

"Aren't you a little tall for five?"

"I'm the daughter he pretends he doesn't have. The

one he abandoned along with his wife and son during the pandemic. Just upped and left one day, never came back."

Walsh let out a low whistle. "No shit."

I was annoyed that I still found myself jumping when people around me swore, expecting the Government's long reach to scoop me up with them just for being in earshot, like the info-casts promised.

"Will anyone respond to that alarm?" I asked.

"Usually, probably. Tonight we may be lucky. I turned it off as soon as it went off, maybe it didn't sound long enough to raise suspicion."

The alarm panel outside blinking at me and then visually silent, I must have been only a few minutes behind Walsh getting into the building.

"You left the doors next door ajar? I thought it was too easy getting in here."

"It might be easy now but to get the connecting door unstuck and unlocked and get the alarm code was anything but."

I nodded in recognition of what he'd done. "Where do they keep the Coralone? Upstairs?"

"There doesn't appear to be any here."

"They ship it all as they produce it?" They were more efficient than I had expected.

"No, there hasn't been any production here for more than three weeks."

Three weeks. When we'd received Sebastian's last bottle, the one I'd broken. I remembered the message on the clinic's computer, 'Coralone withdrawn', the A & E dispensaries being out.

But why would they stop producing it? While it wasn't quite like leaving the asthmatics short of inhalers, Coralone was a brilliant medicine designed to be a one solution fits all for anyone with an auto-immune disease. It didn't make any sense.

"You saw the machine downstairs, the one in bits?" Walsh asked. "I'm not that mechanically minded but from what I can tell, it's being decommissioned."

"Maybe they're moving production somewhere else?"

"That's what I figured, at first. That's what I'd still be thinking, if it wasn't for the deaths."

My mind filled with the image of the bodies in the hospital mortuary. "The red crosses."

"You've seen them? The toe tags?"

I nodded, my mind struggling to make some sense of what Walsh was telling me. "Just now, in the hospital near here."

"Christ, you're a better investigator than me. You've done all this in one night?"

"My brother's dying, it's a hell of a motivator."

"So I'll level with you. Total honesty, okay? I have a friend who works in that hospital. She told me a lot of people have suddenly started dying. The pharmacy doesn't have any more Coralone, and the staff have been told not to use heroic measures to keep these patients alive."

Which would explain the strange reaction to me trying to revive Niall in the Casualty Dept. And Mum, she would have been told the same thing. And I'd kept on at her to get Sebastian admitted, thinking she was just being bloody-minded but she knew no one would fight to keep him alive. Now I understood.

"When they die," Walsh was saying, "they're marked with that red cross and kept separate from other corpses. Army trucks take them away."

Red crosses, the Army taking away corpses. All a scary echo from everyone's past.

"No Coralone here anywhere?" I couldn't believe after everything that had happened I was right back where I'd started at the clinic.

"I haven't checked out all the labs yet," Walsh said. "There may be the odd bottle kicking around in there. I've been looking for a paper trail, but a lot of the stuff is way over my head."

"What about the top floor?"

"Couple of offices up there, nothing helpful in any of them. Staff room, toilets."

"Could you get me in the labs?"

"Why should I help you out?"

I didn't say what I was thinking, that he owed me for my bruises. "You get me in to check for sample quantities of Coralone, I'll have a look at some of the stuff you've found."

"Seriously, kid—"

"My name's Maya."

"Seriously, Maya, it's way above what they must be teaching you."

"So am I, way above. Let me look at it."

"You know scientific stuff, formulae?" Walsh sounded as though I'd said I could sprout wings and fly.

I nodded. "You should probably make up your mind quickly."

He pulled a small dark wallet out of one of his jacket's inner pockets and extracted two long thin instruments that looked like they belonged in a nightmare dentist's practice. He squatted down next to the first lab door and began to jiggle them around in the lock. "This can take a while. Sit."

"I'm fine."

"The US Marines have a saying, don't stand if you can sit, don't sit if you can lie, don't lie awake if you can sleep because you don't know when your next rest may come."

I sat. "Is that where you're from, the US?"

"Yep."

"Why didn't you go back when the pandemic started? I thought everyone who could leave the UK did." I didn't expect him to answer, giving away anything personal didn't seem like the kind of thing he'd do willingly.

"Pretty much. It wasn't that simple for me, I had . . . reasons for staying. Besides, I thought your Government had things under control."

"They probably did until Michael Irvine slaughtered

most of the MPs."

"That Great British spirit they're always talking about should have made them rally round. I don't think anyone could believe that they would all fall apart."

"You're very honest."

"And you're not?"

"Mostly it's not . . ." I was struggling with the word I wanted to say and the word I knew I should.

Walsh swivelled round and looked at me. "It's not wise to say anything against the Government?"

"So I'm told."

He turned his attention back to the lock. "Do you think making people obedient through fear is a responsible way to rule?"

"Do you think they're just as scared as we are?" I countered him with another question.

He didn't answer for a few minutes, his attention on what he was doing as if I hadn't said anything. "Initially," he finally said. "Maybe. After Irvine's bullet spraying. Maybe they were brave then being prepared to pick up the pieces. They did stop us descending into chaos. There's a saying that a civilised society is only ever nine meals away from anarchy. We were almost there when they rallied their new military. People had started to turn on each other. Your mum must have told you about this stuff, right?"

"She doesn't talk about anything from before. You had so much, how did it all disappear?"

"Fear. It was a constant, people would have killed each other for a pack of cookies and there was no one to stop them. Every service collapsed, water, power, the phones, the police, because no one would hang around to run them. Why would you if your family was in danger, if you had to scrap for your next meal? Staying uninfected and finding food was all that mattered to anyone. We were barbarians again. It was a miracle they did restore order."

Finally someone who would tell me what it had been

like, fill in the gaps of what I knew, the gaps of my own history. "Why didn't things go back to normal, you know, the phones, TV, internet?"

Walsh shrugged. "I guess we were all so grateful that someone was taking charge we just accepted what they told us. Initially safety and food distribution were everyone's priority, so what if we couldn't check our emails? Then they told us the infrastructure had been badly damaged in the riots, that it'd take time for things to get back to normal. Then their rehousing programme began and people who were rehoused didn't have computers or routers or phones in their new places."

"What about those who still had all those things?"

"It didn't mean anything because nothing was ever reconnected, not a priority we were told. At the time no one really cared because we were mostly safe, we had food and water, enough that we wouldn't starve at least. No communication was a small price to pay for all that. There were a few pockets of resistance, when the military crackdown was aimed at everyone, not just the ricters. But for most people if they lost some freedoms, it meant they didn't have to worry about where their food was coming from and that they probably wouldn't be stabbed in their beds. They deserved our respect then. Now?" He looked at me. "Well, hindsight is a wonderful thing. What do you think about them?"

"That they're bullies and cowards." The words were out there for Walsh to use against me.

With a tiny click that I'd have missed if I'd been breathing, the lock gave way to his attentions and he pushed the door open.

"You have a look in there while I work on the next one."

CHAPTER SEVENTY-THREE

I shone the beam of my torch round the lab. A bona fide place where proper science was done. I touched my fingertips to the long white table, bench I reminded myself. I perched on the lab stool behind it. Imagine if I was supposed to be here. Imagine coming to work here, somewhere like this, every day. What was I thinking? I had more chance of getting back to Milton Keynes in the next five minutes to a red carpet welcome from Mum.

I had deliberately not thought about her, about our argument, her disappointment in me, the way she'd virtually cut me out of our family. The painful list went on and on, such a long list could we ever get past it all? Maybe getting back with the Coralone in time would be enough. If I got there too late, how would she be? Would she even let me stay?

They'd make career decision early for me then and it'd have to be something that would give me somewhere to live. The military seemed the obvious. How ironic if I ended up being drafted in place of Jace. Jace. I couldn't think about him now either. Maybe in time he'd stop appearing in my thoughts every five minutes when I was used to living my life without everything being referenced back to him. But right now, just the thought of the huge hole his absence would leave was too much. I busied myself reading the labels on the row of brown bottles on a shelf on the back wall instead.

"Find anything that makes sense?" Walsh appeared in the doorway.

"Not yet."

I reached up to the shelves behind me, causing a landslide of papers to flap down to the floor. Damnit, if they were in order, they'd know someone had been in here. I bent down to pick them up, my torch beam searing the back wall.

"How good are your lock-picking skills exactly?" I asked.

"That depends, why?"

"I think I've found the best place to start."

Walsh squatted down beside me and let out a low whistle at the sight of the safe. From his backpack he pulled out a small box with two wires dangling from it. He attached the electrode at the end of each wire to the safe front and began reading the monitor they were hooked up to. Within what seemed like a ridiculously short space of time, the machine cracked the code and the safe was open.

"This seems like it might be important." He pulled out a document wallet and handed it to me. "What?"

I knew I was staring but didn't know what to say. I could hardly ask him if he was a thief. And really if he was, so what? I'd learnt the hard way sometimes those you thought were looking out for you were the ones to fear.

I scanned the top sheet of the papers in the folder then the next. Production schedules they seemed to be.

"What is it?" Walsh asked.

"Give me a minute."

I looked over the next couple of pages but everything else was in a sealed pouch. I held it out to him. "Any way you can get that open without actually breaking the seal?"

"Not a chance." He snapped it open and pulled out

the documents. "But they're in a safe, in a locked room, in a secure building. Whoever finds them will think someone just forgot to seal them up."

I wasn't sure if I was jealous of his lack of respect for authority or whether I was petrified that he might take me with him in his apparent death wish. I turned my attention to the papers.

It appeared to be the formula for the Coralone preparation. It was a little above my level of comprehension but after telling Walsh I could figure out what was in here, I wasn't going to admit that to him. Unless I had to.

The second page was a mirror of the first. But something stood out. "This can't be right."

"What is it?"

I shook my head. I reread the page again, slower this time, comparing it with the first one. How could this be? A clammy sweat crawled over my skin.

"Maya, you look like you're about to throw up. What is it?"

"This here," I gestured at the first page. "Looks like the original formula for Coralone and this one," I waved the second page at Walsh. "it's almost identical but there's an extra element to it."

"An extra element, like what?"

"Like something that definitely shouldn't be there. It looks as if there's some kind of radioactive isotope in the medicine."

"Radioactive, that can't be good."

"No, well, yes, some of them are, they help out in all sorts of ways in nuclear medicine. At least they did, before everything, I don't know how much of that they can still practice now, it's not the area I study in."

Radioactive. A memory knocked at my consciousness. Strands of Jasmine's hair, then Niall's, coming out in my fingers. Everyone's hair falling out, the paranoid porter had said. "They've been dying from radiation poisoning." I half-whispered as though the truth was so awful it couldn't bear to be spoken out loud.

I pulled the first sheaf of pages from the safe towards me again, trying to ignore how much my hands were shaking, how close I felt to throwing up. The production schedules made sense now. They detailed when the Government had started messing with the Coralone formula.

"It started there, look, three years ago. They introduced that," I pointed at the long name, not bothering to try and pronounce it. "And then," I rifled through the schedules, searching for the next change. "There, about eighteen months ago. And now, this last one, only in the last production run."

And then I realised. "L/d on the toe tags is the last dose of Coralone, that's why they're noting the time between last dose and death. They're collecting data. Like for a science experiment." Why did I not work that out earlier? "That's why there's no heroic measures with these victims, it's pointless trying to save someone who's dying from the inside out."

Walsh looked as appalled as I felt. I stared at the pages on my lap. The truth answered all the questions but I didn't want to believe it.

"You're sure about this?" Walsh asked.

"I'm not a scientist but I don't think there's any doubt. That's why they stopped producing Coralone, because no one who needs it will be left alive—"

"Crap. Jesus." Walsh looked like he might throw up too.

"I've got to get back to Milton Keynes. I've got to stop my mum giving my brother any." I staggered to my feet. Walsh grabbed my arm, steadying me. "Sssh, I hear something."

He led me to the stairwell door and cracked it open. I heard it too, below us somewhere, the unmistakeable sound of someone calling my name.

CHAPTER SEVENTY-FOUR

"That must be Jace." I whispered. "He was with me when we came to your flat. We parted company when I found out he's a GI."

"You told him where you were going?"

"Kind of, when I thought I could trust him."

"We have to hide these papers, we don't know who he's brought with him." Walsh looked back at the unlocked lab.

"We have to get them out of here otherwise no one will ever know what's happened."

"Maya, we can't take on the Government like that." He was shoving the papers back into their wallet.

"You think it's right what they've done? You think they should be able to get away with it?" I lowered my voice. I didn't want Jace to hear me. "Don't you think we should at least try to get them held accountable?"

"Accountable to whom? You're forgetting they hold all the power."

"Yes, they do, but what about the ordinary people? Together we have to count for something, don't we?"

"I like your idealism, kid. Okay, tuck these in your waistband." He handed me the papers. "Let's hope the soldiers he brought with him are gentlemen."

Soldiers? Jace wouldn't have brought soldiers with him. He might be a GI, but he wouldn't betray me like that.

Walsh turned his back while I fussed to tuck the papers around my middle as neatly as I could. I watched the beam of his torchlight as it lit up the row of bottles on the back wall of the lab. They gave me an idea. I studied the names of the chemicals.

"What're you doing?" he asked.

"I'm looking for a pyrophoric chemical."

"A what?"

"A chemical that'll burn on exposure to the air, it might come in handy."

"I've got a couple of flares, they'd do kinda the same. Probably makes sense to share them out." He fished in his backpack. "Hold it like this." He held the tube near the base. "It's a strike action, slide the lid off, like you were striking a match and it'll ignite. It burns hot so make sure you hold it near the bottom."

I pocketed the flare just as I heard my name right behind me.

Jace was standing in the lab doorway.

My sarcastic comment about turning me in died in my throat. He held his torch, beam pointed downwards onto the floor. We stared at each other. He didn't look any different. Godamnit, he looked as he always had, like he'd just come over to keep me company, or to ride to school with me, good looking as hell now I'd thought of him that way. Except there was now a huge chasm between us.

"Would you just let me explain?" he asked as if no time had passed since I'd overheard him.

"I don't think there's anything to say, is there?" my voice trailed away. What I really wanted was for him to pull me towards him, to kiss me, to tell me I'd got it all wrong, that of course he wasn't a GI, how could he be? He'd made it up to get us away from the security guard, a ridiculous tale to bluff our way out.

Why couldn't he have just kept lying to me?

"Maya, I know I've hurt you. I wouldn't do that for anything but—"

"You couldn't tell me, Jace. I get that, otherwise I might not have given you anything to report on. I hope I gave you enough that you earned a good wage. I understand now why you don't like Toby, because he dares to go against the Government. But I bet you didn't know that they blackmail him."

"I hate to interrupt this lovers' spat, but we need to get out of here." Walsh said.

"There's no lovers anything here." I walked out of the lab, turning sideways so I could pass Jace without touching him.

I was almost to the stairwell when he grabbed my arm. "Did you ever wonder why we've had so few raids in our street, our neighbourhood?"

I shrugged. I'd always thought Dixon next door was just ineffectual, but all the while I'd been looking in the wrong direction.

"I know as much about our neighbourhood as you do, Maya, but I haven't reported anything major on a single person. I know all about the papers that Toby gets you, all your secret reading but I haven't told a soul. In all the years we've lived there you must have realised we only had a few token raids. Why do you think that is?"

By the light of the criss-crossed torch beams I saw Walsh relocking the lab leaving everything mostly as we'd found it. I looked at Jace. I didn't want to be mad at him. I wanted things to be as they had been so badly. As much as I wanted to save Sebastian, maybe more. But how could I pretend I didn't know?

"Jace," The longing in my voice was breaking my heart. "God, Jace, I—"

The stairwell door slammed open and the sharp beam of a gun-held light split the torch-warmed darkness, stabbing through my vision. Shouted orders collided with each other, but I didn't need to understand the individual words. I put my hands on my head. Surrendering.

CHAPTER SEVENTY-FIVE

The weapon-mounted light flicked from me to Walsh to Jace, splitting the darkness into pulses that beat against my eyelids when I blinked. It was impossible to see beyond it.

The soldier took our torches from us and his light swung towards the stairwell. "Downstairs, I'm right behind you. I won't hesitate to shoot if any of you do anything I don't like."

I led the way down by touch. The door to the ground floor space opened as I reached for the handle. Another soldier waiting for us. He grabbed me by the arm and pulled me into the room.

"Hey, hands off her." I felt my heart lift a little at Jace's shout.

"We didn't give any guarantees about what would happen to any prisoners." The soldier snapped back, his weapon and torch swinging towards Jace's voice. Jace blinked at the light's intrusion. He was standing with the soldiers, his hands by his side. His hands by his side?

He didn't have his hands on his head. Oh my God, Jace had brought them with him. Just like Walsh said.

"She's off limits, like I told you." Jace's tone sounded like my father's, authoritative, used to being obeyed.

"I need to search her." The soldier sounded whiny in comparison.

"I will." Jace stepped forward to me. I put my hands out to push him away, but he grabbed my wrists gently. "Play along, Maya," he whispered. "This was the only way I could get here, to help you." He leant in against me, felt around the back of my jacket.

He ran the edge of his hands, little finger side against me, down between my breasts, across my stomach, over the papers that I knew he could feel. As his hands swept down my sides, I felt an absurd rush of tears. Earlier that night I'd wanted him to touch me, to caress me, but not like this, like I was a criminal, in front of coldly appraising soldiers.

His hand knocked against the flare in my pocket but he didn't pause, brushing right past it, bending to pat down my sodden jeans.

"She's clean." He spoke up for the benefit of the soldiers. "Hands back on your head." Dropping his voice, he added. "Please, just for a few minutes more, okay. I've got a plan, you won't be arrested, don't worry."

He moved over to Walsh and patted him down. I heard Jace murmuring but his voice was too low for me to make out individual words. "Clean."

"Night vision." The lead soldier snapped out the command. The lights on their weapons vanished, plunging the space into a deep, dark blackness.

"Hey," Jace protested. "What're you doing?"

"This is a military operation, I'm in command."

"That's not what we agreed."

"It doesn't matter what we agreed, we're in the field, I have jurisdiction, plus I have a little persuasion on my side." In the pitch black I heard the clink of what could have been the soldier's wedding ring against the metal of his gun.

"You're not hearing me," Jace still sounded calm. "I'm not just any GI. I have special status. Do you want me to take this up with Simon Bessick? He'll jail you just on my say so. Put your weapons down."

"You're bluffing."

"Why don't you get him on your radio and we can see who's bluffing."

"I can't."

"Your clearance not high enough?" I could hear a grim smile in Jace's voice. "Give me the radio, I take my orders directly from him, he'll speak to me."

From my experience with the military I knew Jace's posturing with the soldier would only end one way. And as mad as I was with him right now, I couldn't bear the thought that something might happen to him. I lowered my right hand slowly, pulling the flare from my jacket, hoping he was still standing in front of me enough to hide what I was doing.

"Stop moving!"

"Stay still!"

I was clearly visible to the soldiers. Doing what I planned was probably our only chance now.

I struck the lid of the flare as Walsh had told me. The pain that shot through my palm nearly made me drop it. The hissing flash of the flare igniting almost blinded me and I knew it was coming. No wonder the soldiers yelled - the burst of red light must have savaged their eyes through their night vision goggles. At least they wouldn't be able to hurt any of us now.

But they still tried. The chink ching of a handful of shell casings bouncing on the concrete floor was almost drowned out by their shouts "Christ, I'm blind,", "She fucking blinded me,".

"Let's go!" Walsh's cry echoed my own.

Jace stood a metre or so in front of me, static.

"Jace, you too." I held out a hand to him.

"Go." He dropped to the floor as though his skeleton had turned to water.

"Jace?" I let the flare go and knelt beside him.

"What's the matter?"

The red light lit up his face, contorted in pain. Above the hiss of the flare, his breathing sounded too shallow and fast.

"They got me." He sounded amazed.

I slipped my hand inside his jacket, startled when I found his chest wet. My fingers came away covered in a warm sticky substance that looked like play blood in the strange light of the flare.

"No, no." I tried to hold the edges of his wound together. He couldn't be shot. He was Jace, solid, dependable, always there.

"You need to go." Jace gasped.

"I'm not leaving you. Walsh can carry you—"

"Maya, the shot's good." He grasped my right arm as if to pull away my hand from his chest.

"Hold on, don't you dare—"my voice cracked, refusing to say the terrible word. "You're with me, Jace. I'm not leaving you here. I'm so sorry I was mad at you. I didn't really, I can't live without you . . ." I pressed harder on his wound, trying to coax it back together, to get the skin to reknit. My fingers were slick with his warm blood. My bandage felt wet and heavy, soaked with it.

"You have to get away. Go now, while you can." He drew in a breath that sounded all wrong. "I love you, Maya, since we were kids, love you so much. All I did, only ever did for you . . ."

"Jace, stay with me, please."

This couldn't be happening.

Walsh pulled at my elbow. "He's right, we're losing our window. We need to go."

I slapped him away.

"Jace, hang on. We'll get help, but you have to fight." He couldn't give up. I willed my life force out of my fingertips into him. "Please, Jace, please, fight it, stay with me." I was shouting at him.

I'd never felt so desperate, never wanted anything so

badly like I wanted to rewind the last couple of minutes, to have Jace stand a few centimetres to the side of the path of the bullet meant for me. "Fight, Jace, you have to fight."

With nothing more than an expiration as ordinary as if he'd breathe in again the next second, Jace's hand lost its strength and his arm slid down to the floor.

He was gone.

CHAPTER SEVENTY-SIX

"No!" I grabbed Jace's arm, putting his hand back on mine but its dead weight slipped off. "No, no, no."

"We need to go now, otherwise he died for nothing." Walsh grabbed hold of me and tried to yank me to my feet. I pushed him away, I couldn't let go of Jace's chest.

There had to be some way to bring him back. I covered his mouth with mine and breathed. One, two, three, four. "I need you to do CPR. Walsh, please, I can't let go of his chest, please," I breathed in, passing my breath to Jace again.

As I sat up to beg him to help me, Walsh slapped me across the face. The sting overlaid the pain from the soldier's beating earlier. What did he do that for?

"Now I've got your attention." He spoke quickly, his words punctuated by the soldiers' moaning. "I'm leaving now, you can stay here and be arrested or shot like your friend, or you can come with me. It's up to you. I don't have a gun to your head but you'll feel worse about it later if he died for nothing. Decide."

Leave him? Walsh wanted me to leave Jace? I bent over and kissed him. He was warm. How could I leave him? What if it was all just a cruel trick and he breathed again as soon as I left the room?

"Maya, would you deny him his last wish for you? He wanted to get you out of here."

Walsh grabbed my elbow again. This time I didn't fight him. The flare sputtered into nothing. A solid darkness dropped over us.

"Get the bitch!"

"Don't let them get away!"

Stacatto shouts replaced the moaning. The chilling clicks of a weapon being readied. Walsh kept hold of me as we ran blindly to where the door had been.

A deafening rattle of gunshot made me jump, even as Walsh and I tried to fit through the door at the same time. The metallic chink of bullet casings bouncing off the concrete sounded almost like music, a symphony of one note.

Down the stairs through a darkness that was just as blinding as the burning light had been. Into the basement, banging against filing cabinets, trying to feel for the gaps between them.

"Slam the door." Walsh barked.

I felt with my foot, kicking aside the wooden wedge and pulled the door tight against the frame.

"We don't have long, they'll be calling for reinforcements. Hurry."

I blundered behind him, arms out like a newly-blind person, cursing each time I stumbled into a box. Then he opened the outside door and the less solid darkness of the night helped me see again. The rain lashed against my jacket as though punishing me for having escaped it for a while. I heard Walsh slam the door behind us.

"Here." He bent down and laced his fingers together to give me a boost over the railings, getting over them as fast on his own. "Let's go."

He ran to the end of the back road and turned right. I fell in behind him. Through a twisting turning maze of streets and back alleys he led me. I had no idea where we were going. I didn't care. Jace was gone. Really lost to me now, not like when I'd run away from him during my hissy fit.

My feet stumbled on the pavement, tripped over each other. Everywhere hurt, an agony that burned more with every step. But I would have welcomed more physical pain if it could replace how much I hurt inside. Inside I was screaming, sobbing, wailing. Inside my heart had been shattered. Inside I'd lost everything.

I pushed myself harder, daring the pain to hurt more, trying to keep my thoughts filled with following Walsh, running one step at a time.

After a while he stopped and I ran straight into the back of him. I staggered beneath the agony that surged through my right side – I must have landed harder than I thought when I fell off the railings. My knees gave way and I dropped onto the pavement. Walsh grabbed my elbow and yanked me up.

"Just around the corner, okay?" He mouthed the words right in front of my face so I could hear him above the screaming wind. I couldn't even nod.

He looked up and down the street. But we hadn't seen anyone since we'd left the factory. The factory. Jace. I breathed in, harder, harder, trying to fill my lungs enough they could stop me thinking. I concentrated on Walsh, describing to myself what I was seeing so I wouldn't have any spare capacity to think.

Walsh fumbling in his pocket. Checking the street again, looking up, down. Guiding me to the end of the road. Turning the corner, looking left and right again. Down the side road. "I'm trusting you a helluva lot."

I nodded. I couldn't say anything.

Wherever we were, it seemed completely deserted. Walsh opened a front door and steered me into a darkness made solid by the boundary of four walls, a floor and a ceiling. He pulled the door closed behind me and dead-locked it. I listened to where he was going in a primitive echo-finding way to keep my mind distracted.

I heard him stop. The sound of another lock being turned, barely registering, even in the deep silence shrouding us. He opened the door, pulling me in behind him, before he closed and locked our escape route. Rasping. A match being struck. The guttery, flickering flame touched the wick on a candle and I could see him.

"Take your shoes off, leave them down here. Noisy, with shoes on." He gestured with the candle at the bare wooden stairs. An even strip of old paint covered the ends of each step. I slipped off my trainers and followed him up. My socks squelched on every stair.

At the top, he paused to unlock yet another door. He really was careful. The same routine, I was scarcely through than Walsh was locking it.

"We'd better stick with the candles, any lights through the skylights'll be too much of a give away. Power's still out everywhere."

I nodded again, afraid if I tried to talk, all that would come out would be the howl of grief I was trying to keep under control.

"Here. You hold it."

Walsh had given me his candle and was unlocking what looked like a full-length cupboard before I was really aware I was holding it. He heaved out a trunk. More unlocking. I'd never met anyone who had so many keys.

He pulled out a battered cardboard box.

I felt a little hiccup deep inside me. "The package we delivered to you."

"Yeah, film. I'm going to photograph the papers you have, to keep the originals safe."

Film, that explained 'don't get it wet', but all the other instructions must have been Lawrence just messing with us. Us. Me and Jace before the night turned everything upside down. I could feel sobs rising up inside me, I tried to swallow them down.

Walsh unlocked yet another door and disappeared

inside.

"What is this place?" I half-whispered.

"A dark room, for developing photos. Kind of redundant at the moment with the power cut, but I can have a brighter light in here without anyone noticing."

I didn't mean just this room but I couldn't ask again. He pulled something off the wall which turned out to be a torch every bit as powerful as the one Jace had liberated from the Army. "You can blow the candle out now."

I did as he asked, swaying violently as though I'd been drinking more of the homebrew Jace and I had shared in the car park. Jace and me again. How was I still standing?

"What's up?" Walsh asked.

"Nothing." I lied. The pain was throbbing worse than ever. Right then I would have welcomed passing out so I wouldn't be able to feel it any more, feel anything any more.

"Christ, you're pale."

"I'm anaemic."

Walsh dragged a stool over to me. "Sit, hold." He thrust the torch into my hands and unzipped my jacket.

"What're you doing?"

"Don't worry, I'm not getting fresh."

I was almost used to his accent, or at least wasn't surprised every time I heard it now but he had a way with words that was different to how I used them. A strangeness that marked him as not English.

He pulled my jacket off my left arm. More carefully slid the sleeve off my right. Taking the torch, he shone it over me. He rummaged amongst the papers on the table and found a pair of scissors.

"What're you doing with those?"

"You're hurt, I need to clip your top a bit, just to see how bad."

"I'm fine."

"Yeah, you said that, I'm still not buying it."

I let the exhaustion I'd been holding back crash over

me while Walsh cut through my jumper and T-shirt. The warm dry space and the snip snip of his scissors lulled me into a doze. I wanted the oblivion sleep promised. There I didn't have to think or remember. Across the distance of a dream I could hear him leaving the dark room. I couldn't drag my eyes open to see why. Nothing could be so important now.

The pain was excruciating. Sleep dropped away from me as if it had broken apart like a smashed mirror. "What the hell—"

"Sorry, I hoped you might sleep through this." Walsh held a brown glass bottle in his hand. "Bit of first aid, you've been shot."

CHAPTER SEVENTY-SEVEN

"Shot?" I parroted the word. I shouldn't be surprised. We'd run the gamut of a soldier blindly firing off his magazine. It'd only be surprising if one of us hadn't been hit. I was okay with it being me.

"You're damned lucky, it's a through and through. I can probably patch you up enough for now."

On the floor at my feet was a first aid kit that made ours at home look ridiculous.

"You a nurse or doctor or something?"

"Something's about right. Here," he handed me a couple of tablets. "Broad spectrum antibiotic and pain killer." When I put them in my mouth he handed me a cup of water.

"You don't have any of the safe Coralone in there, do you?"

"If I did, it'd be yours."

In a perverse way I was glad of the pain, glad that it filled my mind, because all while it dominated everything I couldn't think of anything else.

"I need to take off your tops to dress your wound properly." Walsh was saying. "Do you mind?"

I shook my head and went to pull my jumper over my

head but as soon as I moved my arm it felt as if someone had stabbed me with a red hot poker. "I can't."

"It's okay, I can cut them off, give you a change of clothes. You okay with that?"

I nodded.

Walsh cut my jumper and then my T-shirt open, laying the papers I'd carried around my middle on the table behind him. He slipped my bra strap down and began wiping the wound. "You were really lucky, just missed that too. This is gonna hurt a bit."

I braced myself against the pain of stitches but either I was getting used to hurting or the tablet Walsh had given me was magic. It was bearable as long as I didn't think about it.

After a couple of minutes he surprised me again. "You asked me earlier, about why I didn't leave the UK when the flu hit? Firstly I didn't think it would be as bad as it got."

"I guess no one did."

"You got that right."

"My mum would never say why she never tried to get us out. She could have, her parents were from Puerto Rico."

"The main reason I stayed was my girl friend." Walsh patted at my wound, surprisingly gently. I laid my head back against the wall behind me and closed my eyes.

"She didn't get the flu," he went on. "We were lucky, neither of us did. When it first hit I wanted to take her with me back to the States but she wouldn't leave the UK. An international relationship, a lot more trouble than you think. Someone always has to compromise and usually it was me. It wasn't until a few months after they banned travel, that I wised up and realised how dumb I'd been. Before the flu it was easy to get distracted with things, jobs, travelling, TV, films, the Internet – you know what that was, right?"

I would have nodded but the effort was too great.

"My mum did talk to me, you know."

"Sorry, it seems such a lifetime ago. My girlfriend didn't fall apart when the pandemic first hit although a lot of people did. It was when she realised nothing was ever going to get back to normal that she lost it completely."

"Did you split up then?" I could hear the sound of dressing tape being ripped from a roll.

"Not for a while, I had to make sure she took her meds, take her to hospital appointments. Despite how things were between us I'd have done anything to help her get a grip again. But nothing was working. In the end the doctors told me we should call it a day, I was a constant reminder of how our lives should have turned out and she couldn't get better with that around her all the time. It took a long time for me to do what they wanted, some kind of twisted survivor's guilt I guess. So I kind of know how you're feeling right now."

"I'm trying not to feel anything."

"I get that. But don't shut it out too long, it won't do you any good."

I snorted. Like I cared about me. "Do you regret not going home?"

Walsh considered my question. "I don't think regret's the right word but if I could go now, I probably would."

"Is it the same there? Did the flu cripple them too?"

"I guess it must have but how can we know? We only have what we're told by the Government, and we've just seen how much they can be trusted. When the Internet and phone lines went down there was no way left to communicate. I don't even know if my parents and my brother are still alive."

I opened my eyes and looked at Walsh but he was busy smoothing something over both sides of my shoulder. How awful for him. Stuck in a kind of limbo in a place he didn't want to be.

"I saw a plane the day before yesterday." It sounded such an outlandish thing to say, I had to justify it. "At least

I'm pretty sure it was a plane, really high it was. It couldn't have been anything else. Maybe the US escaped the worst. Maybe that's where it was going, or where it was from?"

"You notice any colours on it?" he asked.

"It was too high, I couldn't even hear it. The sun glinted off it, made it look like a silver bullet, that's how I noticed it." I could practically see Walsh filing away that information.

"Above Milton Keynes?"

"No, I was up north, somewhere." I gave him the briefest summary of why.

"I've done my best but I'm not professionally trained, you should still get it looked at."

"Matching pair." I went to flap my bandaged hand at him but just that tiny movement set off flames of pain which had a really long reach. Everything hurt everywhere.

"I'll change that." He unbandaged my hand. I kept my eyes shut tightly while he washed Jace's blood off me.

Jace, Jace, Jace. He'd been reduced to a red swirl in a bowl of water. The last piece of him gone from me. I couldn't hold the tears back anymore.

"It's okay." Walsh held me while I sobbed myself quiet.

"I loved him." My throat was raw. "But I never told him." I wiped at my face with my left hand.

"I'm betting he knew."

I really hoped so.

With my hand rebandaged, Walsh slipped a sling over my head and gently lifted my right arm into it. He left the room and I heard him moving the trunk around.

"Here you go, best I could do." He helped my left arm into the sleeve of a black cardigan, wrapped the right side over my sling and buttoned it up. "You wouldn't win any fashion awards, but at least it'll keep you warm."

"Thanks, Walsh, for everything."

"Welcome." He packed away the first aid kit. "Back in a minute."

When he reappeared he carried two mugs, one of which he held out to me. "Coffee, thought you could use the caffeine."

"Real coffee?"

"Uh-huh. Saved for emergencies."

I sipped the sweetened black liquid, burning my top lip. "What is this place? Is it yours?"

He perched on the edge of the table. "Bolt hole, I guess."

"From what?"

"You need me to tell you?"

I shook my head. "I don't even know your first name," I realised.

"Walsh is okay, once I got out of High School never used my first name much. Talking of names, what was your dad called, when you knew him?"

"Back when he was a decent human being? Jeremy Flint."

I sipped the coffee again, welcoming its sharp taste, the clarity that was breaking through the wreckage in my mind. "Do you know how I could contact him?"

"Why would I?"

"You're a GI, but you're playing both sides, aren't you?"

Walsh sipped his coffee, watching me while he swallowed. "Wasn't aware there were two."

"Not exactly." I kind of got him, but I didn't know quite how to put it into words. "You're investigating the Coralone factory, you have this place."

"Could just be I'm nosey. Before the pandemic I was a journalist, old habits are hard to break."

I shook my head. "You said it yourself you had to turn me over to the authorities in case they had you under suspicion, unless you've been doing something they wouldn't like, you'd have no reason to do that." I looked at him over the rim of my mug. He didn't deny anything. "So do you know where my father lives?" I asked again.

"I have a good idea where he'll be."

"Can you take me to him?"

"I'm sure that you taking this to him is the worst choice you could make."

"Why? I have an 'in' with the guy at the top. I'd be stupid not to use it. But I'm being selfish too. My father must be able to get a message via the military anywhere he wants. He can tell my mum not to give Sebastian any Coralone."

"Do you think he will?" Walsh asked softly.

I took a deep breath. He had to. "I don't know. But I have one thing to bargain with that he'll want very much so he just might."

CHAPTER SEVENTY-EIGHT

Once more out in the filthy night, I followed Walsh. If I never saw another storm, felt another raindrop on my head, it would be too soon. The caffeine buzz was amazing, despite it being after 4am, I'd never felt so awake. Even my mind was co-operating with me, thinking only about what I would say to my father, about putting one step in front of the other, about the ache that radiated out from my wound like a spider's web, along nerve endings, down my arm, into my chest, up my neck, into the opposite side of my body. For the first time I could feel the networks that linked everything inside me together.

I tried to hold in my mind the image of going home to see Sebastian. My mum smiling at me I walked through the door. But then my jazzed-up brain filled in one image too many and the illusion dissolved.

Esther.

How was I going to tell her?God, she'd be heartbroken. The only member of her family to have survived the flu and I'd got him killed. That bullet had been meant for me, not him. It would have been way fairer karma for everything I'd done wrong over the last two weeks if it had hit me. It should have hit me. Oh Jace.

Walsh stopped. "Their offices are two streets away."

I could see a lightening in the darkness at the bottom of the road as though the sun was rising round the corner. "How do you know they'll even be there? It's the middle of the night."

"Trust me, they'll be there. The Barrier's at risk. Their offices are all geared up to withstand pretty much anything. And they're all cowards at heart."

"Barrier?" The nurse at the hospital had mentioned it too.

"The Thames Barrier, a flood defence to protect London from a storm surge but I don't know how successful it's gonna be under this onslaught." He looked up and the rain splattered the little bit of his face that showed between his jacket collar and hood.

"And if it isn't?"

"Let's just hope it doesn't get to that."

I hesitated. I made myself say the words. "You ought to stay out of things, maintain your cover or whatever you want to call it."

"But it'll be hard for you."

"Hard was what happened in the factory." My voice cracked but I rushed on. "This won't even figure on that scale."

"You're sure about this?" Walsh asked.

"Absolutely." I managed to sound convincing. "You need to stay out of their way, because if I 'disappear' someone has to tell the truth. Just tell me how to get in."

He nodded. "Okay, at the end of the street, take a left, there's another turning about half way down, it'll have a patrol guarding it, two soldiers usually this end, two at the other. The entrance door's guarded too."

I shivered, although it was nothing to do with the storm. The two run-ins I'd had with the military weren't anything I wanted to repeat ever. And now I was going to walk up to them and effectively hand myself over. "And getting past them?"

"I don't really know, I've never heard of anyone wanting to break into a Government building before. But they're probably not likely to just shoot you in front of their offices. That'd take too much explaining."

"That's not very reassuring." I looked at where I was supposed to go. Apart from the light it wasn't a street corner different to any other, but I could feel the threat it represented from where I was standing.

"Look, let me take you in, I can say you've got information you won't give me."

"And what if they do know you've been snooping around at the Coralone factory? They're really not stupid."

"Maybe not but I don't see how else you're gonna get past them."

"Let me try and bluff my way in first." I said with way more confidence than I felt. "If it doesn't work, then you'll have to come too."

Before I could change my mind, I marched to the end of the road. I turned left and was almost blinded by the sudden wall of light that hit me. Power cuts clearly didn't extend to Government - it was like daylight. My feet drifted to a stop while I struggled to see. Damn my shoulder, my chest, my neck, my arm, my everything, it all hurt like hell. I couldn't even think straight.

Variations of what I could say tangled up my mind until I couldn't remember how to pronounce a single word. The soldiers both turned to face me as I crossed the few feet between them and me. All I could see were their guns. Big and black and deadly. I swallowed, but my mouth seemed to have forgotten how to produce saliva.

"Hands in the air." One of them yelled.

"I can't," I shouted back, holding my left arm up. "I'm injured."

"Stay where you are, get your hands in the air, both of them."

"I can't, my arm's in a sling, you can search me and see."

"Don't make me ask again," the soldier yelled. He levelled his gun at me.

Oh God, don't shoot me.

Icy water gushed over my trainers, soaking my feet. The tug of a current pulled at me. Where had the water come from? A wall of sandbags to my right had become a slick waterfall of shiny black liquid.

"Fuck!" the soldier yelled, "the Barrier's gone!"

CHAPTER SEVENTY-NINE

The world went mad. Everything happened at once. The soldiers forgot me, shouted at each other as they ran up the road. The floodlights went out.Water rampaged past the sandbag defences, coiling around my ankles now.Bitingly cold, it pulled and tugged at me, trying to drag me down the street with it.

"Move, Maya! That wall won't hold for long." Walsh grabbed my left arm and propelled me up the side turning. Water rushed and gurgled and boiled around our feet, ankle high, knee high, its force irresistible.

The pavement ran uphill just enough to keep the churning blackness shallow so we could get through it. My feet were numb, my legs felt as though they were balancing on nothing. My shoulder was killing me, each step reverberated through every stitch.

Walsh pulled me up the steps of a double-fronted building. Lights blazed from most of the windows. It was like something from a Christmas display in a book. A soldier barred the open doorway. "You can't come in here."

"That's where you're wrong." Walsh said.

"I have my orders, you can't come in."

"You're making a mistake, soldier." Walsh practically growled.

"Get away from the door or I will shoot." The kid pulled his gun around so it pointed directly at Walsh.

Walsh seemed unfazed. "Get me your commanding officer."

"Get away from the door. Last warning."

I caught the slight waver in his voice – he was unused either to issuing commands, or people not obeying them. From his baby-faced look he probably hadn't been giving them long. Walsh pushed himself so far into the soldier's personal space, I was surprised he didn't impale himself on the gun. "I'm a Government Informant. Let us in."

I checked behind us. The water had swallowed the first couple of steps already. If they argued much longer, Walsh and I would be swept away and the soldier's problem would be solved without him having to fire a shot. I hoped he hadn't realised that.

But worse than that, the longer we were held out here, the more chance Mum would have to give Sebastian poisoned Coralone. I found myself pushing Walsh's back. I needed to get in to see my father now.

"I don't have time for this crap." Walsh pulled something out of his pocket and I heard a metallic click. "We're coming in."

The soldier folded inwards and we nearly fell into the warmth and sanctuary of the building. Others appeared from nowhere bizarrely not interested in us, wanting only to barricade the entrance with sandbags.

"What's going on? Who let the civilians in?" An older man in a badly crumpled suit appeared at a door on the other side of the large room in which we were standing.

"We're not civilians. GI 259642." Walsh walked over to the man and flashed his ID. All the times I'd seen Jace's ID and I'd never noticed anything different to mine on it. I guessed his GI number couldn't be readily identifiable – GIs only had their worth through their anonymity.

"Her?" The man flopped a hand at me almost as if he couldn't be bothered.

"She has information."

"You're not usually quite so brazen about your identity, I trust."

Walsh sighed like he wanted to punch the man. "Obviously not. But if we'd stayed out there much longer, we wouldn't be here period."

The man gestured at the young soldier. "Take them up to the library, until we can verify their identities."

"No one wants to hear the information we have?"

"I'd have thought it obvious that we have more pressing matters. You just slipped right down the list."

CHAPTER EIGHTY

A staircase hugged the back wall of the room, the complicated scrollwork of the banisters was unlike anything I'd ever seen before. Each stair was so wide and low I would have preferred to take them two at a time, but our escort seemed happy to plod up each individual step.

Lights blazed from wall lights and ceiling lights up the staircase and along the corridor. Didn't these people listen to their own info-casts?

On the first floor he unlocked a door at the back of the building, flicked on a light switch and gestured us inside another grand room, filled floor to high ceiling with dark wooden shelves. But they needed to rename it. The shelves were mostly empty as if the residents had packed to move out. The musty smell of old books lingered, but only a few volumes leaned against each other in the corners as though looking for moral support.

"You, sit." The soldier gestured to me and then to a huddle of chairs with his gun. "You," he pointed to Walsh. "Up against the door."

"Sure. No hard feelings?" He held out a hand. The soldier studied it as though he didn't know what to do with it.

"The gun isn't loaded. Where would I get bullets? Don't get excited. Just getting it out for you." Walsh put his hand in his jacket and with careful, exaggerated movements, drew the weapon out, held it up by its handle with his thumb and forefinger and put it on the empty shelf next to him.

"You have any more?"

"Comedian."

"Backpack off, slowly."

Walsh shrugged it off and held it out. I felt myself tense as though subliminally he'd passed me a message that he planned to take out the soldier and his gun with a well-placed swipe of his backpack. The soldier took it, Walsh let him and the moment passed.

Walsh spread his legs, put his hands on the shelf edge in front of him and waited for the soldier to search him. The soldier seemed satisfied that he hadn't been lying.

"Can I sit now?" Walsh asked.

The soldier nodded slowly, as if he wasn't sure it wouldn't turn out to be a trick. I wasn't either.

Where I perched on the edge of the seat, Walsh sat right back in his, stretched his feet out, crossed his ankles and put his hands behind his head. After a while he began whistling softly.

"Stop it." The soldier moved his gun. He looked uncomfortable, shifted his weight from one foot to the other.

"So the Barrier's gone then. Wonder why you didn't get radioed to tell you?" Walsh asked. "Must have gone some time ago for the water to be here now."

The soldier glared at him and then looked at a spot above his head. Walsh began whistling again. "What if there wasn't anyone left to call it in?" he spoke as though he were thinking aloud. He sat up straight in his chair. "No, some of them would have survived. I guess they've just got their hands full, that's why they didn't radio."

He let his observations trickle into the soldier's mind.

I could almost see the soldier's brain connecting the dots. He glanced at the door then turned back keeping his gun trained on Walsh.

"You wanna go check things out, you can leave us in here. The door locks, we can't go anywhere. It'd be a perfect time to get a little shut-eye."

Walsh reassumed his position as the most relaxed prisoner in the world, and closed his eyes. I took his lead and tried to curl up but any way I moved hurt. I settled in the end for scrunching down in the chair, supporting my slinged arm on my chest.

The room was warm and stuffy. I wanted to take off my jacket but the thought of the pain any movement would trigger was enough to make me happy to swelter. I concentrated on trying not to let the pain hiccup my breathing, trying to keep it slow and regular as though I was falling asleep. Silence stretched out around me.

And then I heard the door open, close very quietly and the lock slid home. I counted five slow breaths in and out before I opened my eyes.

"Thought you'd actually gone to sleep." Walsh was taking off his belt.

"Not until I've had more painkillers. What're you doing?"

"Getting us out of here and into Bessick's office." From the underside he pulled out two long thin metal strips. "Lucky for me they never think to check here."

"You still think he'll see us, with the Barrier gone and everything?"

"Now's probably the best time." Walsh began working his metal strips in the door lock. "Better than I hoped, soldier boy's taken the key with him."

It was only a few minutes before he had us out of the library, the door relocked and we were walking down the carpeted corridor. "My accent kind of gives me away here, you wanna ask where his office is?"

"You don't know?"

"I'm never allowed to meet him here. He likes to keep his dirty laundry out of sight."

A harrassed looking man in a suit came out of the door just in front of us, almost barging right into me. "Sorry."

"No harm done. Simon Bessick's office? I always get lost here, can you remind me?" I stayed in his personal space, holding his eye contact hoping he wouldn't notice anything about me that could give me away as not supposed to be there. Anything like my sopping jeans, only one filled sleeve of my jacket. At least it was an army jacket.

"Top floor, office at the front end." He stepped around me, rushing off before he finished his sentence.

"Nicely done." Walsh gripped me by the elbow, turning me around back towards the library. "Stairs are this way. I'm bringing you in if we're stopped."

I wasn't sure if I was expecting soldiers to be barring the way to the top floor or if I just wanted them to be, so I'd have a reason not to confront my father. As it was the stairs were deserted, the crisis management all happening on the lower levels.

"I've got this. You can stay here. You can get my back." I added when he appeared to be wavering. "That kid won't stay out of the library forever."

"Okay, but if you need me, yell."

"Absolutely."

Walsh gave me a half-smile. "You're doing great, Maya."

I tried to smile back but I seemed to have forgotten how.

I opened the stairwell door and walked towards the front of the building. The carpet was so thick it was like walking on cushions and it almost threatened to tip me over. At least he wouldn't hear me coming. The lights seemed to blaze even brighter up here in defiance of the elements that had robbed the rest of the city of its power.

The door to what had to be his office was open. I lengthened my stride so I couldn't change my mind and walked through it.

CHAPTER EIGHTY-ONE

My father was sitting behind a big shiny desk facing the door, staring into space. He jumped slightly as I interrupted his field of vision. His expression changed when he recognised me, but not in a good way. "What happened to you?"

"This?" I pointed at the bruise on my face. "One of your soldiers questioned me, but you saw that. Oh, you mean this?" I flapped the empty sleeve of my jacket. "One of your soldiers shot me."

"They're not my soldiers."

"Whose are they then? You're the Government, aren't you? You're the ones who give them their orders."

"I'm not the Government, I'm a cog in a machine."

"I'm not eight-years-old anymore, don't treat me like I'm a kid. You might be one person in the Governmental machine, but you're not a cog. You're right at the top, aren't you." It wasn't really a question.

He adjusted a pen. A sudden flash of memory superimposed itself over him and his desk. I could see the prison warden straightening out invisible kinks in the things on hers. Another office where I didn't want to be, in front of another someone I'd rather not see, another hostile holding everything I wanted.

A loud ringing sound split the tense silence. I jumped. He snatched up the receiver of the phone. "Bessick."

The Government had phones! This was better than I'd hoped – he could get a message to Mum almost instantly.

He dropped his voice and turned slightly away from me. He was still as handsome as I remembered. I hadn't really appreciated that when I'd seen him earlier, the shock of seeing him had masked everything else. The greying of his hair didn't detract from him at all, neither did the lines around his eyes, one drawn down on either side from the corners of his nose to the ends of his lips, outlining the contours of his face. He was dressed in a nice suit, I hadn't noticed that before either, his shirt crisp and white, his tie perfectly knotted. He looked as though he was about to go out for dinner.

Despite what I'd said, I was surprised that a part of me did still feel like I was a kid. Still made me want to walk across the room and hug him, have him hug me back, tell me it had all been a big mistake and that he wanted to come home with me to reunite our family.

"Yes, darling, I love you too." His glance at me as he mouthed the words left me in no doubt as to who was on the other end. "Put me back onto Mummy."

I pushed aside the image of him as an extension of the man I'd known. He wasn't that, he didn't deserve that. I let the rage at him replace the nostalgia and the wishful thinking that had plagued me once I'd found out the truth about him leaving us. I stoked it with the memories of how long I'd stared out of the windows in those early months in Milton Keynes, watching the road for hours in case he came walking down it and wasn't sure which house was ours.

When I ran out of hurtful memories, I conjured up a picture of Sebastian, of Jasmine, of Donna, of Niall, of Jace.

He finished speaking and put the phone back where it had started. "Sorry about that."

"About the interruption or the fact that you wanted a new daughter?"

At least he had the grace to look pained. "It wasn't like that."

"Tell me how it was then."

I didn't know if I was strong enough to hear the truths he might share but I wanted him rocked, off balance. I wanted to intrude into his sheltered, well-structured privileged life and shake him enough that he would be reasonable and do the right thing.

He stared at his desk top, straightening things that didn't need straightening. I wanted to throw it all over the carpet.

"You know abandoning those you 'love' isn't a normal way to show affection." I couldn't bear the silence. "Is your new family prepared for when you do it to them?"

My words cut him, I could see the pain twist over his face. He locked it away quickly. "It was a time you didn't know, Maya, a terrible time. I'd spent eight years protecting you and your brother and longer protecting your mother yet there was nothing I could do against that terrible disease. I was completely powerless."

"So you took the coward's way out."

He shrugged slightly, the tiniest movement. "It might look like that to you but it was the hardest thing I've ever done, walking away from you all. But I couldn't bear to be there to watch—"

"Watch what?"

He took a slow breath before continuing. "Your mother and I didn't know from one day to the next if we'd still be healthy enough to care for you and Sebastian, we had no idea how we'd cope if one of us got the flu. What would we do if we both got it? What would you do if we both died? It was a truly terrifying time. I did everything I could to protect you but you still caught it."

I'd had the flu? I didn't remember and Mum had never told me. Why would she keep that a secret? What was the big deal, most of the population had had it and I'd been lucky, I'd survived.

"I got Sebastian vaccinated because I couldn't watch him fall as sick as you were. I didn't think you'd live and I couldn't lose two children. I did it without telling your mother, she was dead against it, she'd heard rumours that the vaccine wasn't safe. But I . . . there was nothing else I could do. She was nursing you 24/7, she was exhausted, she had no idea what day of the week it was, let alone what I was doing. I had your brother vaccinated against her wishes and you must be able to guess the rest."

I gripped the back of the chair in front of his desk. I desperately wanted to sit down but I wouldn't, not while I could still stand. "Tell me anyway."

"It was the faulty vaccine batch, the one rushed out when the flu mutated. Those it didn't kill it crippled with auto-immune diseases. I curtailed Sebastian's life and I couldn't bear to see what I'd done to him. I knew it was better for me to get out."

"So you walked away from him when he needed you most, when Mum needed you most. You're right it does look like you chose the coward's way out."

"I did what I did. I can't change it."

"But you could have made it up to us, you could have brought us down here with you, we could have been a family again. But you traded up for a newer more perfect version. How do you sleep at night?" He held my gaze as though he had nothing to feel ashamed of, which just made me feel madder than ever. "How do you live, knowing you're killing your son now?"

"What're you talking about?"

I took a breath and concentrated on lowering my voice. "The Coralone. I know all about how you've messed with its formula. How you included a radioactive isotope in the last batch and that's why all the people who take it

328

are dying and not being resuscitated because hospital staff know they've been poisoned. And that's why there's no more production because why would you need a medicine when you've killed off all the weaklings who were taking it and being a drain on resources, ruining the Government numbers because they needed care."

His face changed. I could see the transformation from the man who had once been my father to the political animal that wielded more power than any one person should be allowed. It was like he'd taken off a mask. "I don't know what you're talking about."

"Really? Maybe these will jog your memory" I pulled the photos from my jacket pocket that Walsh had taken of the papers we'd stolen and laid them out on his desk. "Do you want me to translate them into layman's terms or are you a bit of a closet scientist?"

He looked genuinely shocked. "Where did you get these? How did—"

"That's not really important. What does matter is what you're going to do now."

"And what would you have me do, Maya?"

"Pick up that phone and get a message to Mum telling her not to give Sebastian any Coralone."

"There's no phone network outside London."

"Then use army radios, send a soldier in a jeep, have someone stand on the roof and do semaphore, I don't care how, just do it." I really didn't want to think about all the families with spare contaminated bottles now their loved ones had been poisoned. And not knowing any better, what was to stop them wanting to help Sebastian?

The look on my father's face told me he wasn't going to help, the stubborn set of his jaw was something I'd seen in the mirror often enough.

"Godamnit, Sebastian is your son, whatever else you tell yourself. You owe it to him to do everything you can to save him."

"Sir, sorry, Sir." A voice from behind me.

I whipped around. Two soldiers stood in the doorway. "This prisoner escaped," one said, "we'll escort her back downstairs."

CHAPTER EIGHTY-TWO

"You'll be making a huge mistake letting them take me." I spoke low enough so only my father could hear me.

"Right now, I can only see advantages." he muttered. "You're forgetting that the art of negotiation is all about strength and you can't give me anything I want badly enough to even bring me to the table."

"That's where you're so totally wrong. I have one thing that no one else does, one thing that you can't get any other way than from me giving it to you. It's probably one of the things you most want in the world but you don't realise it. At least not yet, but when you do, it'll be too late."

The soldiers crowded me, one taking my left arm, the other trying to get hold of my right, seizing the empty sleeve.

He had to give in. He had to. I tried to hold eye contact with him but the soldiers pulled me round, frogmarched me to the door.

"Stand down." My father spoke when we reached the hall. "This woman is here at my request."

I ducked back into his office. "And the informant I tricked to get in here, if they've found him, they should let him go too."

"Was there a man with her?" My father called after the soldiers.

"Yes, Sir."

"You can let him go."

"Yes, Sir."

And as simply as that Walsh and I were no longer under suspicion and in need of locking up.

"So, Maya, you got what you wanted. Now what's this thing that only you can give me that I need?"

"That wasn't what I wanted. You have to get a message to Mum first to not give Sebastian any Coralone."

"I'm not going to grant any more wishes until I know what you're threatening me with."

I wanted to shake him. How could he be so cruel to his own sick child? How could he not have broken his precious rules to warn us not to give Sebastian any of the poisoned medicine? "Saving your son isn't a wish, it should be your priority. I realise it probably doesn't matter much to you whether he lives or dies but to me and Mum and to him it matters a hell of a lot. And what will it cost you? The few minutes of a phone call or a radio message, a few minutes of a soldier's time to drive to our house to tell Mum."

"I don't have carte blanche to do exactly what I want, despite what you may think. There are people even I'm accountable to."

"And what would they think about you killing off the citizens? "

He looked down at his desk and his voice dropped. "You have no idea what it's like trying to keep everything in balance."

"Nothing can excuse what you've done."

"What about appeasing those we borrowed money from when the financial crisis first hit, what about keeping them happy so they don't enslave the population or would you rather I let them?" His tone picked up a 'you'll do as I say and not as I do' edge that stoked my temper.

"We're pretty much slaves now." I snapped. "We can't do anything we want, we can't go anywhere, we can't choose our own lives."

"But you're safe—"

"Who from? Not your soldiers. They killed my best friend." My voice cracked. Those words were so painful I couldn't finish what I wanted to say.

"The military don't fire unless there's extreme provocation."

My mind played back the horrific moment on the motorway when the soldier gunned down the woman he'd just used. "You don't know your military very well, do you? Or is that just a ploy so you can retain, what's it called, plausible deniability?"

When he didn't fill the silence, I rushed on. "You're doing it all wrong, you know, how you rule us. You think you have absolute control because you tie us down so much, but the tighter you squeeze, the more of our individual freedoms you take away, the more you ought to watch your backs because a day of reckoning will come."

"Most of the population need telling when to blow their noses – how can they be expected to look after themselves?" Did he really believe that? That he was doing us a favour?

"We should have the chance to try, even if we mess up, we should be allowed to do it for ourselves. How else will our lives have meaning?"

He pinched the bridge of his nose with two fingers then released it. "It's been a long night, Maya. Get to the point."

"I want you to begin production of Coralone again, untainted Coralone."

"There's no point, there's no one left to take it."

My heart beat doubly hard. Of course there were people left alive. Sebastian, for a start. I gripped the back of the chair tighter. "How can you know that? You don't

333

know that."

"No, I don't, not for sure, until the data comes in. What I do know is that everyone who took Coralone will have taken doses from the last batch already so for them it's too late. It's a fluke that Sebastian hadn't taken any but he's probably the only one. I can't authorise reproduction of the drug for one person."

Not even for his son? In my childhood memories of him he'd been a loving father, what had happened to turn him against us? "But Sebastian needs the Coralone to stay alive."

"Not as much as you might think. The propaganda machine works very well."

"What do you mean?"

"If doctors tell people they need to take a medicine, they take it. If they're told it's keeping them alive, they'll do anything to make sure they keep on taking it. That mentality is very useful."

I felt my mouth drop open. I stared at my father not knowing what to say, what to think. "You lied?" I managed. "But why would you want to hold them in a position of fear like that?"

He shrugged. "It works."

"You're saying all this time Sebastian didn't need to take the Coralone?"

"Some of them did, he could be one of those, but he might be luckier."

He pushed himself to his feet and strolled over to a highly polished cabinet behind him. Pouring a golden liquid into a glass, he downed it. He inclined an empty glass to me. I shook my head.

"I'll go public with this." I waved my hand at the photos spread over his desk.

"Who are you going to tell?" He looked amused, not worried at all.

I ran through the different scenarios in my head while he refilled his glass and sat back down behind his desk. I'd need someone in authority to explain the data, someone the public couldn't doubt. "I'll take it to the Science Academy."

Now his smile made me want to wipe it away with my own hands.

"And do what exactly?" he asked. "Do you know what the Science Academy is?"

I nodded. "Everyone does."

"Everyone knows the public version, the version that keeps people happy and feeling safe. In reality it's a puppet industry designed to do research and development into what sells abroad for the highest prices. It's the only way to get this economy kick-started so that we can get off our godamned knees."

What was he talking about? Maybe I'd banged my head when I fell off the railings, scrambled my brain. How could Science Academy be a puppet industry? It was going to be our country's saviour. Which is exactly what he'd said, only not in the way we thought. Nothing to benefit us, to improve our lives. Only things to sell to the highest bidder.

And I knew what they would pay the most for. The hints had been there in the paperwork but I'd tried not to see it. I wanted to drop into the chair I was hanging on to.

"This was never about putting these people out of their misery, never about saving resources." My voice shook. "It's about testing some sort of bio weapon, isn't it?"

Even as I said it, I hoped he'd look appalled and jump up and shout at me for thinking so badly about the Government. But he only sipped his drink and said, "You're very astute, Maya. I could find you a position working for me. I could use a brain like yours."

How could he play so heartlessly with people's lives? I wanted to scream at him, to hurt him back, but I knew that wouldn't get me anywhere. I straightened my spine. I had to play his game, be as emotionless as him. There had to be something I could do, some advantage this information could give me.

"I'll keep quiet about the Coralone but I have a couple of conditions."

He looked even more amused. "And they are?"

I clenched my fist against my side. "I want to go to Science Academy but I want to be moved with Mum and Sebastian, so I can help with his care." I kept my face nonchalant, tried to blank out my eyes so they wouldn't betray my thoughts. If I couldn't stop the Government killing off the population blatantly, maybe I could do something from the inside. "And Mrs Esther Anderson, if she wants, she should come too, as an extension to our family. It's her grandson your soldiers killed."

"Jason Anderson was killed?"

I nodded warily. "How do you know his name?"

"I put him there, next door to you, not long after you moved in, to watch you. It was his report that told me you were in prison."

I scrabbled to hold onto my anger. I didn't want him to tell me he'd been looking out for me. I didn't want to know if he'd done nice things for me. I wanted to stay mad at him. Because any other feeling would make it too hard to be abandoned by him all over again.

He sipped his drink. "That's a long shopping list."

"I want Jace taken back to Milton Keynes for a proper burial. And I want Jennifer Randle released from prison immediately and her record expunged."

"Who's she?"

"My teacher."

He shook his head. "You're asking too much."

"That's my price." I tried to keep my voice deadpan.

"It's too high."

Godamnit, why did he have to make me call his bluff? "If you're willing to gamble everything else for the sake of these small things, that's your choice."

I pressed my lips together, certain that the next one to

speak would be the loser. The silence spun out between us. The effort of fighting the pain in my shoulder, of fighting him was becoming too much.

Finally he spoke. "Tell me why I would agree to all this."

I pulled in a breath. This wasn't so hard, it wasn't as if I was throwing away something I'd ever really had, something that I treasured. It was just hard to say the words out loud. Probably because I was in pain, because I was exhausted, because I was grieving, because I wanted to go home to see my brother. Or because they were words I'd never dreamt I would ever say.

"Because if you do I will never tell anyone else that I'm your daughter."

He retaliated with words that hurt more. "No one would believe that anyway."

"I know people who could get a DNA test done. And while you may be faceless to the population, I think your new family would care very much. Your wife probably won't be impressed that you're a bigamist." I paused to let the words sink in. It had to work, it was the only thing I could offer him that he couldn't take.

He stared at the bottom of his glass, tipping it this way and that, watching the liquid lap one side, then the other. He had to agree. He had to.

"Okay, you can have your wish." he said slowly as though he was looking for a way to get what he wanted without giving me any concessions.

My brief flash of jubilation faded as I realised he would give me what I wanted to protect his new family from the ugly truth of his past. Even now I wished he'd loved me that much. I swallowed hard. I could have the tiny satisfaction of not letting him see how much this was hurting me. "All of it?"

He nodded. "But I have a condition of my own. You can't use this against me again, this is your one time. I don't want to have to fight you, Maya, but I will if you don't keep your end of our deal and you've had a glimpse of the kind of power I can wield. I'll get a message to your mother, arrange transport back to Milton Keynes, look after your friend's . . . arrangements and get your teacher freed."

"And she'll need transporting safely back to MK." I interrupted. "You can't have her released into the no-go zone."

"I'll get her taken back. You get what you've asked for today but that's it. And I'd appreciate it if you would keep us meeting a secret from your mother and your brother."

"If he's still alive." The words slipped out but I didn't make any effort to stop them.

He ploughed on like he hadn't heard. "Is that understood? I'm placing a great deal of trust in you."

"I'm honourable." The accusation that he wasn't filled the silence between us but he didn't try and defend himself.

"Then you'll have no problems promising me that this is it."

"I won't ask anything more of you and I'll keep the secret about your real family to myself."

I was glad he didn't ask for any other clarification because I couldn't have promised him anything else. I had no intention of letting him get away with genocide, I just couldn't tell him that yet.

CHAPTER EIGHTY-THREE

The army transport pulled up outside my house and the driver killed the engine. My ears rang with the sudden silence. A few faces peered out of their front windows, the kids stopped their games up and down the street. All watched the army truck with wary expressions and controlled actions. How sad that so young they'd already learnt to be careful, to fear other humans.

My house looked the same, as it should do – I'd only been away for four days, even if it felt like forever. The lounge curtains were open. I felt my heart do a double-take. Was that because Sebastian was having a good day or because . . .

I couldn't finish the thought. My father had told me the message had got through to Mum about the Coralone but he hadn't said whether it had been in time. His apparent disregard for his son was something else I found it difficult not to hate him for.

"Where should . . .?" The soldier who'd driven me home nodded towards Jace's coffin in the rear.

"Can you wait for a while. I need to tell his grandmother, she doesn't know."

"Okay, I'll be here." The soldier leant his head back

and closed his eyes, reminding me of Walsh talking about the Marines, 'don't rest if you can sleep.'

I'd stopped wondering how long it would be until I didn't think of everything in terms of what had happened during the last two weeks. I felt so changed by everything, it would probably always define me.

I paused outside our front door, feeling like an unwelcome stranger. How would Mum be with me now? Despite myself, I looked at next door, at Jace's house. It looked so normal I could almost have expected him to come slamming out at any minute.

It wasn't really selfish to not tell Esther the terrible news first, was it? Wasn't it kinder to leave her believing everything was all right, enjoying that peace, just for a while longer?

I knocked at our front door. As hard as it felt to be just a few seconds from knowing the truth about Sebastian, it was harder to be standing where Esther might suddenly look out to see what the army truck had brought.

Mum opened the door. "Maya!"

"Is he okay? Is he still alive?"

"He seems to be fine." The smile on her face looked to be genuine. The rush of relief that cascaded through me was every bit as powerful as the water that had rampaged through London when the Barrier went. Somehow I staggered into the house, into the lounge where he was sitting in a chair, reading. And then I was laughing and crying and hugging him and my shoulder felt like someone had set fire to the bullet hole but I didn't care.

"You're okay, really okay?" I asked when I could let him go. I could see our father in his features, as if his face had been projected over Sebastian's. It probably wouldn't be easy for Mum when Sebastian grew into himself to be looking at her husband's face every day. It would be hard for me, knowing what I did about him now.

"I'm good, Maya." He grinned at me. I couldn't remember the last time I'd seen him do that.

"But that cough?"

"It must just have been his body taking charge," Mum said, "expelling all the rubbish that had collected in his lungs. Where did you go? What did you do?"

"I went to London."

"London? No way!"

"Yes, way." I ruffled Sebastian's hair.

"Cool! Why did you take so long to come back?"

"They had a big flood, because of the storm. I had to wait till the waters went away. But it wasn't really that cool."

Being marooned in the office building hadn't been too bad, we'd been protected and dry at least. They'd had food and water stockpiled like Walsh said and he'd turned out to be easy to get along with. But I'd spent the whole time desperate to know whether Sebastian was safe and my father had been cruelly unavailable every time I tried to see him to find out.

"What happened to your arm?" Sebastian noticed my sling.

"I was shot."

"Shot?" Mum's exclamation was almost crowned by Sebastian's "That's too cool."

"It's fine."

"What about your face?" Mum asked.

"It's nothing." I said it with enough conviction that I might have believed it myself.

"Why couldn't I give him any Coralone?"

I'd only been home two minutes and Mum had to ask the one question I couldn't answer.

I shifted my arm slightly in my sling, still grateful for the pain, for the perfect excuse as to why I couldn't sign the convoluted agreement my father had had drawn up. Another little dagger that he hadn't trusted me to stay silent about the Coralone, about him and everything. I still felt good that the kak-handed scribble I'd managed with my left hand could have been written by anyone.

Around Mum and Sebastian I'd honour it though. No sense in adding to her grief over him, no sense dampening the mood around Sebastian's apparent recovery.

"I can't tell you exactly," I hedged, "let's just say it's part of the deal I made to get the message to you but what I can say is that you must never take another dose." I gave Sebastian my own version of his hard stare. "You understand? Never. It's important. Not one drop, ever. You won't need it now anyway."

"You were right about the cure." Sebastian looked at me with such pride and innocence, I felt the savagery of our father's betrayal worm its way a little deeper into my heart.

"Maya, I owe you a great deal."Mum looked uncomfortable.

I nodded. All the recriminations I wanted to throw at her, all the things I'd been practising but I wasn't saying any of them. There'd been enough upset in our lives to last a millennia.

"I didn't handle things very well when you went," she glanced at Sebastian, "away and for that I'm sorry. I lost sight of the fact that you're my daughter too and what that means . . ."

"It's okay." I tried to say it like I meant it. Whatever we said wouldn't be enough and with more certainty than I wished, I knew things would never be the same between us again but the least said now might be the best way to patch things over.

"I just need to go and see Esther a minute." I laid a hand on Sebastian's knee. "When I come back, you want to play a game?"

"Yep and you don't have to let me win anymore."

"Get ready for an epic battle then, you can choose what we play." I looked at Mum. "I won't be long."

I stood outside the back door of Jace's house – I'd hardly used the front door while he was alive, I didn't want to start now. I took a deep breath and pulled my spine straighter. Knocking on the door, that was all, I could do that. My trick didn't help – I just couldn't get past how I was about to ruin Esther's life. But I couldn't stand on the doorstep forever. I knocked on the door.

"Maya, love, how are you? Come on in, sit down." Esther pointed at the table and chairs with the potato peeler in her hand. She picked up another muddy potato. "Spit it out, child. That's the best way with bad news."

"How—"

"It's written all over your face and you're in here and Jason isn't. For the last seven years he's never been far away from you."

"I'm so sorry. I never meant for this. I never wanted anything to hurt him. I wish it had been me."

"What happened?" Esther patted her hands on a tea towel and sat opposite me.

"He was shot, by a soldier. He'd . . ." I forgot what I was supposed to be saying, did Esther know what Jace had been?

"You can tell me everything, Maya, I know about his special status." She was beginning to freak me out. In all the scenarios I'd run through in my mind in the days I'd been trapped in London and on the journey back to MK, I'd never dreamt Esther would be so calm, so collected, so reasonable, or so apparently psychic.

"When I found out about . . . his status, I was angry and hurt. We argued. He followed me to the factory that made Sebastian's medicine but he brought soldiers and there was no other way for us to escape so I tried to disable them so we could get away. They shot at me but Jace took the bullet."

Esther shook her head. "That poor boy, he had it bad for you, you know. There was nothing he wouldn't do for you."

I hadn't thought I could cry anymore but slow tears spilled down my cheeks. I didn't try to stop them – one of us should be crying for Jace and Esther remained remarkably dry-eyed. "I didn't get the chance to tell him that I loved him too." I whispered.

"There's your penance," Esther said. "Hardest thing to be the one left behind with all the regrets." She went back to peeling potatoes.

"If there's anything I can do," I wiped at my eyes. "I brought him home so he can be buried here."

"You'd best make the arrangements, I'll probably be reassigned shortly."

"Reassigned?"

"He didn't tell you the full story? I'm not really his gran, we were put together as a family unit by the Government and placed here to report back on you, Anarosa and Sebastian. Jason was too little when we were first assigned so I was the appointed GI. As he's grown and spent so much time with you, he gradually took over. He was a revolutionary in his own quiet way, the price of reporting on you was that he wouldn't report on anyone else, that this street at least, could live a reasonably normal life."

Oh Jace, that's what you were trying to tell me, that's what I pig-headedly wouldn't listen to. The thing that would have made all the difference.

"I'll miss that." Esther was saying. "And him, we may not have been blood related but I was fond of him. I practically raised him, after all."

"He loved you very much." I couldn't help that it came out like an accusation.

"He got too emotionally involved too easily to do this job properly."

"Has this life only ever been a job for you?" Was this woman really Esther? Someone I'd known practically forever but who I apparently didn't know at all.

"Not always, but it doesn't do to forget who you really are." She looked out of the kitchen window. "Your mum's coming to see what's going on. I'll have to play the part of the grieving grandmother now. You'll keep my little secret, won't you? It may make a difference to me one day, somewhere, that you do. It's a dangerous job this calling, after all."

I couldn't have said one word about who Esther really was to anyone at that moment. Shell shocked wasn't the word. I watched Mum peer around the door, saw Esther wail 'Jason's dead' and burst into anguished tears.

Had all the times Esther been kind to me over the years been play-acting too? But Jace hadn't been like that, had he? He'd been a real genuine person, I'd believed him when he said he cared for me, I believed our friendship meant as much to him as it did to me.

My painkillers were wearing off, my shoulder reminding me that no one would ever know the truth of what had happened, of what I'd uncovered down in London. I felt as if I might throw up. Wasn't I as bad as Esther? My own silence and secret-keeping were implicitly reinforcing the Government's position, keeping the status quo of what amounted to a dictatorship, where my own father was the dictator.

Secrets and lies. I had a horrible feeling the price of carrying them would only grow over time, a burden I could never share or ever put down.

CHAPTER EIGHTY-FOUR

SIX MONTHS LATER

"Maya, there's a letter for you." Sebastian walked into the kitchen and handed me a pale pink envelope. "Is it career decision?"

"Probably, looks like Government." I held out my plate of dry toast to him and he took a piece. "There's jam in the fridge if you want."

Even now, so many months later, it was strange and fantastic seeing him almost like other kids. He carried an air of fragility about him, the mark of years of sickness, but he had a shot at a real life now, as real as any of us.

I wasn't sure if he and Mum had made the connection that the Coralone had been keeping him sick for all that time. In a way I was grateful we didn't talk about it because then I didn't have to tell any more lies, vet everything I said. For my own sanity I tried not to think about any of it. I was beyond grateful that by fluke and accident Sebastian hadn't taken any of the poisoned medicine. That was almost enough for me.

"Thanks." He mumbled around the food like any other twelve-year-old. "Aren't you going to open it?"

"In a minute." I took another bite of toast and studied the envelope.

The piece of paper inside would tell me more than what I would spend the rest of my life doing. When I'd first got back from London I'd expected my father to send me something almost immediately. When nothing arrived I'd told myself it'd take time to arrange, even for him. Maybe he'd had to wait for the normal time to release career decision to not arouse suspicion. Damnit I was still making excuses for him. He'd done the other things I'd demanded but what was inside the envelope would reinforce what kind of man he was.

"Don't you want to know?" Sebastian was keener than me.

I wasn't sure I did. "I'm going to the cemetery." I needed to talk to Jace. "You've got homework to do."

"Maya, it's Saturday." He whined just like a normal kid too but it was so good to hear, it still made me smile.

"You want to explain to school why you haven't done it then? Let me know when you do because I'd love to watch how inventive you can be. I'll be an hour or so, back before Mum gets up and back after you've done your homework."

My shoulder protested as I threw my coat on. How long would it take before there were no physical reminders of that awful night in July? I slipped the letter into my pocket and pulled on gloves and a hat as I strode down the garden. The ground crunched under my boots, and I could feel the air sucking the warmth from my face. I grabbed my bike from where it leant against the back fence. Even through my gloves the metal felt cold. A really hard frost last night, temperatures at a record low. The planet was falling apart.

There was no sign of movement from the young family who'd moved into Jace's house. They seemed pleasant enough but I kept my distance. I'd finally stopped wondering where Esther had been reassigned, if she'd been 'given' another grandchild.

I didn't think I'd ever stop feeling guilty about how I'd treated Jace when I heard him admit he was a GI. And as for how I felt about causing his death, it would be years before I could go there. Maybe once it stopped haunting my dreams . . .?

I paused at the back gate. Should I go out the front? No, that was being childish. Besides I'd made my point before. I pulled the gate open, pushed my bike out and looked up and down the back lane. The soldier fell in behind me, probably cursing that he'd pulled babysitting duty again. I'd stopped wondering what brief they'd been given, how my father justified this waste of their time. When I'd first noticed my 'escort' I'd been so angry I'd wanted to walk down to London and take it out on him. How dare he? My word meant something – I'd said I'd stay away and I would. If for nothing other than self-preservation, to not have to be reminded of his betrayal every time I looked at him.

When I'd lost the soldier tailing me in that first week back at home, the panic on his face when he burst into my classroom and found me doing nothing worse than reading had reinforced how seriously my father took me as a threat. From then on I let them follow me, at least it meant they'd leave my family alone.

The cemetery was empty, as I'd expected. I left my bike at the entrance along with my escort and crunched down the paths.

"Hey, Jace." My breath puffed out in tiny white clouds.

I didn't touch his ice-covered headstone as I usually did, too cold today even with gloves on. Esther had left me to make the decisions for his funeral. I had agonised over what to have etched in the stone and in the end settled on simple words that seemed to sum him up best, 'Jason (Jace) Anderson, beloved'. Maybe it would go some way one day to alleviating the guilt I felt at not having told

348

him I loved him before he died.

I picked a stray twig off his grave and threw it behind me. "Got career decision." His headstone remained as impassive as ever.

I pulled the envelope out of my pocket and studied it. I'd always imagined this moment would be more momentous, that I'd be more interested in what I would spend the rest of my life doing. It didn't seem right finding out on my own. I'd always imagined this moment with Jace. A lot of my life was measured like that these days. Things we'd always done together, that I'd taken for granted, were so much harder without him.

I looked at the skeletal trees that marked the boundaries of the cemetery, blinking hard. The anger that I'd felt at the waste of his life was gradually fading to a permeating sadness that I didn't expect would ever leave me. I missed him so much.

The soldier bobbed into and out of my line of vision at the entrance. Only one way in and out, they never bothered to follow me right in. I turned my back on him, hoping he'd get the message.

I tapped the envelope against my hand. Sebastian would tell Mum it had arrived and she would want to know what it said right away. I could just see her lips pressing together when he told her I was at the cemetery again. Our arguments about it were getting worse. She should cut me some slack, she knew how painful it was to be left behind when your best friend left you.

"You planning on opening that? Or you just hoping to read it through the envelope?" I jumped. I'd been so lost in my thoughts I hadn't realised someone else was here.

"Walsh?" Even though he was wrapped up in a scarf and hat that made him impossible to recognise, he was right, his accent gave him away. "What are you doing here?" I looked at the entrance but there was no sign of my army escort.

"He's outside, talking to another one. Change of shift?"

I shrugged. "Maybe, they do it at all different times so I don't get used to any pattern. They get bored watching me in here, I come here a lot."

"Visiting Jace?"

I nodded. "How did you get here, how did you get out of London? What are you doing here?"

"That's not a very nice welcome to someone who's gone to so much trouble to say hi."

"Well, obviously it's good to see you." And surprisingly it was. I didn't have to pretend to be anything else or to not know the things I did with Walsh. I stepped forward and before I realised I was going to do it, put my arms around him in a hug made less awkward by the layers of winter clothing between us.

"You'll blow my cover, you know." Walsh muttered, but I could feel him hug me back.

"What's your cover today?" I asked when we stepped apart.

"Just a regular mourner, same as you. How's your brother?"

"He's good, thanks. Better than we ever expected. So why are you here?"

"Came to see how my favourite rebel is."

I rolled my eyes. "That's such a corny line."

He unwound his scarf enough that I could see him grin. "Yeah, I knew you'd see right through it. Go back to what you were doing, I'll look like I'm paying my respects here, in case your escort peeks in." He stood at the end of the grave on the other side of Jace's and bowed his head as if he were praying.

I listened to the crisp silence around us, playing with my letter, running my gloved fingertips down one side, turning the envelope and running them along the next.

"I've been thinking about what you said," Walsh began after a long minute. "About how normal people could make the Government accountable again. And I think you're right. I think things have gone far enough and it's time to make that stand."

Wow. "And you came all the way from London at great personal risk to tell me that?"

"I came all the way from London at great personal risk to ask you to join me."

I forgot I was supposed to be performing a charade and looked straight at him. "I'm sixteen, Walsh, how can I make a difference to anything?"

He held my gaze. "Sixteen going on thirty. You have a hell of a brain, you're resourceful, determined, loyal and you have an innate sense of justice so strong you're willing to put your life on the line to uphold it."

I didn't know quite what to say to that. "Answer me something honestly?"

"Sure."

"Do you really think we, or anyone else, has a chance against the Government machine? Realistically." I added.

"Sure we do. Might not be a chance with very good odds but we have a shot, and you're right, all it needs is for a few to make a stand to get others believing, prepared to do the same. I'm not gonna lie to you, it won't be easy. It also carries the risk of great danger, they have more ways they can hurt you than you can dream of. But nothing worth anything's easy."

"You really know how to sell it."

He smiled. "Propaganda speech over. No pressure, you decide what you decide, no hard feelings."

"If I say no, you just turn round and go back to London?"

"Well, I was kind of hoping Lawrence's cousin would feed me and put me up for the night first, it's a bloody long way on a bike."

"And if I say yes?" I hardly dared say the words out loud.

"Hey, I'm making this up as I go along. If you say yes

351

I'm hoping you'd come to that dinner and we can figure out where we go from there."

I looked at Jace's headstone. He'd died to save me so I owed it to him to make my life mean something. I ran my fingers down the side of the envelope in my hands again. My future all mapped out for me where I didn't need to think, just obey. But what if it was a future I didn't want? What about all those who were given futures they didn't want, futures that were all wrong for them?

Somewhere deep within me I'd known why I'd sidestepped my father's demand that I not fight against him. I'd only agreed not to tell anyone I was his daughter. I hadn't made him any other promises.

Movement near the cemetery entrance caught my eye. My escort was marching towards me. What now? I glared at him but he kept on coming.

I looked at Walsh and felt a rush of excitement, nerves, a feeling that this was so right and fit so perfectly with what had gone before in my life. There was no other answer. I faced away from Jace's headstone, there was no way he'd approve, no way I could have gone against him like that if he'd still been alive.

I smiled at Walsh. "I'm in."

THE END

ACKNOWLEDGMENTS

I always read acknowledgements with interest because it fascinates me how many people help in bringing a book to life. At the coal face there is the writer alone with the words and the empty screen or page but there so many others become a part of it along the way.

It's been a long road for me to reach this point so there are lots of people who need thanking and having been mentioned in someone else's acknowledgements (thank you, Prof Colin Pillinger!), I have seen how important it is to get it right and so, hoping I do, my heartfelt thanks go to :

My family and friends who never stopped believing.

To my beta readers for your insight and questions and keeping me on the story path - Dave Guyler, Makenna Guyler, Cerys Lloyd-Roberts and Jade Dicerbo.

To Estelle Gillingham who taught me to get out of my way. To Shannon Austin for unswerving belief and for giving me the floor far too often at Buttons. To my fellow scribblers for your patience and encouragement, Richard Barker, Judy Deveson, Ruth Goodridge, Lisa Greaves and the late Colin Webb.

To Lauren Dane for the quote that sits by my shoulder as I write.

To John Berlyne for taking the time and trouble to give me the kind of feedback I could use and without whose insightful comments I may have kept missing the mark.

To Laura Latham for your friendship and savvy and for your understanding of what this really means – now it's your turn.

To Juliet Mushens for believing that I can do this.

That you're holding this copy is also thanks in no small part to Carole Matthews, friend and role model supremo.

A special thanks to my number one fan for extraordinary belief and encouragement.

And to Tempest, for trusting Maya's story to me, may I always be able to reach the gap in the clouds where the stories are waiting.

If you have enjoyed this story, please do leave me a review – honest feedback is how we authors grow and produce better stories next time and how we know to do more of the same!

All good wishes

Karen

www.karenguyler.com
@originalkaren
https://www.facebook.com/karenguylerauthor

Printed in Great Britain
by Amazon.co.uk, Ltd.,
Marston Gate.